LONG LIVE THE KING

To save two worlds, she must kill the king

-or lose everything.

Maryse Marullo

This work is a work of fiction. The characters, events, and storyline are entirely products of the author's imagination. Any resemblance to actual persons, living or deceased, or real-life events is purely coincidental. While the narrative draws inspiration from various sources, it explores complex and challenging subject matter. The author has made every effort to approach these themes with care and sensitivity. However, given the limitations of available information, certain aspects of the story have been shaped creatively. This book is a fictional creation and should be understood as such.

Trigger Warning

This book, Long Live The King, contains themes, scenes, and content that may be distressing or triggering to some readers. Topics explored in this story include, but are not limited to:

Abduction and Captivity: Depictions of a character being forcibly taken from their home and held against their will.

Abuse of Power: Themes of control, manipulation, and exploitation by figures of authority.

Blood and Violence: Graphic descriptions of battles, injuries, and violent encounters.

Death and Grief: The loss of life, emotional aftermath, and survivor's guilt.

Emotional Manipulation: Characters being deceived or coerced into actions they might not willingly take.

Graphic Violence: Explicit depictions of combat, torture, and other physical harm.

Oppression and Tyranny: The consequences of living under an authoritarian regime.

Psychological Trauma: Characters experiencing fear, anxiety, and other emotional struggles.

Rape and Assault Mention (Not Depicted): References to the possibility of assault, though not graphically explored.

Religious and Ritualistic Sacrifices: Themes of sacrifice tied to prophecies and mystical rituals.

Sexual Content: Detailed depictions of sexual intimacy between characters, including intense and emotionally charged moments. Kink and Power Dynamics: Exploration of themes related to dominance, tension, and control in consensual sexual relationships. Sexually Charged Dialogue: Use of explicit, sexually suggestive, and provocative language in character interactions. Sexual Tension: Prolonged and deliberate slow-burn buildup of romantic and sexual tension between characters.

Toxic Relationships: Complex and morally gray dynamics between characters.

War and Rebellion: Depictions of societal unrest, rebellion, and its toll on individuals.

Reader Discretion Advised:

This book is intended for mature audiences and explores dark, gothic, and emotionally charged themes. Please proceed with caution if you are sensitive to any of the topics listed above.

Characters

Elira (eh-LEE-rah)

Damien (DAY-mee-ehn)

Kael (KAY-el)

Veylan (VAY-lahn)

Lyric (LEER-ik)

Keylan (KEE-lahn)

Eryndor (Eh-rin-door)

Malevolent (Muh-lev-uh-luhnt)

DEDICATION

To those who crave stories that make your heart race, your cheeks flush, and your imagination run wild.

This is for the ones unafraid to explore the dangerous edges of desire, where love is both a battle and a surrender.

May this remind you that passion, even in the darkest moments, can light the way.

For you, who dare to feel deeply and live boldly.

NOTE FROM MARYSE

I'm so sorry.

Embers of a Lost World
Young Elira

The hospital smells funny—all sharp and clean, but not in a nice way. The walls are cracked and stained, like they've been sick too. Everything feels too quiet, except for the beeping of the machines and the low hum of the lights. Outside the window, the sky is red, like fire, and the air smells like it's burning. The sun is so bright it makes everything look tired.

It's so hot everywhere.

I swing my legs under the chair, but it squeaks every time I move, so I stop. Mom's lying in the bed, her face pale and her eyes heavy. Her hair used to be shiny and black, like mine, but now it's all dry and thin. She smiles at me, though, just a little, and I feel like I want to cry and hug her at the same time.

"Elira Veyastra," someone calls from the door, saying my whole name like it's a rule. I look up and see a tall man in a white coat. His eyes are dark and tired, like he hasn't slept in forever. He doesn't smile.

"I need a moment," he says, his voice serious. He looks at Mom, then back at me. "It won't be long now."

I don't know what to say, so I just nod. My chest feels tight, and I grab Mom's hand, holding it even though it's cold.

"You don't have to stay here, love," she says, her voice scratchy. She sounds so small, and I don't like it. "This isn't fair for you."

"I want to stay," I say quickly. My voice wobbles, but I don't care. "I want to be here with you."

Her hand squeezes mine just a little, but it feels like a lot. "You're stronger than you think, Elira. Don't let this world change that. Promise me."

I nod again because it's hard to talk when my throat feels all tight. "I promise," I whisper, even though I don't know if I can keep it.

The room is too bright and too dark at the same time. Outside, the city looks scary, with tall broken buildings and streets that don't have cars or people anymore. Everything is cracked and dry, like the whole world is falling apart.

"What happens when you're gone?" I ask her, my voice so small I almost don't hear it.

Her eyes look at me like she's trying to tell me something important. For a second, she looks like the Mom I remember, the one who always knew what to do.

"You keep going," she says softly. "You fight. You live. For me, for yourself. Promise me you'll try."

I promise again, but my chest hurts because I don't want her to go. I want her to tell me it's going to be okay, even if it's not.

The doctor comes closer, and his hand rests on my shoulder. I don't look at him. I just keep holding her hand, even when it gets colder, even when she stops breathing. The machine makes a long, flat noise, and the doctor turns it off. Everything is quiet except for the sounds outside—the wind, the crackling air, and the city that's still burning.

I press my forehead against her hand, wishing I could make her warm again, but I can't. I don't move, even when the sky outside goes dark, swallowing the red sun. The world feels too big and too small all at once, and I don't know what to do.

A Dying World
Elira

The city's falling apart. Literally.

The buildings look like they're holding each other up, leaning at awkward angles, their windows shattered and vines crawling up the walls like they're reclaiming what's theirs. The sky's the same dull gray it's been for months, and the air smells like smoke.

Not the comforting kind, like campfires or roasted chestnuts. No, this is the sharp, acrid tang of something burning that shouldn't be.

Plastic, maybe. Or something worse. It hangs in the air, clinging to my clothes, my hair, and my lungs.

The city groans around me, a living, dying thing. Buildings loom like skeletons, their windows shattered and walls scorched with blackened streaks. The streets are cracked, uneven, littered with broken glass and discarded scraps of things people no longer have the luxury to care about.

I tug my coat tighter around me as the wind picks up, carrying with it the faint sound of sirens in the distance. Sirens are always distant now. No one comes when you need them.
Sometimes, I wonder how long it's been like this.

The days blur together, and the world has been falling apart for so long that I've almost forgotten what it was like before. Before the shortages, before the riots, before the city started swallowing itself whole.

I used to have a life here. A good one.

I remember the way the streets used to hum with life, filled with people who didn't have to think about whether their next meal would come from a ration line or a dumpster. I remember the sound of music drifting out of cafés, the laughter of children playing in the parks, the glow of lights that didn't flicker or die out without warning.

Most of all, I remember my parents.

My chest tightens at the thought, and I push it aside. This city doesn't leave room for memories. It barely leaves room for survival.

"Hey, you got anything?"

The voice snaps me out of my thoughts, and I stop short, my grip tightening on the strap of my bag. I turn to see a man standing at the mouth of an alley, his face half-hidden beneath a hood. His eyes are sharp, hungry, darting to the bulge in my coat pocket where the edge of a loaf of bread peeks out.

I don't answer. I don't dare. Instead, I adjust the strap on my shoulder and quicken my pace, ignoring the way his gaze follows me down the street.

The apartment I call home is on the third floor of a building that should've been condemned years ago. The elevator doesn't work, of course, and the stairwell smells like urine and mildew. By the time I reach my door, my legs are aching, and my breath comes in shallow gasps.

Inside, it's not much better. The wallpaper is peeling, the furniture is secondhand, and the light flickers ominously when I flip the switch. But it's mine, and that's all that matters.

I drop the bag on the counter and pull out the bread, placing it beside a half-empty jar of peanut butter. It's not much, but it'll get me through the next few days if I ration it right.

The worst part isn't the hunger or the cold or the fear of stepping outside—it's the loneliness.

I used to have friends. A boyfriend. People who cared about me, who would laugh at my stupid jokes and listen to me rant about the things that didn't matter. But they're gone now, scattered to the wind like everything else.

Sometimes, I wonder if I should have left too. If there's something better waiting beyond the city limits. But I've heard the stories. The endless highways, the empty towns, the scavengers who would kill you for a can of beans.

At least here, I know what to expect. The city doesn't care about me, but at least it's consistent. Days bleed into nights, and nights bleed into moments like this—quiet, still, where I can almost forget the apocalyptic world outside my walls.

I curl deeper into the threadbare blanket, letting the faint hum of the broken heater fill the silence. It doesn't do much to warm the apartment, but it's enough to remind me that I'm still here. Still alive.

My eyes drift shut, my thoughts a blur of ration lines, endless gray streets, and the nagging question I can never seem to answer: How much longer can I do this?
And then, a sound.

Faint at first, almost like a whisper, but it pulls me back from the edge of sleep. A scrape, followed by a low creak, like metal bending under pressure.
I sit up slowly, my heart pounding. The window.
I left it cracked earlier to let out the stale air. Now, the thin battered curtain flutters faintly, the cold night breeze slipping through the gap.

I tell myself it's nothing. Just the wind. Maybe

the frame shifted again, like it always does when the temperatures drops.

But then I hear it—a soft crunch, like glass breaking beneath a boot.

My stomach twists as the realization hits me.

Someone's here

The sound of shattering glass wakes me.

My eyes snap open, and for a moment, I'm disoriented, unsure if the sound came from inside or outside. But then I hear it again—the crunch of broken glass underfoot—and my blood turns to ice.

I sit up slowly, my heart pounding as I scan the room. The door is still locked, the chain in place, but the window—

A figure moves in the shadows, and I freeze.

"Nice place," a voice says, low and smooth, with just a hint of something mocking.

The man steps into the dim light, and my breath catches. He's tall, with brown hair that falls just past his ears, and eyes that seem to gleam a light brown in the darkness.

His clothes are neat, almost too neat for someone in this part of the city, and the way he moves is unsettling.

"Who are you?" I demand, my voice breaking the silence.

He smiles, slow and deliberate, like he's savoring the moment. "No one you need to worry about. Yet."

"Get out," I say, rising to my feet.

His smile widens. "I don't think so."

Before I can react, he moves—fast, impossibly fast—and suddenly he's in front of me, his hand wrapping around my wrist. His grip is firm but not painful, and his touch sends a shiver down my spine.

"You're coming with me," he says, his tone leaving no room for argument.

"Like hell I am," I snap, twisting my arm in an attempt to break free.

His grip tightens just enough to stop me, and his expression hardens. "You don't have a choice, Elira." The way he says my name makes something inside me twist, and I realize two things in that moment.

One: He knows exactly who I am.
And two: My life will never be the same again.

The Stranger's Bargain
Elira

The first thing I feel is the ache.

It radiates through my head, sharp and relentless, dragging me out of unconsciousness. My arms are stiff, and there's a faint metallic taste in my mouth that makes my stomach churn.

The second thing I notice is that I'm not in my apartment anymore. The floor beneath me isn't the cracked linoleum I'm used to—it's cold, damp earth. The air smells different too, fresher but tinged with something sharp, like pine and wet leaves.

I blink against the faint light filtering through the canopy above me. Trees. There are trees everywhere.

"What the—"

"You're awake."

The voice is low, smooth, and instantly infuriating.

I twist toward the sound, and there he is. The man from my apartment—the one who broke in, the one who grabbed me—is leaning against a tree a few feet away, looking annoyingly smug.

"Nice nap?" he asks, his green eyes gleaming with amusement.

"Where the hell am I?" I demand, sitting up too quickly and wincing as my head protests.

"The better question," he says, pushing off the tree and taking a slow step toward me, "is how you managed to sleep through the transition. Most people find it… unpleasant."

"Transition?" I repeat, my voice rising. "What are you talking about?"

"You'll see," he says, his lips curling into a slow, infuriating smile.

My fists clench as I glare at him, but before I can spit out another question, I notice the faint glow behind him.

It's subtle at first, like the shimmer of heat rising off pavement, but as I focus, I realize it's coming from a jagged tear in the air itself. The edges ripple like water, and beyond it, there's nothing but darkness—an endless void that makes my stomach twist.

"What the hell is that?" I ask, my voice barely above a whisper.

"That," he says, glancing over his shoulder, "is how we got here. Impressive, right?"

"No," I snap, scrambling to my feet. "What the hell did you do to me?"

His smirk doesn't falter. "Relax, sweetheart. You're fine. Better than fine, actually. You're alive, which is more than I can say for most people in your position."

"Don't call me sweetheart," I say through gritted teeth.

"Fine," he says, shrugging. "What should I call you then?"

"How about not at all?"

He chuckles, crossing his arms as he watches me. "I'll admit, you've got a bite to you. I like that."
"Good for you," I say, taking a cautious step back. The ground feels uneven beneath my boots, the damp earth sinking slightly under my weight.

Every instinct I have is screaming at me to run, but there's nowhere to go. The forest stretches out in every direction, dark and endless, and the tear in the air— whatever the hell that is—sits between me and my only apparent way out.

"I want to go home," I say, my voice firmer now.

His expression shifts slightly, the amusement in his eyes dimming. "That's not an option." "Why not?"
"Because home doesn't exist anymore," he says, his tone flat.

words hit me like a punch to the chest, and for a moment, I can't breathe.

"What are you talking about?" I ask, my voice barely above a whisper.

He sighs, raking a hand through his dark hair. "You crossed over, Elira. This isn't your world anymore."

I stare at him, trying to make sense of what he's saying. "You're lying."

"I'm not," he says simply. "And you're going to have to trust me sooner or later if you want to survive."

"Trust you?" I laugh, the sound bitter and sharp. "You broke into my home, dragged me here against my will, and now you're telling me I can't go back? Why the hell would I trust you?"

"Because I'm the only one who knows the rules," he says, his voice dropping.

"Rules?"

He steps closer, his brown eyes locking onto mine. "Every world has rules, sweetheart. Break them, and you don't last long."

We don't say much after that.

The fire crackles softly between us, its glow casting flickering shadows on his face. I stay silent, my hands clenched in my lap, as the weight of his words settles over me. What can I even say? He's out of his goddamn mind.

He leans back against a fallen log, his posture relaxed, like he doesn't have a care in the world. I hate him for that. For acting like this is normal, like this is fine.

"What happens now?" I ask eventually, my voice quieter than I'd like.

He opens one eye, glancing at me with that infuriating smirk. "We move. It's not safe to stay in one place too long."

"Move where?" I ask, my frustration bubbling to the surface. "You keep talking about rules and danger, but you haven't told me a damn thing that makes sense."

"You'll figure it out," he says, standing and stretching like we're about to go for a leisurely stroll.

I groan, dragging a hand down my face. "You're impossible." "Thanks," he says with a wink. "That wasn't a compliment," I mutter, pushing myself to my feet.

The fire sputters and dies as he kicks dirt over it, plunging us into a darkness that feels colder than it should.

He leads the way through the forest, his movements quick and precise, like he's been here a thousand times before. I follow reluctantly, the damp earth sucking at my boots with every step. Because. Do I even have a choice not to?

My mind races, trying to piece together what the hell is happening. The trees seem to close in around us, their branches forming a canopy so thick that the faint light of the stars barely filters through.

And then it hits me—there's no smoke here. No exhaust fumes or burning plastic or the metallic tang of the city's decay.

I stop walking, my chest tightening as I take a deep breath. The air is clean. Cleaner than anything I've ever known. It smells of pine and damp earth, with faint hints of something sweet, like flowers blooming somewhere in the shadows.

The forest stretches endlessly around us, the trees towering and ancient, their bark rough and dark. Moss blankets the ground in patches, soft and spongy underfoot, and somewhere in the distance, water trickles faintly over rocks.

For a moment, I forget everything else—his smirk, the fear clawing at my chest, the uncertainty of whatever the hell this is.

The forest is beautiful, almost painfully so, and it feels like I've stepped into another world.

"What's wrong now?" he asks, glancing over his shoulder, his tone half-annoyed, half-amused.

"It's…" I hesitate, searching for the words. "It's just… different here."

"Different how?" he says, stopping to turn toward me, his arms crossing over his chest.

I look around, gesturing vaguely at the trees.

"The air. The sky. Everything. It's like…"

"Like it hasn't been ruined yet," he finishes, his voice softer than I expect.

I nod, swallowing the lump in my throat. "Yeah."

He watches me for a moment, his smirk fading slightly. "Get used to it. It's not all pretty flowers and fresh air out here."

The moment passes, and we keep moving. The forest is darker now, the shadows deeper, and I can't shake the feeling that we're being watched.

I quicken my pace, stepping closer to him despite every instinct screaming at me to keep my distance.

"So," I say, my voice sharper than I intend, "are you planning to kill me, or…"

He glances at me, raising an eyebrow. "Or what?"

"You know," I say, the words sticking in my throat. "Rape me. Torture me. Whatever it is creeps like you do."

He stops walking so suddenly that I nearly bump into him.

"Wow," he says, turning to face me. "You've got a hell of an imagination, sweetheart."

"Don't call me that," I snap, glaring at him.

"Fine," he says, his smirk returning. "But for the record, if I wanted to hurt you, I wouldn't be dragging you through the forest right now. I'd have done it already."

"That's not comforting," I mutter, crossing my arms.

"It's not meant to be," he says, turning and continuing down the path. "It's just the truth."

I hesitate, my stomach twisting, but I have no choice but to follow.

"You're an ass," I mutter under my breath.

"No argument there," he calls back, his tone maddeningly smug.

He doesn't say much, and I don't bother asking any more questions. The few answers he's given have only made things worse.

"Keep up," he says over his shoulder, his tone light but pointed.

"I'm trying," I snap, stumbling over a root and barely catching myself.

"Try harder," he says, his smirk audible even in the dark.

"God, I hate you," I mutter under my breath.

"No, you don't," he says, his voice annoyingly smug.

I don't respond. Mostly because I don't have

the energy to argue.

He leads the way through the forest, his movements quick and precise, like he's been here a thousand times before. I follow reluctantly, my mind racing as I try to piece together what the hell is happening.

The forest feels alive somehow, the air humming with an energy I can't name. Shadows shift in the corners of my vision, and every now and then, I catch glimpses of something moving between the trees—something big.

He doesn't seem bothered, which only makes me more nervous.

"You've got a name?" I ask, my voice sharper than I intend.

He glances over his shoulder, his smirk visible even in the dim light. "Kael."

"Kael," I repeat, testing it. "Sounds fake."

"It's real enough," he says, turning back to the path ahead. "Why? Thinking of naming me something else?"

"How about 'jackass'?" I mutter.

He chuckles softly. "Creative. But I think I'll stick with Kael, thanks."

"You could at least tell me where we're going," I say finally, breaking the silence.

He glances back at me, his smirk returning. "Would you believe me if I did?" "Try me," I say, narrowing my eyes.
"Fine," he says, his tone light. "We're heading to the nearest safe zone. Think of it as a temporary pit stop before the fun really begins."

"Fun," I mutter under my breath. "Sure. This is a blast."

He chuckles, shaking his head. "You're not bad company, you know. For someone who complains so much."

I glare at him. "You're not bad company either—for a kidnapper."

"I aim to please," he says, winking.

"God, I hate you," I mutter, but there's no heat in it.

Into the Unknown
Elira

The forest grows darker the deeper we go.

The thick canopy above blocks out most of the light, leaving only faint beams of moonlight to guide our way.
Every snap of a twig or rustle of leaves sets my nerves on edge, and I can't stop glancing over my shoulder, half-expecting something to lunge out of the shadows.

Kael, of course, looks perfectly at ease. His steps are steady, his movements confident, and his stupid smirk hasn't faded once since we started walking.

"What's the plan, Kael?" I ask, breaking the silence.

My voice sounds meaner than I intended, but I'm too tired and too angry to care. "Or are we just wandering aimlessly until something eats us?"

"Relax, sweetheart," he says without looking back. "Stop calling me that," I snap.

He chuckles, his tone maddeningly smug. "You've got a lot of rules for someone who doesn't know where they are."

"I don't need to know where I am to know I don't like you," I mutter under my breath.

"Noted," he says.

The path ahead opens into a small clearing, the moonlight brighter here. The air feels colder somehow, the kind of chill that sinks into your bones and makes your skin prickle.

Kael stops abruptly, holding up a hand to

silence me before I can ask what's wrong.

"What now?" I whisper, my fingers tightening instinctively around the strap of my bag.

"Quiet," he murmurs, his eyes scanning the treetops.

I freeze, my breath catching in my throat as I follow his gaze. The forest seems impossibly still, the usual rustling of leaves and chirping of insects gone, replaced by a heavy, suffocating silence.

Something's wrong.
"Stay close," he says, his voice low.

"To you?" I ask, raising an eyebrow. "Not a chance."

"Fine," he says with a shrug. "But don't come crying to me when you get eaten."

The silence stretches on, broken only by the sound of our footsteps crunching softly against the forest floor. The trees seem to grow taller and more twisted as we walk, their branches reaching out like skeletal fingers.

"Why does it feel like we're walking into a haunted forest?" I mutter, glancing around nervously.

Kael grins, his tone light. "Maybe we are."

"Great," I say, rolling my eyes. "Do you have a plan for when something jumps out and tries to kill us?"

"Run faster than you," he replies, his smirk widening. "You're a real piece of work, you know that?" I snap.

He doesn't answer, but I catch the faintest chuckle as he continues ahead.

We reach another clearing, this one smaller and more open. Kael stops again, this time crouching low to the ground as he inspects something I can't see.

"What are you doing?" I ask, staying a safe distance behind him.

"Tracking," he says simply.

"Tracking what?"

He looks up at me, his expression unreadable. "Something that's been following us."

My stomach drops, and I glance over my shoulder instinctively. "You couldn't have mentioned that sooner?"

"I didn't want to scare you," he says, his lips twitching into a faint smile.

"Too late," I mutter, my grip tightening on the strap of my bag.

Kael straightens, his movements slow and deliberate. "Don't go to far from me," he says again, his tone more serious this time.

I hate that I listen to him, but the fear clawing at my chest leaves me no choice.

As we move forward, the air seems to grow heavier, almost suffocating. My steps feel slower, each one taking more effort than it should, and the faint whispers of doubt in my mind grow louder.

"Keep moving," Kael says, his voice cutting through the fog in my head.

"Easy for you to say," I mutter. "You're not the one who feels like they're about to pass out."

"It's the forest," he says. "It gets into your head if you let it."

"How do I not let it?" I ask, my voice shaking slightly.

He glances back at me, his expression oddly serious. "Focus on me."

"On you?" I ask, raising an eyebrow. "What, am I supposed to stare at your stupid face and hope for the best?"

"If it works," he says with a grin.

I glare at him, but I can't argue. My options are limited, and as much as I hate to admit it, he's the only thing keeping me grounded right now.

The forest begins to thin out, the oppressive shadows giving way to faint glimmers of light ahead. Kael's pace quickens, and I follow, my heart pounding in my chest as we step into another clearing.

This one is different.

The trees form a perfect circle around the edges, their branches tangled together like they're trying to keep something in—or out. In the center stands a stone archway, its surface carved with symbols I don't recognize. The air hums faintly, a low vibration that makes the hairs on the back of my neck stand up.

"What is this?" I ask, my voice barely above a whisper.

"Safe zone," Kael says, stepping toward the archway. "For now."

"For now?" I repeat, following reluctantly. "That's not exactly reassuring."

"It's better than nothing," he says, glancing back at me. "Come on. We're not alone out here."

The Village
Elira

A stone archway hums as we pass through it, the vibration sinking into my chest and making my pulse stutter.

I glance back over my shoulder, half-expecting the forest to rush in behind us, but the tangled trees stay where they are, dark and menacing.

"Does it always feel like that?" I ask, my voice quieter than I'd like.

Kael shrugs, his usual smirk firmly in place. "You get used to it."

"I'm super relived," I mutter, rubbing my arms as the hum fades.

The air on the other side feels different—less oppressive but still heavy with tension. A narrow dirt

path lined with scattered stones, and in the distance, faint wisps of smoke curl into the sky.

"Where are we?" I ask, quickening my pace to catch up to him.

"You'll see," he says, not bothering to look back. "You love being cryptic, don't you?"
"It's a talent," he replies, the corner of his mouth twitching upward.

The village appears suddenly, like it's been waiting for us to stumble upon it.

The houses are small and crooked, made of wood and stone with thatched roofs that look like they've seen better days. Smoke drifts lazily from the chimneys, and the faint murmur of voices carries on the wind.

It's not much, but it's more life than I've seen in my twenty-six years of life.

"Stick with me," Kael says, his tone sharper now.

"Why? Think someone's going to kidnap me again?" I snap, crossing my arms.

"More like they'll kill you if they think you're a threat," he replies evenly.

"Would it be so bad," I mutter, but I stick closer to him anyway.

As we step into the village, the voices quiet, and I feel eyes on me from every direction. People peer out from behind curtains and doorways, their expressions a mix of suspicion and curiosity.

A group of kids playing near the edge of the village stops to stare, their laughter dying in their throats.

"I don't think they like me," I whisper.

"They don't like anyone, and your looks… well, let's just say you stand out," Kael says, his voice low and pointed.

He waves casually to a man with a scar running down his face, but the man only glares in response before disappearing into the shadows.

"Stand out?" I repeat, frowning. "What's that supposed to mean?"

Kael glances at me, his smirk fading slightly. "It means you've got the kind of face that makes people uneasy."

"Uneasy?" I ask, narrowing my eyes.

"You're rare," he says simply, like that's supposed to explain everything.

I stop walking, planting my hands on my hips.

"Rare how?"

"Look around, Elira. How many people do you see with hair like yours? Or eyes that color?"

I glance at the people watching us from behind curtains and half-closed doors. Most of them have darker hair—shades of brown or black—and their eyes range from deep browns to muted hazels. No one else has the striking contrast of jet-black hair and vivid blue eyes.

"I don't see how that's a problem," I say, crossing my arms.

"It's not a problem," Kael says, his smirk returning. "It's an advantage. People pay a lot for things that are… different."

A chill runs down my spine, and I glare at him. "You make it sound like I'm some kind of object."

He shrugs. "You're not. But that doesn't mean people won't try to treat you like one."

"Fantastic," I mutter, rolling my eyes. "This is going to be fun."

Kael chuckles, starting to walk again. "Fun for me, maybe."

I glare at him, crossing my arms. "And how the fuck do you even know my name?"

Kael raises an eyebrow, his smirk returning. "You're not very good at keeping a low profile, sweetheart."

"That's not an answer," I snap.

He shrugs, his tone maddeningly casual. "I know more than you think. Enough to find you. Enough to keep you alive."

"Alive for what?" I demand, my chest tightening.

Kael doesn't answer right away. Instead, he steps closer, his green eyes locking onto mine. "Gods, you're annoying. You'll find out. Soon enough."

Kael leads me to a large building near the center of the village. It's sturdier than the others, with stone walls and a roof that looks like it might actually hold up in a storm. The sound of raised voices echoes from inside, and my stomach twists as he pushes the door open.

The room falls silent the moment we step in.

It's filled with people, all of them armed and all of them staring at me like I'm something they scraped off the bottom of their boots.

"Kael," a woman says, stepping forward. Her dark skin hair is pulled back into a braid, and her golden eyes are sharp enough to cut glass. "Who's this?"

"She's with me," Kael says, his tone casual.

"She looks like trouble," the woman replies, crossing her arms.

"She is," Kael says with a grin. "That's why I brought her."

"Fantastic," I mutter, glaring at him.

The woman's gaze shifts to me, and I straighten under the weight of her scrutiny. "What's your name?"

"Elira," I say, my voice steadier than I feel.

"She's not one of us," another voice says, deeper and rougher. A man steps forward, his arms crossed and his eyes narrowing at me. "Why should we trust her?"

"Because I do," Kael says, his tone firmer now.

The man snorts. "That's not much of an endorsement."

I open my mouth to respond, but Kael holds up a hand to stop me. "Relax. She's not here to cause problems."

"Then why is she here?" the woman asks, her eyes narrowing.

"Because she's important," Kael says simply.

The room erupts into murmurs, and I shoot him a glare. "What are you doing?" I whisper.

"Helping you," he whispers back, his smirk returning.

"You're making it worse," I hiss.

"Trust me," he says, and for some reason, I hate that I almost do.

The meeting drags on, the rebels arguing over whether or not I should stay. Kael defends me with his usual infuriating charm, but it's clear not everyone is convinced.

In the end, the woman—Lyric, as I later learn—makes the final call.

"She stays," Lyric says, her tone leaving no room for argument. "But if she causes any trouble, she's out."
"Fair enough," I say, lifting my chin.
Kael grins, leaning closer to me. "See? Told you it'd work out."

"Shut up," I mutter, but I can't stop the faint flicker of relief that warms my chest.

The First Lesson
Elira

The next morning, I wake up to shouting.

It's sharp and relentless, breaking through the fragile peace of sleep like a hammer. For a moment, I forget where I am, my mind scrambling to piece together the jumbled fragments of yesterday—the forest, Kael, the village.

Groaning, I sit up, wincing as the rough fabric of the cot scrapes against my skin. The room they stuck me in is small and plain, with stone walls that feel more like a cell than a bedroom.

A single wooden chair leans precariously against the wall, and the faint light from a small, square window casts long shadows across the floor.

At the foot of the bed, a bundle of clothes sits neatly folded, the dark fabric standing out against the weathered wood.

I frown, pushing the blanket aside as I reach for them.

My current outfit isn't much to speak of—faded jeans with holes in the knees, a thin, oversized hoodie that's frayed at the cuffs, and scuffed sneakers that barely hold together.
It's all practical, or at least it was back home, but here it feels… wrong. Like it doesn't belong in this strange, ancient world.

The new clothes are different.
The pants are made of supple black leather, fitted but flexible, with strange straps crisscrossing over the thighs and down the legs, their purpose as much a mystery as everything else here. The shirt is plain and black, its fabric thick and sturdy, and the jacket—

The jacket catches my attention immediately. It's a mix of leather and soft, sheep-like wool, the fur lining the inside and peeking out at the collar and cuffs. It feels warm, solid, like armor against the cold air that seems to cling to this place.

I run my fingers over the material, a small part of me wondering who left these here—and why.
The shouting grows louder, and curiosity wins out over exhaustion. I grab my new boots and shove them on, stumbling toward the door.

Outside, the square is buzzing with activity.

The early morning light casts everything in a pale, golden hue, illuminating the mismatched buildings and cobblestone paths. People are scattered everywhere, their movements purposeful and sharp. A group of men huddle near the edge of the square, sharpening weapons on makeshift grindstones, the rhythmic scrape of metal against stone mingling with the low hum of conversation.

Others haul crates, their shoulders straining under the weight of supplies, while a few bark orders at anyone within earshot. It's chaotic, but there's a strange sense of unity in it all, like each person knows their role in this strange, cobbled-together machine.

In the middle of it all stands Lyric.

She's impossible to miss, her long brown locks catching the light as she turns sharply to face a man towering over her. Her golden eyes burn with intensity, and her posture is a mix of elegance and unshakable authority.

Even in the plain, functional clothing she wears—a fitted white tunic and dark trousers—she looks like she belongs in a painting.

"You think that was acceptable?" she demands, her voice sharp enough to cut.

The man mumbles something I can't hear, and Lyric steps closer, her frame slim but radiating strength. She moves with the kind of precision that makes you believe she could snap someone in half without breaking a sweat.

"Try that excuse again," she snaps, her tone low and deadly, "and I'll make you run drills until your legs give out."

Kael appears at my side, leaning casually against the doorframe. His smirk is firmly in place, as usual, and he looks far too amused by the scene unfolding in front of us.

"Morning, sweetheart," he says, his voice dripping with mock cheerfulness.

"Don't call me that," I reply automatically, not taking my eyes off Lyric.

"She's something, isn't she?" he says, nodding toward her.

"Something terrifying," I mutter.

Kael chuckles, crossing his arms. "That's why she's in charge."

"In charge of what? Making grown men cry?"

"Among other things," he says, his grin widening. "This is a rebellion village. People here are rebels."

I blink, turning to him fully. "Rebels? Against what? Against who?"

"Don't ask more," he says, holding up a hand. "I'm not explaining. Not yet. Too soon."

"That's not cryptic at all," I mutter, rolling my eyes.

"Good," he says with a smirk. "I like keeping you curious."

I glance at him, narrowing my eyes. "Why is she in charge? Where are we? Why does everyone look at me like I've got two heads?"

Kael tilts his head, his smirk softening into something almost amused. "One question at a time, sweetheart."

"Fine," I say, crossing my arms. "Why do they look at me like that? Is it my hair? My eyes? What's so special about me?"

"It's definitely not your charming personality," Kael quips, but his smirk falters slightly when I glare at him.

"Kael." My voice is sharper now, and he sighs, raking a hand through his hair.

"Your looks are... uncommon," he says finally. "People around here don't see a lot of black hair. Or blue eyes."

"So?" I ask, exasperated. "What does that mean? Why am I here?"

Kael's gaze flickers, like he's debating whether to answer. Finally, he shrugs. "You'll find out soon enough."

"Not helpful," I mutter, scowling.

Lyric's gaze snaps to us suddenly, and I swear I feel the weight of her stare pinning me in place.

"You," she says, pointing directly at me.

"Me?" I squeak, trying not to shrink under her scrutiny.

"Yes, you," she says, striding toward us with a purposeful grace that makes me want to bolt. "If you're going to stay here, you need to earn your keep."

"I—what?"

"Training," she says, stopping just in front of me. She's shorter than I expected, but the intensity in her golden eyes makes her feel ten feet tall. "You need to learn how to fight."

"I don't—"

"You don't get a choice," she says, cutting me off. "Kael, take her to the field. Start with the basics."

Kael raises an eyebrow, clearly enjoying my discomfort. "You sure she's ready for that?"

"She doesn't have to be ready," Lyric says, her tone as sharp as her gaze. "She just has to do it."

Before I can argue, Lyric spins on her heel and stalks away, her long braid swinging behind her.

Kael claps a hand on my shoulder, his grin infuriatingly wide. "Welcome to the rebellion, sweetheart."

"This is going to be fun."I mutter, shrugging off his hand.

Breaking the Mold
Elira

The field is a disaster.

Patches of dirt and dead grass stretch out in uneven clumps, surrounded by a low wooden fence that looks like it might collapse if someone so much as sneezes on it.

A few crude targets made of straw and fabric are propped up at one end, their surfaces riddled with arrows and slashes.

"This place is a mess," I mutter, taking it all in.

Kael leans against the fence, his grin as infuriating as ever. His brown hair is messy, curling slightly at the ends, and his warm brown eyes glint with amusement.

He's wearing a loose gray shirt that clings to his broad shoulders, the sleeves rolled up to reveal strong forearms scarred from what I assume are years of fighting. He looks to be in the same group age as me. Despite his cocky attitude, there's something boyish about him—he's attractive in a way that feels unpolished, more rough edges than perfection.

"What? Not impressed?" he asks, his grin widening.

"This is where you're going to teach me to fight?" I ask, raising an eyebrow.

"Everyone starts somewhere," he says with a shrug. "And you're about as 'somewhere' as it gets."

I glare at him, crossing my arms. "I've never held a weapon in my life."

"Exactly," he says, straightening up and grabbing a wooden sword from a pile near the fence. He tosses it to me, and I barely catch it before it smacks me in the face.

"Hey!" I snap, fumbling with the weight of it.

"Rule number one," Kael says, smirking. "Always be ready."

He steps into the center of the field, motioning for me to follow.

"Okay, sweetheart, let's see what you've got," he says, planting his feet and holding the sword loosely in one hand.

"What I've got?" I repeat, staring at him. "I told you, I've never done this before."

"Exactly," he says, his grin widening. "Which means there's nowhere to go but up."

I groan, gripping the sword tighter as I step toward him. "Fine. But if I break something, it's your fault."

"Deal," he says, shifting his stance. "Now, try to hit me."

"What?"

"Hit me," he says, gesturing with his free hand. "You're kidding."
"Do I look like I'm kidding?"

I hesitate, eyeing him warily. "What if I actually hurt you?"

His laugh echoes across the field, loud and

sharp. "Sweetheart, you couldn't hurt me if you tried."

"Oh, I'm trying," I mutter, raising the sword awkwardly.

I run to him, and he sidesteps effortlessly, his movements quick and fluid.

"Not bad," he says, grinning. "For someone who swings like they're holding a broom."

I grit my teeth, adjusting my grip and trying again. This time, he blocks me easily, the wooden swords clacking together with a dull thud.

"Better," he says, his tone almost approving. "But you're still too stiff. Loosen up."

"Loosen up," I repeat, glaring at him. "Easy for you to say, Mr. 'I've Been Doing This Forever.'"

He chuckles, stepping back. "Trust me, you'll get the hang of it. Eventually."

The practice continues for what feels like hours. Kael blocks every swing I make, his smirk never faltering, while I struggle to keep up, my arms aching and my frustration boiling over.

"Come on," he says, dodging another clumsy attempt. "Is that all you've got?"

"I hate you," I snap, panting.

"No, you don't," he says, grinning.

"Yes, I do!" I swing again, putting every ounce of energy I have into it.

This time, he doesn't move fast enough, and the wooden sword connects with his side. It's not a hard hit, but the look of surprise on his face is enough to make me grin.

"Got you," I say, lowering the sword.

Kael chuckles, shaking his head. "Not bad, sweetheart. Not bad at all."

I roll my eyes, but I can't help the faint flicker of pride warming my chest.

As the sun dips lower in the sky, Kael finally calls it.
"Good work today," he says, clapping me on the shoulder. "We'll pick this up tomorrow."

"Tomorrow?" I groan, dropping the sword. "I'm going to be sore for a week."

"You'll live," he says, smirking.

I sit on the edge of a wooden bench near the fence, catching my breath as he leans casually against the post next to me. His hair is a mess of sweat and dirt, and yet he still looks entirely too pleased with himself.

"So," he says after a beat, his tone lighter. "What's your plan, then?"

"My plan?" I ask, frowning up at him.

"Yeah," he says, gesturing vaguely toward the field and the forest beyond. "You're here now. No way back. What are you going to do about it?"

I shrug, picking at a splinter on the edge of the bench. "It's not like I have much of a choice, do I?" "Not really," he admits, his grin widening.

"I mean," I say, sighing, "it's not like I left anything behind. Back home, it's just… nothing. Dead city, dead air, dead everything. I guess staying here isn't much worse."

Kael tilts his head, watching me with an expression that's almost curious. "That why you're not fighting harder to go back? Because there's nothing waiting for you?"

I glance at him, narrowing my eyes. "Don't act like you care."

"Who says I don't?" he asks, his smirk softening.

I scoff, shaking my head. "You're such an ass."

I roll my eyes, standing up and brushing off my hands. "Maybe I should go back just to get away from you."

Kael chuckles, following me as I head toward the edge of the field. "Sorry, sweetheart. You're stuck with me now."

"My biggest dream," I mutter, gripping the wooden sword tightly as another low growl rumbles in the distance.

"Relax," Kael says, though his gaze flicks toward the shadows at the tree line. "It's probably nothing."

"Probably?" I ask, narrowing my eyes. "That's not exactly reassuring."

"You're fine," he says, waving a hand dismissively. "The safe zone keeps most things out."

"Most things?"

He shrugs, his smirk back in place. "Keeps things interesting, doesn't it?"

I glare at him. "You're the worst guide ever."

"Guide?" He laughs, shaking his head. "You think I'm guiding you? I'm barely keeping you from getting yourself killed."

"Great. Good to know I'm in capable hands."

"Very capable," he says, his grin widening.

Before I can respond, another growl echoes through the clearing, this one closer. My grip tightens on the sword, my pulse racing as I take an involuntary step back.

Kael's smirk falters, and he steps in front of me, his posture shifting into something sharper, more defensive.

"Stay behind me," he says, his voice low. "What is it?" I whisper, my heart pounding.
He doesn't answer immediately, his gaze locked on the shadows just beyond the fence. The growl comes again, deeper this time, and the hairs on the back of my neck stand on end.

"Whatever it is," he says finally, "it's not friendly."

The shadows shift, and for a moment, I think I see something move—something big and dark, its form blending into the trees.

Kael curses under his breath, reaching for the real sword strapped to his side. "Get ready."

"For what?" I hiss, clutching the wooden sword like it's going to do anything against whatever's out there.

He doesn't respond, his attention fixed entirely on the figure emerging from the shadows.

When it steps into the clearing, I freeze.

It's massive—easily the size of a horse, with sleek black fur that seems to absorb the light around it. Its amber eyes gleam in the dim light, sharp and intelligent, and its lips curl back to reveal sharp, white teeth.

"A wolf?" I whisper, my voice trembling.

Kael doesn't move. "Not just any wolf."

The creature stalks closer, its movements slow and deliberate, like it's sizing us up. Its gaze locks onto me, and I feel an odd shiver run down my spine—not fear exactly, but something else.

Before Kael can step forward, the wolf lets out a low, rumbling growl that seems to shake the ground beneath us.
And then, impossibly, a voice echoes in my

"You're her."

I stumble back, my eyes widening. "What the fuck?"

Kael looks at me sharply. "What is it?"

"You didn't hear that?" I ask, my voice shaking.

"Hear what?"

The wolf steps closer, its gaze never leaving mine. Its voice is clear in my mind now, low and rough, like the sound of gravel shifting underfoot.

"You're her. The one we've been waiting for."

I don't know what to say. My throat feels tight, and the air around me seems to hum with something I can't name.

Kael raises his sword, his stance defensive. "Elira, stay behind me."

But the wolf doesn't move toward him. It moves toward me.

"Don't be afraid," the voice says, softer now. *"I won't hurt you."*

"I…" My voice falters, and I lower the wooden

sword slightly.

"Don't," Kael snaps, his tone sharp. "Don't trust it."

The wolf stops just a few feet away, its massive frame towering over me. Its eyes seem to bore into mine, and for a moment, everything else fades—the field, the tension, even Kael's warnings.

"You're stronger than you think, Elira," the voice says. *"And you're going to need me."*

Before I can respond, the wolf turns sharply, its ears pricking at some distant sound. It lets out a low growl before disappearing back into the shadows as quickly as it appeared.

The silence that follows is deafening.

"What the hell was that?" Kael demands, turning to me.

"I…" I shake my head, my legs feeling like jelly. "I don't know." But even as I say it, a part of me does know. It wasn't just a wolf. It was something more. And somehow, it knew me.

Shadows and Secrets
Elira

Kael hasn't stopped pacing since we got back to the village.

He moves back and forth across the room like a caged animal, his hands running through his hair every few seconds. The usual smirk is gone, replaced by something sharper, more agitated.

"What the hell was that?" he says, stopping abruptly to glare at me.

"You think I know?" I snap, slumping into the chair by the window. My legs are still shaky, and my head hasn't stopped buzzing since the wolf disappeared.

"You were the one it was talking to," Kael says, crossing his arms. "If anyone knows, it's you."

I groan, pressing the heels of my hands into my eyes. "I told you, I don't know. It just… said things."

Kael narrows his eyes. "What kind of things?"

"Like…" I hesitate, my stomach twisting as I remember the wolf's voice in my mind. "Like it knew me. Like it's been waiting for me."

He exhales sharply, dragging a hand down his face. "That's not good."

"You think?" I glare at him. "If you know something, now would be a good time to share."

Kael opens his mouth to respond, but the door creaks open before he can get a word out. Lyric steps inside, her expression sharp as her golden eyes scan the room.

Lyric looks as poised as ever, her long braid swaying as she moves toward the table. Her gaze lands on me, and for a moment, I feel like I'm under a microscope.

"What's this about a wolf?" she asks, her tone calm but carrying an edge.

"It wasn't just a wolf," Kael says, finally stopping his pacing. "It spoke to her."

Lyric's eyebrows raise, and she turns to me. "Spoke to you?"

"In my head," I say, shrugging helplessly. "I don't know how. It just… did."

Lyric steps closer, studying me intently. "What did it say?"

"That it's been waiting for me," I admit, my voice quieter now. "That I'm strong. I don't know what it meant."

Lyric exchanges a glance with Kael, and frustration bubbles up inside me.

"Enough," I snap, standing. "What the hell is going on? Where am I? What is this place? And why does everyone act like I don't belong here?"

Lyric sighs, motioning for me to sit back down. "You're in the kingdom of Atheran," she says simply. "Atheran," I repeat, sitting slowly. "And?"

She leans against the table, her golden eyes steady on mine. "It's one of the four kingdoms in this realm. Atheran is ruled by King Damien." Her tone hardens at the name. "The others—Rivath, Caloré, and the Wildlands—are technically independent, but they're all under his influence."

"And Damien is the one you're rebelling against?"

Lyric nods. "He's a tyrant. Ruthless, manipulative, and completely without mercy. He's destroyed anyone who's dared to challenge him."

Her words send a chill down my spine, but I push through it. "What does that have to do with me? I don't know this place, or this king, or…" I trail off, running a hand through my hair.

Kael's voice cuts in, quieter now, the usual smugness stripped away. "You don't think you belong here, but you do. Somehow, this place is connected to you—it's your home, or it was, a long time ago." He pauses, his gaze flicking to the window, where the forest looms in shadow. "And that wolf… it's a sign."

"A sign of what?" I ask, my voice barely above a whisper.

"That you're here for a reason," Kael says, turning back to me. "This isn't just about being in the wrong place at the wrong time. You're here to fix something. To stop what's coming before it destroys everything—the past, the present, and whatever's left of your future."

I stare at him, my chest tightening. "Destroy everything? What does that even mean?"

"It means," Lyric says, cutting in as she steps forward, her golden eyes steady, "that this isn't just about King Damien's reign of terror. It's about what happens if he's not stopped. He's not just a tyrant, Elira—he's a gateway to something worse."

Kael nods grimly. "If he keeps his throne, the destruction in this time will affect your timeline, and it'll be the end of everything."

My stomach churns, and I lean back in the chair, shaking my head. "You're saying I'm supposed to… what? Kill him? Save the world? I don't even know how to hold a damn sword. AND what the fuck are you talking about with your timeline?"

"That's why you're here," Lyric says firmly. "To learn. To fight. And to stop this before it's too late." "What does that mean?" I ask, narrowing my
eyes.

Lyric hesitates, her jaw tightening. "Wolves like that were part of the old magic," she says finally. "Magic that hasn't existed in this world for centuries. If it's back…"

"If it's back, what?" I press, my heart pounding. She doesn't answer, and Kael crosses his arms, his brow furrowing. "It means something's changing," he says. "Something big. And it probably has to do with you." The room falls into a tense silence, and I sink back into the chair, my thoughts racing.

"So, what do I do?" I ask finally. "Just wait for something else to find me?"

"You train," Lyric says firmly. "You need to learn how to fight. Whatever that wolf wants from you, it's not going to be easy. You need to be ready."

I swallow hard, nodding slowly.
"First thing tomorrow," Lyric continues, turning toward the door. "Kael will take you back to the field. And Elira?"

I glance up, startled by the intensity in her gaze.
"Don't trust anything," she says quietly. "Not the forest, not the wolf, and definitely not Kael."

Kael snorts, but Lyric ignores him as she leaves the room.

Once we're alone, Kael leans against the table, his expression unreadable.

"You're making waves," he says.
"Yeah, well, I didn't ask to be here," I mutter, my voice lacking its usual bite.

Kael studies me for a moment, then nods toward the cot in the corner. "Get some rest. Tomorrow's going to be a long day."

I don't argue. As the door closes behind him, I stare out the window at the shadowy forest, my thoughts circling back to the wolf's voice.

Exhausted.

Threads of the Past
Elira

I wake up to the sound of birdsong this morning, soft and melodious. It's something I've never experienced before—or at least, not that I can remember. The light gently filters onto my face, and I know it's time to get up.

The village is quieter now, the frenetic energy of yesterday replaced by a subdued focus. People move with purpose, their faces grim, as if the weight of what's coming hangs heavy over them.

Kael is waiting for me by the edge of the square, leaning against the same fence from yesterday's training session. His dark hair is slightly disheveled, and he's chewing on a piece of dried meat, his eyes scanning the horizon like he's searching for trouble.

"Ready for round two?" he asks as I approach, his tone lighter than I feel.

"Do I have a choice?" I mutter, stopping a few feet away.

Kael smirks, tossing the remains of the dried meat into the grass. "Not really. Come on."

We head back to the field in silence, the tension between us simmering just under the surface. The wolf's appearance yesterday is a question neither of us seems eager to answer, and yet it hangs over everything like a storm cloud.

Kael hands me the same wooden sword as before, his expression unreadable. "Let's see if you remember anything from yesterday."

I grip the sword, the rough wood biting into my palms. "You're not exactly inspiring confidence, you know."

"I'm not here to inspire you," he says simply, stepping into his stance.

"Shocking," I mutter, raising the sword awkwardly.

The lesson begins much the same as before— Kael blocking every swing, dodging every clumsy attack, his movements smooth and calculated. But today, there's an edge to his tone, a seriousness that wasn't there yesterday.

"You're still too stiff," he says, stepping aside as I miss another strike. "Your body knows how to move. Stop fighting it."

"My body doesn't know a damn thing," I snap, adjusting my grip.

"Maybe not this one," he mutters under his breath, but it's loud enough to make me pause.

"I don't get it?" I ask, lowering the sword.

Kael sighs, running a hand through his hair. "It means you're more connected to this place than you realize. Your instincts—they're buried under all that noise in your head, but they're there. You just have to trust them."

I stare at him, my chest tightening. "If I'm connected to this place, then why the hell don't I remember any of it?"

"Because it's not about remembering," he says, his tone quieter now. "It's about what's in your blood. You're tied to this world in ways you don't understand yet."

"That's vague and unhelpful," I mutter, raising the sword again.

Kael smirks faintly. "You're catching on."

The practice continues until my arms feel like they're going to fall off. By the time Kael finally calls

it, my hands are blistered, and my shirt is soaked with sweat.

"Not bad," he says, leaning casually against the fence. "You're improving."

"I hit you once," I say, glaring at him.

"It's a start," he says with a shrug.

I groan, dropping the sword and slumping onto the bench. "If I don't die saving the world, I'm definitely going to die from this."

Kael chuckles but doesn't respond. Instead, his gaze shifts to the forest, his expression darkening.

"What?" I ask, sitting up straighter.

He shakes his head. "Nothing. Just… this place. It's restless."

"Restless how?"

Kael doesn't answer immediately, his eyes scanning the treetops. "The wolf. The magic it's tied to. It's waking things up. Things that have been sleeping for a long time."

A chill runs down my spine. "Like what?"

"Like the past," he says, his voice quiet. "And the things we've spent centuries trying to bury."

The walk back to the village is silent, the weight of Kael's words pressing heavily on my chest. The forest seems darker now, the shadows deeper, and every snap of a twig makes my pulse race.

When we reach the square, Lyric is waiting for us. She stands near the center, her golden eyes scanning the village like a hawk surveying its territory.

"How did she do?" she asks as we approach.

"She's getting there," Kael says, his tone neutral.

Lyric looks at me, her gaze steady. "Good. We don't have much time."

"For what?" I ask, crossing my arms.

"To prepare you," she says simply. "The magic in this world is shifting, Elira. The wolf wasn't just a coincidence. It's a warning. Things are moving faster than we anticipated."

I swallow hard, my throat dry. "And what happens if we're not ready?"

Lyric's jaw tightens. "Then we lose everything. Past, present, and future." Lyric gestures for me to follow her, her long braid swinging behind her as she moves toward the far end of the square.

I glance at Kael, who's already wandering off in the opposite direction, before jogging to catch up with her.

The village is alive with quiet activity. People carry bundles of firewood or baskets of herbs, their heads down and their expressions focused. A group of children plays near the edge of a weathered fountain, their laughter soft but bright in the otherwise somber atmosphere.

Lyric pauses as we pass the children, crouching slightly to greet a little girl clutching a stuffed toy that looks like it's seen better days. "Take care of that, Nella," Lyric says with a warm smile.

The girl nods solemnly, clutching the toy tighter before breaking into a shy grin.

I watch, caught off guard by the softness in Lyric's demeanor. For someone who radiates strength and command, she carries a surprising gentleness when she's with the villagers.

"You're good with them," I say as we start walking again.

"They deserve something to believe in," Lyric replies, her golden eyes scanning the narrow streets. "Even if it's just a moment of kindness."

As we move through the village, people greet Lyric with quiet nods and murmured words of respect. She returns their gestures with a calm authority that feels as natural as breathing. I catch a few curious glances thrown my way, but no one says anything.

"Do they all know who I am?" I ask, lowering my voice.

"They know enough," Lyric says. "That you're different. That you're important. Beyond that, it doesn't matter."

"Different how?" I press. "Because of my hair and eyes? Kael mentioned something about that."

Lyric sighs, her pace slowing as we turn down a quieter path. "There are old beliefs, Elira. Stories about people with hair as dark as the night and eyes as bright as the sky. They were seen as… chosen. Marked by the gods."

"That sounds dramatic," I say, frowning.

"It was," Lyric replies with a faint smirk. "But dramatic or not, those beliefs shaped this world for centuries. People with your features were rare, revered—and feared. Some saw them as saviors, others as harbingers of destruction."

"Great," I mutter, crossing my arms. "So, which one am I supposed to be?"

Lyric stops, turning to face me. "That's for you to decide."

Her words sit heavy in my chest as we resume walking, the quiet hum of the village filling the silence between us.

We pass a small chapel, its stone walls covered in moss and its arched windows dark with age. Lyric pauses, resting a hand on the worn wooden door.

"This is one of the few places left where the old faith still lingers," she says quietly. "The belief in the gods, the prophecies—they've faded over time. But for some, it's still very real."

I glance at the chapel, its presence looming like a ghost of the past. "And you? Do you believe in any of it?"

Lyric doesn't answer right away. "I believe there's truth in every story. Even if it's buried beneath centuries of fear and superstition."

I nod slowly, the weight of her words settling over me. "Kael mentioned that I'm connected to this place. That it's in my blood. What does that mean?"

Lyric's expression hardens slightly. "It means you're part of something bigger, something older. But even I don't fully understand it."

"Then how did Kael know to find me?" I ask, my voice sharper now. "How did he get to my world?"

"That," Lyric says, her tone firm, "is a question I've been asking myself since he returned. Portals like the one he used aren't supposed to exist anymore. The magic needed to create them was lost generations ago."

"Then how did he do it?"

Lyric shakes her head. "I don't know. But he's not the type to stumble into something like that by accident."

Her words send a shiver down my spine. "So, you needed me because of some prophecy about people who look like me?"

"Not just the prophecy," Lyric says, her voice softening. "We needed you because you're the only one who can bridge the gap. You're tied to this world and your own, Elira. If anyone can stop what's coming, it's you."

We stop at the edge of the village, the forest stretching out in front of us like an endless maze. Lyric crosses her arms, her gaze distant.

"This place holds so many answers," she says. "But it also holds dangers you can't begin to understand."

I swallow hard, my throat dry. "And the wolf? What's its connection to all of this?"

Lyric's jaw tightens. "The wolf is part of the old magic. It's bound to you somehow, just as you're bound to this world. But why it's returned now... I don't know."

Her words hang in the air, heavy with implication.
"Whatever it wants," she continues, her golden eyes locking onto mine, "it's tied to your purpose here. And if you fail, it won't just be this world that falls."

The chill in her voice sends a shiver through me, and I turn my gaze back to the forest.
For the first time, the weight of what I've been pulled into truly sinks in.

Echoes of Destiny
Elira

The days feels longer than it should, the weight of Lyric's words pressing on me like a storm waiting to break. I keep catching glances from the villagers as I walk back through the square, their eyes flicking to my hair, my face, and then quickly away, like they're afraid to linger too long.

By the time I reach the small stone building where they've let me stay, my thoughts are a tangled mess. The idea of being tied to this world—of being responsible for saving it—feels impossible.

But the wolf's voice, low and certain, echoes in my mind: "You're her. The one we've been waiting for."

I slump onto the cot, staring at the ceiling, trying to make sense of the pieces Lyric gave me.

The old faith. The gods. The prophecies. And Kael—how did he even find me? How does someone just… jump between worlds, between time?

My restless thoughts are interrupted by a soft knock at the door. Before I can answer, the door creaks open, and Kael steps inside, his usual smirk faint but present.

"Settling in?" he asks, leaning against the wall. I glare at him. "If by settling in, you mean
spiraling into existential dread, then yeah. I'm doing great."

Kael chuckles, folding his arms. "You're handling it better than most would."

"Tell me more, Kael." I ask, my voice sharper than I intended. "Not the vague 'save the world' bullshit. I want the truth."

His smirk fades, and for the first time, I see something like hesitation in his expression.
"You're here," he says slowly, "because we needed you. Lyric told you about the prophecy, right?"
"Yeah, chosen by the gods, blah blah blah," I say, waving a hand. "But that doesn't explain how you found me. Or why me, specifically."

Kael exhales, running a hand through his hair. "You're not the first person with those features, Elira. The prophecy's been around for centuries, but it's always been more myth than reality. Until you."
"Okay," I say, sitting up straighter. "So, how did you find me? You don't just trip and fall into a portal."

"You're right," he admits, his tone darker now. "It took years of searching. The magic needed to create that portal—it's old, forbidden. Dangerous."

My chest tightens. "But why my world? Why now?"

Kael steps closer, his eyes locking onto mine. "Because your world is tied to this one, more than you realize. What happens here ripples there. If we don't stop Damien, the destruction you know in your future becomes permanent. Both worlds fall."

I swallow hard, his words settling over me like a lead weight. "So, no pressure."

Kael smirks faintly. "None at all."

The conversation is interrupted by another knock at the door, this one brisk and impatient. Lyric steps in without waiting for an answer, her gaze flicking between the two of us.

"We've got a problem," she says, her tone clipped.

"What kind of problem?" Kael asks, his smirk fading.

"Scouts spotted movement near the outer edge of the forest," Lyric says. "Too organized to be animals. Too erratic to be anything friendly."

Kael straightens, his posture immediately shifting into something more defensive. "Damien's soldiers?"

"Possibly," Lyric says, crossing her arms. "Or worse."

"Worse?" I echo, my stomach dropping.

Lyric's gaze lands on me, her expression unreadable. "There are things in this world that don't align with any kingdom. Creatures that don't answer to anyone but themselves. If they've been stirred up by the magic returning, they'll come looking for its source."

"Me," I say quietly. Lyric nods. "You."

The three of us step into the square, the sun already sinking low on the horizon. The tension is palpable, the usual hum of the village activity replaced by quiet murmurs and the occasional clatter of weapons being prepared.

Kael and Lyric exchange a few quick words with one of the guards, and then Lyric turns to me. "We're going to the perimeter," she says firmly. "You need to see what's out there."

I hesitate, my heart pounding. "What if it's dangerous?"

"It is," Lyric says bluntly. "But if you're going to survive this, you need to understand what you're up against."

Kael claps a hand on my shoulder, his smirk faint but reassuring. "Don't worry, sweetheart. I won't let anything eat you."

I glare at him.

The walk to the perimeter is tense, the forest growing darker with every step. The air feels heavier here, charged with something I can't name.

When we reach the edge, the guard stationed there nods grimly. "It was here," he says, pointing to the faint indentations in the dirt.
I crouch down, studying the tracks. They're large, too large to be human, and clawed.

"What the hell made these?" I ask, standing quickly.

"We don't know," Lyric says, her tone tight. "But whatever it was, it wasn't hiding its presence. It wants us to know it's here."

Kael scans the treeline, his hand resting on the hilt of his sword. "This isn't just random movement. It's testing us."

"Testing us for what?" I ask, my voice barely above a whisper.

Kael doesn't answer, but his grip on his sword tightens.

Lyric's golden eyes flick to me, her voice low but steady. "Stay sharp, Elira. Whatever's coming, it's only the beginning." My fingers curl around the hilt of the wooden practice sword still strapped to my side. It feels inadequate—like a toy against whatever left those tracks.

"What happens if it comes back?" I ask, breaking the heavy silence.

Lyric glances at me, her golden eyes sharp. "We deal with it."

"That's not exactly a good plan," I mutter, but my voice lacks its usual bite.

Kael smirks faintly. "You'll get used to it. Or not. Either way, you're here."

I shoot him a glare, but Lyric interrupts before I can respond. "This isn't the time for bickering. If whatever this is decides to attack, we need to be ready."

Kael nods, his expression unusually serious. "We should send out a small team to track it. Find out where it's coming from and whether it's working alone."

Lyric's jaw tightens. "Agreed. But not tonight. It's too risky in the dark."

"What if it doesn't wait?" I ask, my voice
quieter now.

Lyric looks at me, and for the first time, I see a flicker of uncertainty in her usually composed demeanor. "Then we fight."

We linger at the edge of the forest as the sun dips lower, casting long shadows that stretch across the village. The guard swaps shifts, another rebel taking his place, and the tension feels like it could snap at any moment.

Kael leans against a tree, his arms crossed, while Lyric moves to the side, speaking quietly with the newly arrived guard. I stay where I am, staring at the tracks in the dirt, my thoughts a chaotic mess.
"Do you believe her?" I ask suddenly, glancing
at Kael.

He raises an eyebrow. "About what?"

"All of this," I say, gesturing vaguely to the forest and the tracks. "The wolf, the magic, the prophecy. Do you believe it?"

Kael's smirk fades, and for a moment, he looks almost… tired. "Does it matter if I believe it?"
"It matters to me," I say, my voice sharper than I intended.

He studies me for a long moment before answering. "I believe there's probably some truth to the story. But I also believe that truth is twisted by the people who tell it. So, yeah, I believe in the prophecy. But I don't think it's as simple as everyone wants it to be."

I frown, his words settling uneasily in my chest. "Explain."

Kael shrugs, but there's something guarded in his expression. "Prophecies are like mirrors, sweetheart. They show you what you want to see. But they don't tell you the whole story."

Before I can press him further, a sound breaks through the quiet—a low, guttural growl that seems to come from everywhere at once.

My heart leaps into my throat, and I instinctively step closer to Kael, my hand tightening on the hilt of the wooden sword.

Lyric turns sharply, her golden eyes scanning the treeline. "It's back."

The guard raises his spear, his knuckles white. "I don't see it."

Kael moves in front of me, his sword already drawn. The blade gleams faintly in the dim light, and his posture shifts into something predatory, almost feral. "Stay close," he mutters, his voice low.

The growl comes again, louder this time, and the trees at the edge of the forest rustle violently. A figure emerges slowly from the shadows—not the wolf from before, but something darker, taller.

Its shape is vaguely humanoid, but its limbs are too long, its movements too jerky, like a puppet on broken strings. Its eyes glow faintly, and its mouth is filled with jagged, uneven teeth.

"What the hell is that?" I whisper, my voice trembling. Lyric steps forward, her stance rigid. "Something old. Something that shouldn't be awake."

The creature lets out a high-pitched screech, and before I can blink, it lunges.

Everything happens too fast.

The guard thrusts his spear, but the creature dodges, its movements unnervingly quick. Kael moves like lightning, his blade slicing through the air as he intercepts the attack, forcing the creature back.

"Get behind me!" Lyric snaps, shoving me toward the tree line.

"I can fight!" I protest, raising the wooden sword.

"Not against that!" she snaps, her voice cutting through my panic.

Kael and the creature clash again, his sword ringing as it meets the creature's claws. Sparks fly, and the force of the impact sends Kael stumbling back.

Lyric moves in, her strikes precise and deadly, but the creature seems to anticipate her every move.

I grip the wooden sword tightly, my heart pounding as I watch the chaos unfold. Every instinct screams at me to run, but something deeper—something primal—roots me to the spot.

The creature lets out another screech, its glowing eyes locking onto me. For a split second, the world seems to freeze, and I hear a voice in my mind, low and raspy: "You cannot save them."

The words snap me back to reality, and I step forward without thinking, raising the wooden sword. "Elira, no!" Kael shouts, but it's too late.

The creature lunges toward me, its claws outstretched, and I swing the sword with every ounce of strength I have. The impact sends a shockwave up my arms, and the creature lets out a strangled cry, stumbling back.

Kael and Lyric seize the moment, their blades striking in unison. The creature collapses with a final, ear-piercing screech, its body crumpling into the dirt.

Silence falls, broken only by the sound of my ragged breathing.

Kael lowers his sword, his gaze snapping to me. "What the hell were you thinking?"

"I—" My voice falters as I look down at the wooden sword in my hands. The edges are splintered, but the weight of it feels different now, like it's become a part of me.

Lyric steps closer, her golden eyes narrowing. "You felt it, didn't you? The magic."

I nod slowly, my chest tightening. "It… it spoke to me."

Shadows of Deception
Elira

I step out of the stone house to find Kael waiting for me, leaning against the doorframe with his usual casual smirk. He's already dressed for another round of training, his sword strapped to his hip.

"Ready for more punishment?" he asks, his voice light.

I shrug, brushing past him. "You're too confident for your own good."

"Maybe," he says, falling into step beside me. "But it's part of my charm."

As we make our way toward the training field, I catch glimpses of villagers preparing for another day.

Women carry baskets of herbs and food, their hands weathered but strong. A group of children runs by, their laughter echoing faintly in the distance.

"Do you ever stop to help?" I ask Kael, nodding toward the bustling activity around us.

He grins, unfazed. "I help by staying out of their way. Trust me, they like it better that way."

"Convenient," I mutter, shaking my head.

We reach the field, and Kael wastes no time handing me the familiar wooden sword. My arms ache at the mere thought of swinging it again, but I grip it tightly, determined not to give him the satisfaction of complaining.

The training is relentless.

Kael doesn't go easy on me, forcing me to repeat the same moves over and over until my muscles burn and my grip slips from the sweat coating my hands.

Again," he says, his tone sharper now.

"I'm trying," I snap, raising the sword for what feels like the hundredth time.

"Trying isn't good enough," he says, blocking my swing effortlessly. "You think Damien's soldiers will let you off because you're trying?"

The mention of Damien sends a chill through me, and I grit my teeth, putting more force into the next swing. Kael blocks it again, but this time he nods faintly.

"Better," he says, stepping back.

I lower the sword, panting. "You're exhausting."

"And you're improving," he replies, his smirk returning. "I'd call that progress."

We're interrupted by the sound of Lyric's voice calling from the edge of the field.

Kael turns, his expression hardening slightly. "What now?"

Lyric strides toward us, her golden eyes sharp and focused. Even in her plain rebel attire, she looks commanding, her every step purposeful.

"We need to talk," she says, glancing at me briefly before focusing on Kael.

"What's wrong?" I ask, catching the tension in her voice.

Lyric hesitates, then shakes her head. "It's not for you to worry about. Yet."

"Great," I mutter, crossing my arms. "More secrets."

Kael follows Lyric a few steps away, their voices too low for me to catch. They exchange quick, clipped words, and though Kael tries to keep his usual nonchalance, there's something different about him—something sharper.

When they return, Lyric's gaze lands on me. "Elira, there's something you should know. We've had reports of increased patrols near the borders. Damien's forces are searching for something—or someone."

I feel my stomach drop. "You think it's me?"

"It's likely," Lyric says. "But we're taking precautions. Kael will take you to one of the safehouses deeper in the forest tomorrow."

"Wait, what?" I ask, my heart pounding. "Why can't I stay here?"

"Because it's too dangerous," she says firmly. "You're too valuable to risk."

The weight of her words settles over me like a lead blanket, and I glance at Kael, who's watching me with an expression I can't quite read.

"Fine," I say finally, my voice tight. "But I want answers. Real ones. No more vague prophecies and cryptic warnings."
Lyric nods slowly. "You'll have them. In time."

As the day stretches into evening, I find myself wandering back toward the forest edge, the wooden sword still in my hand. The faint hum of the magic in this place is stronger here, like a heartbeat beneath the ground.

I pause, staring into the shadows, half-expecting the wolf to emerge again.

But the forest remains still, its secrets locked away.

Kael's voice pulls me from my thoughts. "You shouldn't wander off alone."

I turn to find him leaning against a tree, his arms crossed. "I wasn't wandering. I was thinking." "Dangerous habit," he says with a faint smirk.

I roll my eyes, but his words linger, a reminder of just how precarious my situation is.

As we walk back to the village together, Kael falls unusually quiet. His gaze flicks toward the forest more than once, and there's a tension in his posture that wasn't there before.

"What's really going on?" I ask finally, my voice low.

He doesn't answer right away, his jaw tightening. "Nothing you need to worry about. Just stick close to me tomorrow. I'll handle it."

I narrow my eyes at him, but before I can press further, we reach the village square, and the moment slips away.

The night feels colder as I step into my small room, the wolf's voice echoing faintly in my mind once again: "You're her. The one we've been waiting for." Whatever's coming, it's closer than ever.

Into the Unknown
Elira

Kael leads the way. He doesn't talk much, but every now and then, his gaze flicks over his shoulder, checking to make sure I'm keeping up.

"You always this cheerful when you're dragging someone through the middle of nowhere?" I ask, trying to keep the edge out of my voice.

Kael smirks faintly but doesn't answer, his attention focused ahead.

The silence stretches, heavy and tense. My thoughts wander back to the village, to Lyric's stern gaze as she explained why I had to leave. "It's not just about you, Elira. If they come for you, they'll destroy everything we've built."

I get it. I do. But that doesn't mean I have to like it.

"Are we close?" I ask finally, my voice sharper than I intended.

"Not yet," Kael replies without looking back.

We reach a narrow stream, and Kael pauses to fill a small flask from the clear, rushing water. He hands it to me without a word, his expression unusually serious.

"Thanks," I say, taking a long drink.

"I've got one question for you."

"Of course you do." He grunts.

"Why are you really doing this for the rebels? Taking me to some random safehouse? What's in it for you?"

Kael tilts his head, his expression unreadable.

"What makes you think I need a reason?"

"Because everyone needs a reason," I say, crossing my arms. "And you don't strike me as the selfless type."

He chuckles softly, pushing off the tree. "Maybe I just enjoy your company."

"Yeah, right," I mutter, shaking my head.

The safehouse finally comes into view just as the sky starts to darken. It's smaller than I expected—a squat stone building tucked into a clearing, the edges overgrown with moss. Kael pushes the door open, and I follow him inside, my unease growing with every step.

The interior is cramped but warm, a small fire already burning in the hearth. A cot sits in one corner, and a table in the center holds an assortment of supplies—bandages, dried meat, a jug of water.

Kael drops his pack onto the table and pulls out a blade, setting it down with a faint clink. "Welcome to your new home."

I glance around, my arms crossing over my chest. "This is it?"

"What were you expecting? A manor?"
"No, but maybe a second cot would've been nice," I say, nodding toward the single bed.

Kael smirks, leaning against the table. "Don't worry, princess. I'll take the floor."
"Gee, thanks," I mutter, dropping onto the cot.

As night falls, the tension doesn't ease. Every creak of the building, every faint rustle outside sends my nerves into overdrive.

Kael sits by the fire, sharpening his sword with slow, deliberate movements. The sound of metal scraping against stone fills the room, steady and rhythmic.

"Do you think they'll come for me?" I ask quietly.

Kael glances up, his expression unreadable. "Who?"

"Whoever's out there," I say, gesturing vaguely toward the window. "Damien's soldiers, the monsters, whoever."

"They might," he says simply.

"And you're okay with that?"

He shrugs, the firelight catching on the edge of his blade. "If they do, we'll deal with it."

"Yeah, because I need a big strong man," I mutter, leaning back against the wall.

Kael watches me for a moment, his gaze sharp. "You'll be fine, Elira. You're tougher than you think."

"Is that supposed to be a compliment?" I ask, raising an eyebrow.

"Take it however you want," he says, smirking faintly.

I roll my eyes, but his words linger, settling uneasily in my chest. The fire crackles softly, the only sound breaking the silence.

Kael's blade catches the light as he continues polishing it it, his focus unnervingly intense.

"You're awfully quiet now," I say, trying to mask my nerves. "Usually, you can't shut up."

Kael doesn't look up. "Some situations call for silence."

"Like what?"

He sets the blade down, finally meeting my gaze. "Like when you're being hunted."

My stomach twists, and I sit up straighter. "What do you mean, 'hunted'?"

Kael leans back in his chair, his expression unreadable. "You think Damien's just going to let you wander around? If he knows you're here, he'll send someone—or something—to find you."

I swallow hard, his words sinking in. "And you're just telling me this?"

"You already knew," he says, shrugging. "I just thought I'd remind you."

"Yeah, you are a thoughtful one" I mutter, pulling my knees to my chest. "That's exactly what I needed to hear."

The tension in the room grows heavier, the fire casting flickering shadows across the walls. I glance toward the window, half-expecting to see something lurking just beyond the glass.

Kael notices and smirks faintly. "Don't worry. If anything comes, you'll have plenty of warning."

"How do you know?"

He tilts his head, his eyes glinting in the firelight. "Because they're not subtle. You'll hear them long before you see them."

"That's sound stupid," I say, though my voice lacks its usual bite.

Kael's smirk fades slightly, and for a moment, his expression softens. "You'll be fine, Elira. I wouldn't have brought you here if I didn't think you could handle it." The rare sincerity in his voice catches me off guard, and I look away, unsure how to respond.

I settle back against the cot, staring at the ceiling as my thoughts race. The danger feels closer now, more real, but so does the uncertainty surrounding Kael. His words, his actions—they don't add up, and the nagging suspicion in the back of my mind refuses to quiet.

"What's your deal, Kael?" I ask suddenly, breaking the silence.

He raises an eyebrow. "My deal?"

"Yeah. You act like you don't care about anything, but you're always there when things go south. Why?"

Kael chuckles softly, shaking his head. "You really want to know?"

I nod, holding his gaze.

"Let's just say I have my reasons," he says, smirking again.

"That's not an answer," I snap, my frustration

bubbling to the surface.

"It's the only one you're getting tonight," he replies, standing and stretching. "Get some rest, sweetheart. Tomorrow's going to be fun."

"Your idea of fun sucks," I mutter, but he's already heading toward the door to check the perimeter.

As the door clicks shut behind him, I let out a shaky breath, the weight of the day pressing down on me.

Whatever Kael's reasons are, one thing is clear: I can't trust him. Not completely.

And in this world, that might be the most dangerous thing of all.

Secrets in the Dark
Elira

The fire crackles gently, its flickering light dancing across the room. I've been fixated on it for what seems like an eternity, my thoughts circling in an endless loop. Kael's silence since our last conversation leaves me wondering if it's a blessing or a warning.

The stillness is broken by a distant howl, low and drawn out, sending a shiver through me.

Kael tenses immediately, his hand dropping to the hilt of his sword. "Stay here," he says sharply, rising from his chair.

I'm on my feet before I realize it. "What is it?"

"Stay. Here." His voice leaves no room for argument, and before I can press him, he's out the door.

The silence that follows is suffocating.

I inch toward the door, gripping a dagger on the little table tightly, every instinct screaming at me to follow him. But I hesitate, the memory of his sharp tone holding me back.

The minutes stretch on, the fire popping softly behind me. Then, just as I start to convince myself that nothing's wrong, I hear it—a muffled thud, followed by the unmistakable sound of metal on flesh.

I rush to the door, throwing it open without thinking.

The forest is alive with movement, shadows darting between the trees. Kael is a blur of motion, his sword flashing in the dim light as he fends off something large and fast.

It's not human—I know that much immediately. Its hulking form is covered in thick, matted fur, and its glowing yellow eyes lock onto me the second I step outside.

"Elira, get back inside!" Kael shouts, his voice sharp and panicked.

But the creature doesn't give me a chance to move. It lunges, its claws slashing through the air, and I barely manage to duck in time.

The world narrows to the sounds of my ragged breathing and Kael's shouted orders as he fights to draw the creature's attention away from me. My hands tighten on the blade, its cold weight the only thing grounding me.

I don't think—I just move. Swinging the poker with all the force I can muster, I aim for the creature's side. The impact sends a shockwave up my arms, and the creature lets out a guttural snarl, stumbling slightly.

Kael seizes the opening, his blade slicing cleanly through its neck. The creature collapses with a thud, its body crumpling into the dirt.

For a moment, neither of us moves. My chest heaves, my hands trembling as I stare at the motionless form in front of me.

"What the hell was that?" I whisper, my voice barely audible.

Kael doesn't answer right away. He wipes his blade clean on the creature's fur, his expression grim. "A reminder," he says finally, his tone clipped.

"A reminder of what?"

"That this place doesn't forgive mistakes," he says, turning to face me. "You could've been killed."
I glare at him, my fear giving way to anger. "I couldn't just stand there and do nothing!"

"You should've," he snaps, his voice harsh. "Next time, you might not be so lucky."

The tension between us weighs heavily as we haul the creature's body further into the woods, every step echoing with unspoken words.

Back inside, Kael leans his sword against the table, his movements slower than before. "Get some sleep," he says, not looking at me.

"Are you serious?" I ask, incredulous. "After all that, you expect me to just lie down and relax?"
He finally meets my gaze, his brown eyes darker than usual. "You'll need your strength. That thing wasn't alone."

His words send a chill through me, and for once, I have nothing to say.

The Breaking Point
Elira

The fire burns low, barely more than embers now, and I hate it. I hate the quiet hum of the flames, the suffocating stillness of this damned cabin, and the endless waiting for the next monster to claw its way out of the dark.

We've been stuck here too long, with no plan, no movement, no signs of anyone—just me and Kael, circling the same four walls like caged animals.

The walls feel smaller every day, closing in, smothering me with every wasted hour. My anger simmers beneath the surface, threatening to boil over with every scrape of Kael's blade on the whetstone.

Outside, the forest feels unnervingly still. The usual rustling of leaves and distant howls have fallen silent, leaving only an oppressive quiet that presses against the walls.

"Something's wrong," I say, breaking the silence.

Kael glances up, his expression unreadable. "What makes you say that?"

"Because it's too quiet," I reply, sitting up on the cot. "Even I can tell that's not normal."
He sets the blade down, his eyes narrowing slightly. "I'll go check it out."

Before I can argue, Kael grabs his sword and heads for the door. He moves quickly, his posture tense, and the heavy wooden door creaks as it swings shut behind him.

The silence presses down, thick and suffocating, as if the air itself has stopped breathing. My heart races as my eyes lock on the door, my fingers tightening around the iron poker still resting against the hearth.

Then, a low growl rumbles through the air, deep and guttural, vibrating through the walls.

I'm on my feet in an instant, the dagger clutched in my hands. My body moves toward the door, drawn by a mix of fear and adrenaline.

The growl comes again, louder this time, and it's followed by the unmistakable sound of Kael shouting.

I push the door open, stepping into the cold night air. The forest is darker than ever, the shadows thick and impenetrable. Kael is a blur of motion in the clearing, his sword flashing as he fends off something massive.

It's not alone.

Another creature, smaller but just as fast, darts toward Kael from the side. He barely blocks its attack in time, his movements quick and precise, but he's outnumbered.

"Elira, not the moment!" he shouts, his voice sharp.

But before I can move, a third creature emerges from the treeline, its glowing eyes locking onto me.

My blood runs cold as it charges, its claws slashing through the air. I swing the poker blindly, the impact jarring up my arms as it strikes the creature's shoulder. It stumbles, snarling, but before it can recover, a black blur slams into it from the side.

The creature crashes to the ground, and I stumble back, my eyes widening as the wolf steps into the light of the clearing.

It's massive, its sleek black fur shimmering faintly under the moonlight. Its golden eyes meet mine for a brief moment before it turns back to the creature, its growl low and dangerous.

The fight that follows is a blur. The wolf moves with terrifying speed, tearing through the creatures with a ferocity that leaves me frozen in place. Kael fights alongside it, his sword slicing cleanly through one of the smaller creatures as the wolf takes down the larger one.

Within minutes, the clearing falls silent once more.

Kael lowers his sword, his chest heaving as he glances at the wolf. "Friend of yours?" he asks, his tone dripping with sarcasm despite the situation.

I can't answer, my gaze locked on the wolf as it approaches me. Its golden eyes seem to pierce through me, and for a moment, the world feels impossibly still.

"*You're her*," the voice echoes in my mind, deep and resonant. "*The one we've been waiting for.*"

I stagger back, my breath catching in my throat. "Did… did you just…?"

The wolf doesn't respond aloud, but the faint hum of its presence lingers in my mind, like a tether I can't ignore.

Kael raises an eyebrow, glancing between us. "You've got some explaining to do."

"Me?" I snap, finally finding my voice.
"You're the one who dragged me into this mess!"

The wolf lets out a low rumble, and I feel a strange sense of reassurance, like it's telling me to calm down.

Kael sighs, wiping his blade clean on his sleeve. "We need to move. Now."

"What?" I ask, still reeling.

"This place isn't safe anymore," he says, gesturing to the fallen creatures. "If these things found us, more will follow."
I glance at the wolf, its golden eyes steady and unflinching. "Are you… coming with us?"

It doesn't answer, but it steps closer to me, its massive form towering over my own.

"I'll take that as a yes," I mutter, gripping the poker tightly.

Kael shakes his head, already heading back inside to gather his things. "This just keeps getting better."

As I follow him, the wolf close at my side. Inside the safehouse, the tension feels like it could snap.

Kael run quickly, tossing supplies into a bag with a precision that borders on frantic. The fire in the hearth sputters low, its light barely reaching the corners of the room.
"We're heading to Lyric," Kael says abruptly, breaking the heavy silence.

The mention of Lyric sparks a flicker of relief, but it's buried beneath a mountain of questions and the lingering fear from the attack.

Kael moves like a man with a mission, slinging his pack over his shoulder and grabbing his sword with practiced ease.

"You want to tell me what's going on?" I ask, my voice sharper than I intended.

Kael doesn't look up. "What's going on is we need to leave. Now."

"Yeah, I got that part," I snap. "But where? And what are these things after me?"

Kael turns, his eyes narrowing slightly. "Do you really want me to explain, or do you want to survive long enough to ask Lyric yourself?"

The beast lets out a low rumble from where he stands near the door, his massive form casting long shadows across the walls. His ember eyes meet mine, and the faint hum of his presence brushes against my mind again.

"Go," the voice murmurs softly, steady and unyielding. *"We cannot stay."*

The wolf's calm certainty does more to steady my nerves than anything Kael has said, and I grab my pack without further argument.

Kael nods curtly and heads for the door, his sword glinting faintly in the firelight.

"Where exactly is she?" I ask, following him outside into the cold night air.

"A day's walk," he says over his shoulder. "If we're lucky."

"And if we're not?"

Kael smirks faintly, though it doesn't reach his eyes. "Then we'll find out what else is hunting you."

The Rebel's Heart
Damien

The throne room smells of fear and desperation. My advisors have been arguing for what feels like hours, their voices grating against my already- thin patience.

"Move the troops west—"

"No, the east flank is vulnerable—" "We can't afford to delay!"

I lean forward slightly, resting my chin on my hand as I study them. "Gentlemen," I say, my tone mild but laced with steel, "if I wanted to listen to incompetent squabbling, I'd attend one of the village fairs."

They freeze, their mouths snapping shut like children caught misbehaving.

"Now," I continue, my gaze sweeping the room, "someone tell me something useful before I start decorating the walls with your entrails."

One of the braver fools clears his throat. "My lord, the rebellion—"

"—is a thorn in my side," I interrupt sharply, standing from the throne. The sound of my boots hitting the stone floor echoes through the chamber, and I let the silence hang for a beat. "Thorns don't concern me. You do. Every minute you waste flapping your jaws, the rebellion spreads."

The man wilts under my glare, but another steps forward, his voice trembling. "There is… another matter. A potential asset."

My brow arches, the flicker of interest enough to make him fidget. "Go on."

"There's been word from our contact," he says cautiously. "He claims to have found… her."

The weight of his words sinks in, and the room feels colder.

"Her," I echo softly, the single word sharp enough to draw blood. "The girl with the black hair and blue eyes?"

"Yes, my lord," he confirms. "He believes she may be the one the prophecy speaks of. He intends to bring her to you."
My jaw tightens, and I step closer, towering over the man. "And you trust him?"

The advisor swallows hard. "He has proven useful in the past. His loyalty is… negotiable, but his results speak for themselves."

I glance toward the window, my reflection faintly visible in the glass. The scars along my cheek itch, a reminder of promises made and broken.

"So," I say, my voice laced with venom, "our dear snitch thinks he's found the key to all this chaos. How convenient."

"Shall I send the hunters to ensure his success?" the advisor asks nervously.

"No," I snap, turning sharply. "He wants her for the coin. Let him think he's in control. But if he tries to play me…" My lips curl into a cold smile. "Remind him who holds the leash."

The advisor bows deeply, retreating without another word.
Alone in the room, I pace the cold stone floor, my thoughts churning.

The girl. If she's real, she's more than a threat. She's an opportunity—a weapon. But only if I can control her.

The informant greed might bring her here, but the question remains: what will I do with her when she arrives? Destroy her? Break her? Or something far worse?

My gaze drifts back to the window, the moonlight illuminating the land that stretches beyond.

"Come to me, girl," I murmur, the words low and dangerous. "Let's see if you can survive the fire."

I cross the room to the alcove that houses the iron door—a relic of the kingdom's older days, etched with runes that twist and shimmer faintly in the dim light.

The door groans as I push it open, revealing a narrow staircase spiraling downward into the dark. The air grows heavier with every step I take, the weight of something unseen pressing against my chest.

The chamber is exactly as I left it: the stone walls damp with condensation, the faint smell of iron lingering like a ghost. In the center stands the mirror—a towering, obsidian pane framed by jagged silver, its surface shifting like black water.

It waits for me.

I stare at it for a long moment, the scars along my cheek burning faintly, as they always do when I'm near it. My fingers twitch at my sides. I should leave. I should walk away. But I never do.

"Speak," I say finally, my voice sharp. "I know you're watching."

The surface of the mirror ripples, and a voice slithers into my mind, low and resonant.

"You're impatient tonight, Damien."

"Spare me the games," I snap, pacing the room. "You already know what I'm going to ask."

"And you ask anyway. Do you enjoy pretending you have a choice?"

I grind my teeth, the ache in my jaw familiar. "The girl. Is it her? Or is it another innocent victim?"

The voice hums, a sound that vibrates through the chamber like distant thunder. *"She is everything. And nothing. A blade or a wound. A salvation or a curse. That depends entirely on you."*

"Fucking with words, like always," I mutter, turning to face the mirror fully. "Why her? What makes her different from all the others?"

The voice laughs, a sound that sends a chill down my spine. "*You already know the answer, boy. She has what you do not. Freedom. Power unclaimed. The choice to burn the world—or save it.*"

I take a step closer to the mirror, not like this evil entity needed it. It always spoke to me, day and night. In my fucked-up mind.

My fists clenching at my sides. "And what choice do I have?"

"*None,*" the voice says smoothly, the word slicing through the air like a blade. "*You belong to me, Damien. Your scars, your pain, your throne—they are all mine.*"

My reflection flickers, and for a brief moment, I see something else staring back at me: a shadowy figure.

"*But her…*" the voice continues, its tone almost reverent. *"She could set you free. Or destroy you, or me."*

I laugh bitterly, the sound echoing through the chamber. "Freedom? You think I care about that anymore?"

The voice hums again, low and knowing. *"You will. When you see her, you will."*

The mirror's surface stills, the voice fading like smoke in the wind. The chamber feels emptier without it, but the weight in my chest remains.

I press my palm to the scar on my cheek, the old wound throbbing faintly beneath my touch. The memory of the pain, of the moment I made my pact, flares bright in my mind.

Freedom. Salvation. Choices.

Threads of Truth
Elira

The morning sun barely pierces the dense roof of green leaf above, but its pale light is enough to make me squint. My legs ache with every step, and I'm starting to think Kael might actually be enjoying this relentless pace.

The black wolf walks beside me, his massive frame a comforting presence. The ember glow of his eyes feels oddly steadying, even though I can still feel the stares of the guards at the gate burning into my back.

We walk in silence for what feels like hours, the tension between the three of us heavy but unspoken. I glance down at it, his stride calm and deliberate, as if he has no trouble keeping up.

"You're…not talking to me?"I   murmur, not expecting a response.

"*Because you have not asked the questions.*" I freeze, my heart lurching. The voice isn't Kael's, and it's not coming from outside. It's in my head.

My gaze snaps to the wolf, who looks up at me with those ember eyes, his head tilting slightly.

"Did… did you just talk to me?" I whisper, my voice barely audible.

"*I did.*"

The world seems to tilt slightly, and I grab a nearby tree for support. "Okay. Great. Add 'talking wolf' to the growing list of things that make no damn sense."

Kael glances back, his smirk faint. "You good back there?"

"Fine," I snap, waving him off. "Just having a perfectly normal conversation with the wolf."

Kael raises an eyebrow but doesn't press the issue, turning his attention back to the path ahead.

I look again in the best direction, my breath coming in short bursts. "You could've said something," I hiss under my breath.

"You were not ready."

"Oh, I'm sorry," I whisper harshly. "Ready for what? The giant wolf with ember eyes who can talk in my head? Yeah, totally something I needed time to prepare for."

"And yet, here we are," he replies calmly, his tone almost amused.

I pinch the bridge of my nose, exhaling sharply. "Okay. Fine. You talk. Great. Anything else I should know about you?"

"Much. But it will take time."

"Fantastic," I mutter, rolling my eyes. "Just what I needed. Another cryptic friend.."

It lets out a soft huff, the sound almost like a chuckle. *"You are strong, but your anger blinds you. Focus, Elira. The path ahead is long."*

I glance at him again, narrowing my eyes. "What's your deal anyway? Why are you even here?"

"I am here for you," he says simply. *"To guide you. To protect you. And, if necessary, to remind you of your purpose."*

His words settle over me like a weight, heavy and undeniable. My mind races with questions, but something about the calm certainty in his tone makes it hard to argue.

"Fine," I say finally, straightening. "But don't think I'm just going to follow you blindly. I need answers. Real ones. Do you even have a name?"

"And you will have them," he replies, his ember eyes gleaming. *"In time. My name is Veylan."*

The connection fades slightly, and I can still feel his presence lingering in the back of my mind, steady and reassuring.

Kael glances back again, his smirk faint but curious. "Talking to the wolf, huh?"

"Shut up, Kael," I mutter, trudging forward.

"Lyric's stronghold," Kael says, glancing back at me and pointing forward.

The wolf growls softly, his ember eyes scanning the scene below.

I frown, glancing between the two of them. "Why does he look like he doesn't trust this place?"

Kael shrugs, adjusting the strap of his pack. "He doesn't trust much. Smart wolf."

"You're not exactly filling me with confidence," I snap, my nerves already fraying.

"Good," Kael replies, his smirk returning. "Confidence gets you killed."

The path down to the village is steep, and my boots slip more than once on the loose gravel. Veylan moves beside me like an invisible force, his presence a constant reassurance even as Kael strides ahead, unconcerned.

By the time we reach the gates, my nerves are stretched thin. The guards stationed there eye us warily, their hands resting on the hilts of their weapons.

"Relax," Kael says, raising a hand in greeting. "We're friends. Sort of."

"Kael," one of the guards says, his tone flat. "You've got some nerve coming back here."

"Miss me, Derrick?" Kael replies, grinning.

The guard scowls but steps aside, muttering something under his breath. I glance at Veylan, whose growl rumbles low in his throat.

The guard scowls but steps aside reluctantly, his hand hovering near the hilt of his sword as he eyes Veylan. "What the hell is that thing doing here?"

"That thing has a name," I snap before Kael can offer one of his annoying quips.

The guard narrows his eyes at me, then at Veylan, whose growl rumbles low and threatening in his throat. The sound vibrates through the air, and the guard's face blanches slightly.

"You're bringing a giant wolf into the village?" another guard asks, stepping closer and eyeing Veylan warily. "Are you insane? What if it attacks someone?"

Kael smirks faintly, gesturing to Veylan. "Relax. He's with us. Think of him as... security."

"Security?" the first guard scoffs, though he doesn't step any closer. "More like a damn liability."

"He's more trustworthy than most people," I say, my tone sharp.

Veylan's ember eyes flick to me briefly before scanning the area, his presence an unspoken challenge to anyone who dares question him.

As we pass through the gates, the tension doesn't ease. People stop what they're doing to stare. Conversations fall silent. Mothers pull their children closer. The weight of their gazes settles on me, but most of their attention is locked on Veylan.

"Is that… a wolf?" someone whispers, their voice barely audible.

"No wolf gets that big," another mutters.

"Where did it come from?" "What's it doing here?"

Veylan keeps his head high, his stride steady and confident, but I can feel the tension rolling off him. His growl rumbles softly, a warning that sends shivers through the crowd.

I glance at Kael, who's walking ahead like he doesn't have a care in the world. "A little help here?"

He glances back, his smirk irritatingly casual. "You're doing great, sweetheart."
"Thanks for nothing," I mutter under my breath.

A group of children peek out from behind a cart, their wide eyes locked on Veylan. One of them whispers, "Do you think it eats people?"

I kneel slightly, meeting their curious gazes with a faint smile. "Only the bad ones."
Their eyes widen further, and they dart back behind the cart, giggling nervously.

Kael laughs softly, shaking his head. "That's one way to win hearts and minds."

stares don't stop as we wind through the village, and I can feel my patience wearing thin.

"Do they always gawk like this?" I ask Kael, gesturing to the onlookers.

"They've never seen anything like him before," Kael replies. "Or you, for that matter. Black hair and blue eyes are rare enough, but throw in a massive wolf with glowing eyes, and you're practically a legend."

"Just what I always wanted." I mutter.

Veylan brushes against my side, his ember eyes scanning the crowd. The hum of his presence flickers in my mind, calm and steady. *"Ignore them. They are irrelevant."*

By the time we reach the center of the village, I'm ready to snap at the next person who so much as glances at us. Lyric's sudden appearance is almost a relief—until her sharp, golden eyes lock on Veylan.

"Interesting company you've been keeping," she says, her tone neutral but curious.

"He's with me," I say quickly, stepping slightly in front of Veylan.

Lyric raises an eyebrow but doesn't comment further. Instead, she turns her attention to Kael. "Trouble?"

Kael shrugs. "Always."

Lyric's gaze flicks back to Veylan, her lips curving faintly. "A wolf this size, with eyes like that... You don't see that every day."

"He's more than just a wolf," I say, my voice firmer than I expect.

"I can see that," Lyric replies, her expression unreadable. "Good. You'll need him."

Revelations
Elira

The village sprawls before us, a patchwork of stone and wood structures nestled into the valley. Smoke curls lazily from chimneys, and the sound of hammering and raised voices fills the air.

Lyric strides ahead with her usual calm confidence, Kael trailing behind her, while I stick close to Veylan, whose massive form draws every eye in the street.

"Relax," Kael says, glancing back at me with that infuriating smirk. "They're just curious."

"Curious feels a lot like judgment," I mutter, my grip tightening on the poker in my hand.

The weight of their stares presses down on me as we weave through the streets. Children peek out from behind barrels and carts, their wide eyes locked on Veylan.

One brave girl steps forward, her tiny hand clutching a stick like it might protect her.

Veylan lets out a soft huff, lowering his massive head to meet the girl's gaze. She freezes for a moment, then giggles nervously before darting back to her group.

"He's making friends," Kael says, his tone laced with amusement. "How cute."

I glare at him. "Shut up."

Lyric leads us into a large building at the center of the village, its reinforced stone walls exuding strength and stability. The air inside is cooler, the faint scent of leather and woodsmoke lingering in the air. Maps and weapons cover the long table in the center, their careful arrangement a stark contrast to the chaos outside.

"Sit," Lyric says, gesturing to the chairs around the table. "We have much to discuss."

Kael drops into a chair with his usual casual grace, propping his feet up on the edge of the table. I hesitate, glancing at Veylan, who positions himself near the doorway.

Lyric sits at the head of the table, her golden eyes sharp as they flick between me and Kael. "The rebels have been preparing for this moment for years. Damien's power is strong, but his control is faltering. The time to strike is coming."

"And what does that have to do with me?" I ask, leaning forward.

Lyric meets my gaze, her expression unwavering. "Everything. The prophecy speaks of one who will bring balance to the kingdoms. One who carries the blood of both worlds. That's you, Elira."

I cross my arms, leaning back in my chair. "So what's your plan? Just throw me at Damien and hope for the best?"
Lyric's lips twitch into a faint smile. "Hardly. First, you'll train. Combat. Magic. Everything you'll need to survive."

Kael grins, leaning back in his chair. "You're going to love it, sweetheart. Nothing like a good fight to—" *"Enough."* Veylan's voice cuts through Kael's teasing like
a blade, deep and resonant in my mind.

"What the heck, I hear him,"

The wolf steps forward, his ember eyes locking onto Kael, who stiffens slightly, his smirk faltering.

"I can choose to spoke with all if I want to. Elira already has everything she needs," Veylan says, his gaze flicking to me.

I blink, startled. "What are you talking about?" *"You carry it within you,"* he replies calmly. *"You simply need to awaken it."*

Kael raises an eyebrow, glancing between me and Veylan. "Awaken it? That sounds ominous."

"Kael, shut up," I snap, more out of nerves than irritation.

Veylan lowers his massive head, his ember eyes boring into mine. *"Trust me, Elira. Press your forehead to mine."*

The room falls silent. Even Kael stops smirking, his gaze sharpening as he watches. I hesitate, my heart racing.

"Are you serious?" I ask, my voice barely above a whisper.

"Completely."

I glance at Lyric, who watches the scene unfold with quiet intensity, then back at Veylan. Taking a deep breath, I step forward and kneel slightly to meet his towering height.

The warmth of his fur brushes against my skin as I press my forehead to his. For a moment, nothing happens. Then everything changes.

A rush of heat floods through me, like fire spreading beneath my skin. It's not painful, but it's overwhelming—bright and powerful, as if every nerve in my body has been set alight. My breath catches, and I feel a strange hum vibrating through me, deep and ancient.

Images flash behind my closed eyes—shadows and light, voices I don't recognize, memories that are not mine, and a sense of something vast and untamed stirring within me.

When I pull back, the sensation lingers, a faint crackle of energy just beneath the surface. My hands tremble, and I stare at them, half-expecting sparks to fly from my fingertips.

"What the hell was that?" I whisper, my voice shaky.

Veylan sits back, his expression calm but pleased. *"Your potential."*

Kael whistles low, leaning back in his chair. "Well, that was…nothing. Feel any different?"

"Stop talking, Kael," I mutter, though my focus remains on Veylan.

"Let's find out," Lyric says, standing. "Kael, take her to the sparring ring. Test her."

Kael grins, his cocky attitude returning. "With pleasure."

The sparring ring is a wide, open area behind the main hall, bordered by rough-hewn logs and scattered with training dummies and weapons. Kael tosses his coat onto a nearby stump, rolling his shoulders as he steps into the center.

"You sure about this?" he asks, drawing his sword.

I hesitate, glancing at the poker still clutched in my hand. Veylan's voice hums in my mind. *"Trust yourself. You already know how."*

Taking a deep breath, I step into the ring, gripping the poker tightly.

Kael doesn't hold back. He comes at me fast, his sword flashing in the sunlight. But something shifts as I move to block. My body feels lighter, quicker— like the energy from before is still coursing through me, guiding my movements.

His strikes are fluid and calculated, but I counter them easily, my reflexes sharper than they've ever been. The sword Lyric just gave me feels natural in my hands, almost like an extension of myself.

"Not bad," Kael says, his grin faltering slightly as I dodge another swing.

"You haven't seen anything yet," I snap, the confidence in my voice surprising even me.

He lunges again, but this time I'm faster. I sidestep his attack and swing the blade in a wide arc, catching him squarely in the side. He stumbles, his sword slipping from his hand, and I press the advantage, spinning with a precision I didn't know I had.

In seconds, he's on the ground, my weapon aimed at his throat.

Kael blinks up at me, stunned. "What the hell?"

I lower the sword, my chest heaving as the adrenaline begins to fade. "I guess I've got a knack for this."

Lyric claps from the edge of the ring, her expression approving. "You're a natural."

Kael groans, sitting up and rubbing his side. "Yeah, great. Someone remind me never to underestimate her again."

Veylan rumbles softly, his ember eyes gleaming with satisfaction. *"You are ready."*

Lines in the Sand
Elira

The training ring empties quickly after my fight with Kael. People who had gathered to watch murmur among themselves, glancing at me like I'm some sort of anomaly.

Lyric steps forward, her golden eyes assessing me with a hint of approval.

"That was impressive," she says, folding her arms. "But one fight doesn't make you ready. You'll need more training."

I bite back a groan, still catching my breath.

My muscles hum with energy, the remnants of whatever Veylan awakened in me, but exhaustion is creeping in fast.

"Can't wait for the next beating."I mutter.

Kael grins from where he's leaning against a post, rubbing his ribs. "Don't worry, sweetheart. I'll go easy on you next time."

"Right," I snap, glaring at him. "That's why you're the one who got flattened."

Lyric hides a smile, but her tone remains serious. "Rest for now. We'll start again tomorrow."

Kael and Lyric move off to the side, talking in low voices, leaving me alone with Veylan.

The wolf steps closer, his eyes steady and calm.

"You're awfully smug," I whisper.

"*You should be too*," his voice hums in my mind. "*You have taken the first step toward what you were meant to be.*"

"Meant to be?" I echo, narrowing my eyes. "You're starting to sound like them. Prophecy this, destiny that. What if I don't want any of it?"

Veylan tilts his head slightly, his expression almost amused. "*It is not about what you want, Elira. It is about what you must do.*"

I sigh, running a hand through my hair as I glance around the ring. The rebels are watching from a distance, their whispers and curious looks grating on my nerves.

"What are they saying?" I ask, not really wanting to know the answer.

"*That you are different,*" Veylan replies. "*That you might be the one to save them.*"

I let out a sharp laugh, standing and brushing dirt off my pants. "No pressure or anything."

Veylan huffs softly, his massive head nudging my side. "*You are stronger than you know, Elira. They will see it soon enough.*"

The walk back to the main hall is quiet, the weight of the day settling heavily on my shoulders. Lyric's words echo in my mind: You're part of this world, whether you like it or not.

Inside, the hall feels colder, the dim light from the lanterns casting long shadows across the stone walls. I drop into a chair by the fire, staring into the flames as my mind churns.

Kael strolls in a few moments later, his usual smirk in place. "You've got them talking, you know. The mysterious girl from another world who tamed the giant wolf and flattened me in a fight. Quite the reputation you're building."

"You can stop talking, Kael," I mutter, though there's no real bite in my words.

He chuckles, leaning against the mantel. "You're welcome, by the way."

"For what?" I ask, raising an eyebrow.

"For giving you a chance to show off," he says, his grin widening. "Don't let it go to your head."

Before I can respond, Lyric enters, her expression
serious. "We need to talk."

Kael straightens, the teasing edge in his demeanor fading instantly. "What's going on?"

"Scouts spotted movement near the northern border," Lyric says, her tone clipped. "Damien's forces are closing in. It's only a matter of time before they find us."

My stomach twists, the reality of the situation crashing over me. "So what do we do?"

Lyric looks at me, her gaze steady. "We prepare. You'll need to be ready, Elira. This fight is coming sooner than we expected."

Veylan steps closer, his presence grounding me as his voice hums softly in my mind. *"You will face it. And you will not face it alone."*

The weight of his words settles over me, heavy but strangely comforting. I meet Lyric's gaze and nod. "Then let's get to work."

"Yes , but first, we need to clean. Eat, sleep." She proclaims.

Shadows of the Past
Elira

The hot springs stretch out like an oasis in the dark village, steam rising in delicate tendrils that blur the edges of the world. The soft glow of lanterns illuminates the jagged cliffs surrounding the springs, casting golden light on smooth, glistening rocks.

The air is thick with the scent of minerals, earthy and tangy, mingling with the low hum of conversation and the occasional burst of laughter.

I sit on the edge of the largest pool, my legs submerged up to the knees. The warmth seeps into my skin, soothing the ache from the sparring earlier. Around me, people wade freely through the water, their bare skin glistening, their movements uninhibited.

Lyric had called this place a reprieve, a haven where the villagers could let down their guard. But to me, it feels like being dropped into someone else's dream—one I wasn't entirely ready for.

Kael, of course, looks like he was born for this. He's chest-deep in the water, arms stretched along the edge of the pool as he leans back, his hair damp and clinging to his face. The steam softens the hard lines of his jaw, but his smirk is as sharp as ever.

"You're missing out, sweetheart," he says, tilting his head toward me.

"I'm fine," I reply, crossing my arms over the damp cotton bra I stubbornly kept on. My underwear—thin, basic, and soaked—clings uncomfortably to my skin, but it's better than the alternative.

Kael raises an eyebrow, his smirk widening. "Afraid someone's going to take a peek?"

I flip him my middle finger, smiling with all my teeth.

He laughs softly, the sound carrying easily over the bubbling water. "Suit yourself. But you look ridiculous sitting there like that. Either commit to relaxing or don't bother."

"I'll pass, thanks," I mutter, though my cheeks burn hotter than the steam rising around me.

Around us, villagers move with an ease I envy. Some sit on the rocks, chatting quietly, while others float lazily in the water.

The lights create a golden haze, reflecting off the rippling surface of the springs and highlighting every curve, every scar, every line of their bodies. No one seems to care about the nakedness, the vulnerability. Except me.

"You're thinking too much again," Kael calls out, his voice dragging me back to the present. "You're here. You might as well enjoy it."

"Do you ever stop talking, seriously?" I shoot back, glaring at him.

He grins, unbothered. "Only when I'm distracted." His eyes flick pointedly toward the thin fabric clinging to my chest.

Veylan's growl rumbles softly beside me, the sound low and warning. Kael's grin falters for a moment, his gaze shifting to the massive wolf.

"Easy there," he says, holding up his hands. "I was just teasing."

"*You do not need him to defend you,*" Veylan's voice hums in my mind, steady and calm. "*You are stronger than you know.*"

I glance at the wolf, whose ember eyes gleam faintly through the steam. His presence is grounding, a tether in the midst of this strange, surreal place.

Lyric emerges from one of the smaller pools, her hair slicked back and damp, clinging to her shoulders.

She's wearing a simple cloth tied around her waist, but her golden eyes are as sharp as ever.

She approaches with the grace of someone who's used to being in charge, her gaze sweeping over the scene before landing on me.

"You're not relaxing," she observes, folding her arms.

"Observant," I mutter, shifting slightly on the rock. "How do you people just… sit around like this?"

"Because we don't have the luxury of carrying shame," Lyric replies smoothly. "Life is hard enough without letting your own insecurities weigh you down."

"Easy for you to say," I mutter, glancing at her effortlessly confident stance. "You look like you belong in a painting."

Her lips twitch into a faint smile. "And you look like someone who's ready to ask the questions that have been gnawing at her all night."

I sigh, running a hand through my damp hair. "Fine. Let's start with the obvious. Damien. What's his deal? Why is he so hell-bent on destroying everything?"

Lyric's expression hardens slightly, and she sits on a nearby rock, the steam swirling around her. "Damien wasn't always the way he is now. He was once the kingdom's greatest warrior—loyal, fearless, respected, beautiful. But something happened during the war against the northern tribes. He disappeared for weeks, and when he returned… he wasn't the same."

Kael's grin fades, replaced by a rare seriousness. "He made a deal," he says, his tone grim. "With something ancient and dark. The scars on his face aren't just from battle. They're marks of the pact he made."

"What did he trade for?" I ask, my chest tightening.

Lyric shakes her head. "Power. Survival. Control. Maybe all of it. Whatever it was, it came at a cost. The malevolent force isn't just inside him. It's woven into the very fabric of this world. To defeat him, we'll have to face it too."

Veylan steps closer, his ember eyes locking onto mine. 'You carry the strength to face what lies ahead, Elira. You simply need to claim it."

His voice hums through my mind, a steady pulse of reassurance. I glance at him, then at the others. The fire within me flickers, not as faint as before.

"Then let's start," I say finally, my voice steady. "If this is what I'm here for, I'm not running from it."

Kael chuckles softly, his smirk returning.

"Feisty. I like it."

"If it breaths, you like it." I rolled my eyes.

A Growing Storm
Elira

The morning breaks over Lyric's village with the kind of quiet that sets my teeth on edge. For a place that felt alive with activity just yesterday, the stillness feels unnatural.

Lyric leads the way through the village, her golden eyes scanning the horizon as she explains the plan. I keep close behind her, my thoughts a tangled mess of questions and half-formed doubts.

Kael walks a few steps ahead, his posture lazy but his eyes sharp, as if he's waiting for something to go wrong.

Veylan keeps to my side, like always now his black furr flicking from little beads of the air's condensation.

I tug at the black leather jacket Lyric gave me last night, the material stiff but protective. The straps around my thighs feel strange, like I'm wearing someone else's life. Maybe I am.

"So," I say finally, breaking the silence. "Are we going to talk about yesterday?"

Lyric glances back, her expression unreadable. "What part of yesterday, exactly?"

"Oh, I don't know," I reply, crossing my arms. "The part where you dropped the whole 'save the world or die trying' speech, the plan maybe?"

Kael snorts, his smirk already forming. "She's got a point, Lyric. Your motivational speeches could use a little work."

Lyric rolls her eyes but doesn't respond, her attention shifting to the path ahead.

The forest surrounding the village is darker than I remember, the canopy so thick it turns the sunlight into thin, gold streaks. The air smells of damp earth and moss, a strange mix of life and decay.

"So where exactly are we going?" I ask, stepping over a twisted root.

"It's one of the last safe havens we have. If Damien's forces push farther south, we'll need their support."

"And if they don't want to help?" I ask, my voice sharper than I intend.

Lyric pauses, her gaze flicking to mine. "Then we'll convince them. But I'm pretty sure we'll be fine."

"Great," I mutter. "Because I'm so good at convincing people."

We walk in silence for a while, the tension between us simmering just below the surface. Veylan moves closer, his massive form brushing against my side.

"You are uneasy," his voice hums in my mind, low and calm.

"No kidding," I mutter under my breath. "This whole thing feels like a death sentence."

"You underestimate yourself," Veylan replies. *"And them."*
I glance at Lyric and Kael, who are deep in conversation ahead. "I don't even know if I can trust them."

"Trust is earned," he says simply. *"But the girl is for sur not your enemy."*

Kael slows his pace, falling back to walk beside me. He tilts his head slightly, his smirk half-hearted for once. "You okay, sweetheart? You've got that look again."

"What look?" I ask, narrowing my eyes.
"The one that says you're about to punch someone," he replies with a grin.

I snort softly, shaking my head. "Maybe I am."

"Relax," he says, bumping my shoulder lightly. "You've already proven you can take me down. No need to make it a habit."

"Don't tempt me," I mutter, though a small smile tugs at the corner of my mouth.

We stop briefly near a stream, the water sparkling faintly in the weak sunlight. Lyric crouches by the edge, refilling her canteen as Kael and I linger a few steps away.

"So," Kael says, leaning casually against a tree. "What do you think of our little rebellion so far?"

"I think you're all insane," I reply without hesitation.

Kael laughs, the sound light and easy. "Fair enough. But you're still here."

"Yeah, well," I say, glancing at Veylan. "Someone's got to keep you idiots alive."

And he laughed, in my head, quietly but it put a smile on my lips.

Kael's grin widens, but Lyric cuts in before he can respond. "Let's move. We don't have time for this."

As we head back onto the path, the air grows colder, the trees darker. Veylan tenses beside me, his growl low and rumbling.

"What is it?" I whisper, my heart speeding up.

"We are being watched."

Lyric stops abruptly, her hand on the hilt of her blade. "Everyone, stay close."

Kael draws his sword, his expression losing all traces of humor. "How close are we to the village?"

"Too far," Lyric replies, her voice tight.

I grip the hilt of my dagger in my hand, the weight of it suddenly feeling too light. My pulse pounds in my ears as shadows shift between the trees, too quick and too deliberate to be the wind.

And then, the first arrow flies.

Chaos erupts in an instant. The arrow embeds itself in the tree inches from Kael's head, and before I can register what's happening, figures emerge from the shadows. Damien's soldiers, clad in dark armor that seems to absorb the dim light, rush forward with blades drawn.

Lyric is the first to move, her blade flashing as she deflects an oncoming strike. Kael follows, his sword meeting steel with a resounding clash. The sounds of battle ring out, sharp and jarring against the stillness of the forest.

Veylan doesn't wait.

A guttural snarl rips from his throat as he launches himself at the nearest soldier. His massive form moves with terrifying speed, and before the man can react, Veylan's jaws clamp down on his arm, the sickening crunch of bone echoing through the air.

The soldier screams, a sound that's quickly cut off as Veylan tears him to the ground. Blood sprays across the mossy earth, dark and vivid against the muted greens and browns. Veylan's pupils grow wider, his fur slicked with crimson as he turns to the next target.

I freeze for a moment, the scene unfolding like a nightmare. One soldier swings his blade toward me, and instinct takes over.

I raise the blade, meeting his strike with a strength I didn't know I had. Sparks fly as our weapons clash, and I drive the blunt end into his ribs, sending him stumbling back.

"Keep moving!" Lyric shouts, her voice sharp over the chaos.

Veylan leaps again, his claws raking across another soldier's chest. The man crumples with a wet gurgle, and Veylan roars, the sound reverberating through the forest.

It's a primal, bone-deep sound that sends a chill down my spine even as it fills me with a strange sense of safety.

Kael fights beside me, his movements precise and efficient. "Stay close!" he barks, deflecting a strike aimed at my side. "This isn't the time to freeze up!"

"I'm not freezing!" I snap back, driving the sword into the leg of another soldier. He falls with a cry, and I step over him, my chest heaving.

The bastard seem endless, their dark forms blending with the shadows. But Veylan is a force of nature, cutting through them like they're nothing. His jaws snap around a soldier's throat, and the man drops, lifeless, before Veylan moves on to the next.

Blood pools around his paws, and his growl deepens, vibrating through the ground.

Finally, the onslaught slows. The remaining soldiers retreat into the shadows, their footsteps fading into the distance. The forest falls silent again, save for the ragged breaths of our group.

Veylan stands amidst the carnage, his fur matted with blood, his ember eyes scanning the trees. He lets out a low huff, shaking himself off before padding back to me.

"They are gone," he says, his voice calm despite the violence he just unleashed. "For now."

I reach out, my hand trembling as I touch his fur. "You… you saved us."

"*We save each other,*" he replies simply.

Lyric wipes her blade on the grass, her expression grim. "We need to move. If they found us here, they'll find us again."

Kael nods, sheathing his sword. "Agreed. Let's not stick around for round two."

Refuge and Reckoning
Elira

We burst through the gates of the new village, breathless and battered, the heavy wooden doors slamming shut behind us with a deafening thud.

The guards at the entrance immediately brace themselves, their weapons raised and their faces hard with suspicion.

"Stand down," Lyric commands, her voice slicing through the chaos. Even after the fight and the desperate run, her tone holds an edge of authority that's impossible to ignore.

The guards hesitate, their eyes darting to me, to Kael, and finally to the blood-drenched wolf at my side. Veylan's fur is still matted with dark streaks, his ember eyes glowing like twin flames as he stands tall, unflinching under their scrutiny.

"Who are they?" one of the guards demands, his grip tightening on his spear.

"They're with me," Lyric replies sharply. "And they just survived an ambush. Let us through."

Reluctantly, the guards lower their weapons, stepping aside. Their eyes linger on Veylan, unease flickering across their faces as we pass.

The village is smaller than I expected, its buildings clustered tightly together as though huddling for warmth. Everything here feels rougher, rawer—the wooden walls are patched with metal sheets, and the streets are uneven, strewn with hay and dirt. Smoke drifts lazily from chimneys, mingling with the scent of damp earth and something faintly metallic.

People pause in their tasks to watch us, their gazes wary and guarded. Some clutch makeshift weapons, others simply stare, their expressions a mix of fear and curiosity. The tension in the air is palpable, thick enough to choke on.

"They don't look happy to see us," I murmur, keeping my voice low.

Kael, walking just ahead of me, glances over his shoulder. "Would you be? We're strangers, and you're dragging a wolf the size of a horse."

I glare at him, but Veylan huffs softly, almost like he's amused.

"Where are we going?" I ask Lyric, trying to ignore the weight of the stares.

"To Eryndor," she replies without looking back. Her tone is clipped, but there's a note of familiarity that makes me pause.

"Eryndor?"

"The leader here," Kael says, smirking. "Big guy. You'll like him. Or not. Hard to tell with you."

"Fuck off, Kael," I mutter, my focus shifting to the largest building at the center of the village. Its walls are reinforced with stone, and its doors are flanked by two more guards, their expressions just as stern as the ones at the gate.

Lyric strides ahead, pushing open the heavy doors without hesitation. Inside, the air is warmer, lit by a roaring fire in a massive hearth.

The room is sparsely furnished, with a long table dominating the center and maps and weapons scattered across its surface.

A man rises from behind the table, his presence immediately commanding. He's tall and broad-shouldered, his long brown hair woven into intricate braids that frame his face. His eyes are dark and piercing, but there's a gentleness to his expression that tempers the sharp angles of his jaw and cheekbones.

"Lyric," he says, his voice deep and steady. "You're late."

She rolls her eyes, but there's a flicker of warmth in her gaze. "We ran into trouble on the way. Damien's soldiers."

His expression hardens, his jaw clenching.

"How many?"

"Enough to make us run," she replies grimly. "But we took care of it."

His gaze shifts to me then, lingering for a moment before moving to Veylan. His brow arches slightly, and he steps closer, his focus entirely on the wolf.

"And who's this?" he asks, his tone lighter, almost teasing.

"That's Veylan," I say before Lyric can respond. "And he's not a pet."

"Clearly," Eryndor replies, crouching slightly. "But he's magnificent."

To my surprise, Veylan steps forward, his massive head lowering slightly as Eryndor extends a hand. The wolf sniffs it briefly before letting out a soft huff, his tail flicking once.

Eryndor grins, standing. "A king among wolves. I like him."

Veylan's voice hums in my mind, amused. *"I like him too. He knows his place."*

I stifle a laugh, glancing at Lyric. She's watching Eryndor with an expression I can't quite place—fondness mixed with something sharper, something guarded.

"We need to talk," she says finally, breaking the moment. "About what comes next."

Eryndor nods, his expression turning serious. "Then let's talk."

A Collision of Fate
Elira

After a reallu long meeting with all of us, explaining everything that happened so far, we've been invited to join Eryndor's people.

The village square is alive with music and laughter, the air heavy with the scent of roasted meat and spiced wine. Lanterns sway gently in the breeze, their warm light casting golden patterns on the stone walls and the dancing crowd.

For a moment, it's easy to forget about the blood and chaos we left behind in the forest. People twirl and clap in time with the music, their movements wild and uninhibited. The rhythm is infectious, the kind of beat that makes you want to lose yourself for just a little while.

I stay near the edge of the square, watching the dancers with equal parts envy and wariness. Veylan lies beside me, his eyes half-lidded but alert, his massive form a comforting weight against my leg.

"You're brooding again," Kael says, appearing at my side with a mug in hand.

"I'm not brooding," I mutter, crossing my arms.

"You're definitely brooding," he replies with a smirk. "Come on, sweetheart. This is your chance to have a little fun."

"I'll pass," I say, glancing at the crowd. "You're clearly having enough fun for both of us."

Kael raises his mug in a mock toast before disappearing into the throng, leaving me to my thoughts.

Eryndor leads us through the bustle, his long braids swaying with every step. He's explaining something to Lyric in low tones, his deep voice calm but firm, while Kael strides a few steps ahead, glancing at every shadow like it's about to jump at us.

"Good boy," Eryndor murmurs, grinning as if Veylan's not a hulking predator who just tore through half a battalion.

The wolf lets out a soft huff, the sound almost a chuckle, and I roll my eyes. "Seriously? He gets royal treatment now?"

Eryndor glances up at me, his grin widening. "He earned it."

Lyric clears her throat, bringing us back to the matter at hand. "We need to debrief again. Now."

Eryndor straightens, his expression turning serious. "Agreed. The council room is ready. Elira stay here, enjoy the festivities. We'll talk with you tomorrow morning."

I open my mouth to argue, but Veylan's voice hums in my mind, steady and calm. *"Listen to them."*

Lyric follows him without hesitation, Kael hot on her heels. I glance at Veylan, who growls softly, his ember eyes narrowing.

"I'm guessing 'stay here' isn't an option?" I ask.

"Not for you."

The music shifts, the tempo slowing into something more deliberate, almost sultry. The dancers pair off, their movements more intimate now, and the energy in the square changes.

"Are you just going to watch all night?"

The voice startles me, low and smooth, with a hint of something playful underneath. I turn to find a man standing a few feet away, his face partially shadowed by the flickering lantern light.

He's tall, his posture relaxed but with a quiet confidence that sets my nerves on edge. His hair is dark and slightly tousled, brushing the collar of his simple shirt, and his sharp features are softened by the warmth of the light.

"I don't dance," I say, my tone sharp.

He smiles faintly, stepping closer. "Everyone dances eventually."

Before I can argue, he holds out a hand, his green eyes gleaming as they meet mine. Something about his gaze makes my breath catch, but I shove the feeling aside.

"I don't think—"

"Just one," he says, cutting me off. "If you hate it, I'll let you go."

It's stupid. Reckless. But before I can talk myself out of it, my hand moves on its own, slipping into his. His grip is firm but not overpowering, and he leads me into the crowd with an ease that feels practiced.

The music flows around us, the low, rhythmic beat syncing with the pulse in my chest. He pulls me close, one hand settling lightly at my waist as we move in time with the melody. His touch is firm yet controlled, the kind that speaks of confidence without arrogance.

Up close, he's even more breathtaking. His green eyes catch the flicker of lantern light, vivid and piercing like freshly cut emeralds. They're framed by lashes so dark and thick they almost seem unreal.

The scars that cut across his cheek and over one eye only add to his magnetism, a rugged edge to his otherwise perfect features. Weird, how every man in this world is scarred. Real warrior.

His jawline is sharp, shadowed with the faintest trace of stubble, and his lips curl into a faint, almost mocking smile. His dark hair is slightly longer than expected, brushing against the nape of his neck and curling faintly around his ears, the strands tousled in a way that feels both effortless and deliberate.
"You're not terrible," he says after a moment, his voice low enough that only I can hear. It's rich and smooth, with a faint rasp that sends a shiver down my spine.

"High praise," I reply dryly, my sarcasm covering the flutter in my stomach.

He chuckles softly, the sound warm and oddly disarming, like it doesn't quite match the sharpness of his appearance. "You always this charming?"

"You always this persistent?" I counter, arching an eyebrow.

For a while, we just move together, the crowd around us fading into the background. There's a strange intensity to the way he watches me, like he's trying to figure me out without asking any questions.

"So," I say, breaking the silence. "Are you from here?"

"Something like that," he replies vaguely, his gaze flicking briefly to the edge of the square.

"That's a vague answer, mister."

He only laughs.

I narrow my eyes at him, but before I can press further, the music shifts again, signaling the end of the dance. He steps back, releasing my hand, but his gaze lingers on mine.

"Thanks for indulging me," he says, his tone lighter now.
"Don't get used to it," I reply, my defenses snapping back into place.

He smiles faintly, but there's something unreadable in his expression as he turns and disappears into the crowd.
I stand there for a moment, trying to shake the strange feeling he left behind. Veylan moves to my side, his presence grounding me as his voice hums softly in my mind.

"He is not what he seems."

I glance at the wolf, my chest tightening. "What does that mean?"

"You will see."

His cryptic reply only deepens my unease, but there's no time to dwell on it as Lyric calls for me from across the square.

The moment is gone, but the memory of his green eyes stays with me, a nagging whisper I can't ignore.

Morning After
Elira

The first thing I register is the pounding in my skull, a rhythmic thud that matches the faint groan escaping my lips. The second is the sound—a deep, rumbling purr that vibrates through the floor and straight into my bones.

My eyes flutter open, and I immediately regret it. The sunlight streaming through the small window is far too bright, slicing into my head like a blade. I groan again, rolling onto my side, and come face to face with the source of the noise.
Veylan.

The massive wolf is sprawled in the middle of the room, his ember eyes half-closed as he emits a sound that can only be described as a purr.

"What the hell?" I mutter, my voice hoarse.

And then I see him.

Eryndor is sitting cross-legged on the floor like a damn child, one hand buried in Veylan's thick fur as he brushes the beast with long, deliberate strokes. His braided hair sways with each movement, and the faintest grin plays on his lips.

"Morning, sunshine," he says without looking up.

"What are you doing?" I croak, forcing myself to sit up. The room spins briefly, and I press a hand to my temple, groaning again.

"Grooming," he replies simply, holding up the brush. "Do you know how much fur this guy sheds? It's like a second wolf."

Veylan huffs, the sound low and rumbling, but he doesn't protest as Eryndor continues his work.

"You're brushing him," I say, blinking at the surreal sight.

"Someone has to," Eryndor says, finally glancing at me. His dark eyes glint with amusement.

"He came to wake you up, but I think he decided I was more fun."

"Traitor," I mutter, glaring at the wolf, who lets out a low, satisfied growl that sounds suspiciously smug.

Eryndor stands, brushing off his hands. "Anyway, you're up now. Lyric's waiting. We've got plans to go over."
I groan, running a hand through my tangled hair. "Great. Let me just die quietly first."

"No time for that," he says, offering a hand to help me up.

I stare at it for a moment before grudgingly taking it. His grip is firm but warm, and he pulls me to my feet with ease.
"You look awful," he says cheerfully.

"Thanks," I snap, my tone dry. "That's exactly what I needed to hear."

As I stumble around the room, trying to piece together what's left of my dignity, Veylan rises gracefully to his feet, shaking out his fur.

"You overindulged," his voice hums in my mind, calm and vaguely judgmental.

"Don't start," I mutter under my breath, grabbing the jacket I discarded last night.

Eryndor chuckles, leaning against the doorframe. "You and Lyric are more alike than you think."

I glare at him. "If you don't stop talking, I'm going to send Veylan on you."

Eryndor grins, clearly unbothered. "Good luck with that. We're best friends now."

The walk to the main hall is mercifully short, though every step feels like a hammer to my skull. The village is quieter this morning, the remnants of last night's celebration lingering in the form of discarded mugs and faint laughter echoing from the far end of the square.

Lyric is waiting in the hall, her golden eyes sharp as she studies the maps spread across the table.

Kael leans against the wall nearby, a half-eaten apple in hand and his usual smirk firmly in place. "You're late," Lyric says without looking up.

"Blame him," I say, nodding toward Eryndor, who shrugs innocently.

Lyric sighs, gesturing for us to join her. "We don't have time for this. Damien's forces are already moving. If we're going to strike, it has to be soon."

The discussion begins, the weight of their words settling heavily over the room. But even as I focus on the maps and strategies, my mind drifts to last night—to the mysterious man with green eyes and scars, and the strange tension that crackled between us.

I shake the thought away, forcing myself to concentrate. Whatever happened last night doesn't matter now.

There's a war to fight, and no time for distractions. Lyric spreads a large map across the table, her golden eyes sharp as she points to several marked locations. "Damien's forces are advancing faster than we anticipated. This village might hold out for now, but the others further south won't be so lucky."

Eryndor leans over the map, his brow furrowed. "We're stretched thin. Even if we send reinforcements, it won't be enough to hold all the territories."

"So what's the plan?" I ask, my voice breaking through the tense silence.

Lyric's gaze flicks to me, her jaw tightening. "We hit him where it hurts. His supply lines, his communication hubs. If we can cut those off, his army slows down."

Kael, lounging against the wall, snorts softly. "Easier said than done. Damien's not stupid. He'll have those routes guarded like a dragon hoarding treasure."

"Which is why we're not going through the obvious routes," Lyric counters. She taps a section of the map, a cluster of jagged lines that look like cliffs. "This pass is dangerous, but it's the only way to bypass his patrols without being spotted."

I study the map, the faint sense of unease creeping back into my chest. "Dangerous how?"

Lyric doesn't look up. "Sheer drops, unstable paths. One wrong move, and you're dead."

"Sounds…like the best plan ever ," I mutter under my breath.

Eryndor straightens, crossing his arms. "It's risky, but it's our best shot. If we can disrupt his supply lines, it'll buy the other villages time to prepare."

Kael raises an eyebrow. "And what happens when he realizes what we're doing? He'll come after us, and we'll be trapped in that death trap of a pass."

Lyric fixes him with a hard stare. "Then we make sure he never gets the chance."

The room falls silent, the weight of her words settling heavily over all of us. Veylan shifts beside me. *"This is not a plan,"* he says in my mind, his tone calm but firm. *"It is desperation."*

"It's what we have," I reply softly, my hand brushing against his fur.

Eryndor sighs, breaking the silence. "If we're doing this, we need to move fast. His scouts won't stay idle for long."

Lyric nods, rolling up the map. "We leave at dawn. Rest while you can."

As the group begins to disperse, I linger by the table, my fingers tracing the lines of the map. The pass looks like a nightmare—a narrow stretch of cliffs with no room for error.
"You all right?"

I glance up to find Eryndor watching me, his expression softer than usual.
"Yeah," I say, though my voice lacks conviction.

He steps closer, his presence calm but steady.
"It's a lot to take in. But you're not alone in this."

I nod, though the weight in my chest doesn't lighten. "I just hope we're not walking into a trap."

Eryndor's jaw tightens, his dark eyes flicking to the map. "If we are, we'll fight our way out. That's what we do."

His words are meant to reassure me, but the knot in my stomach only tightens.

I leave the hall, Veylan pads silently beside me, his warmth grounding me against the chill of the night. I glance at him, his ember eyes glowing faintly in the darkness.

"You are stronger than you know, Elira," he says softly in my mind.

I don't reply, but his words echo in my thoughts as I stare up at the stars. Whatever lies ahead, I'll face it. And I'll survive.

Because I have to.

The Devil's Deal
Elira

Barely five minutes after our discussion ended, Kael insisted on showing me a cave just outside the village. I asked Veylan to stay behind, as the entrance is supposedly very small. I like the idea of distracting myself and seeing something I've never seen before. Especially before leaving for their suicidal plan.

I follow Kael through the narrow paths, his steps steady and deliberate, like he's done this a thousand times before.

"Where is it?" I ask, the unease creeping up my spine making my voice sharper than I intended.
"Somewhere quiet," he says casually, his tone light but hollow.

The back of my neck prickles. I glance over my shoulder, but the village behind us is dark, the few remaining lights casting long shadows that feel like they're reaching for me.

He stops abruptly, turning to face me with a grin that makes my stomach churn. "You're wound tight, sweetheart. Relax."

"Relax?" I echo, crossing my arms. "You dragged me out here in the middle of the night, and you want me to relax? We have a lot to do with the others and, YOU, want to show me something, alone may I add."

His smirk sharpens, and something cold flashes in his eyes. "Don't make this harder than it needs to be."

Before I can process his words, he moves. The blade presses against my throat, the steel biting into my skin just enough to draw a thin line of blood.
My breath catches, and the world seems to tilt.
"Kael… what the hell are you doing?"

"What I've always done," he replies, his voice low and smooth, like he's explaining something simple. "You didn't think I was just tagging along for the fun of it, did you? There's a price for everything, Elira. And you? You're worth more than you know."

My blood turns to ice, but the fury bubbling beneath it ignites just as quickly. "You're selling me out," I hiss, my voice shaking with rage.

"Bingo," he says, the smirk never leaving his face. "Black hair, blue eyes—you're a goldmine. The crown's been paying me to keep their little prophecy problem under control for years. You're just another paycheck."

Something snaps inside me. "You bastard," I spit, struggling against his grip.

His laugh is soft and cruel, the sound slicing through the night. "Don't take it personally. It's just business."

The air shifts, and a guttural roar tears through the silence.

Veylan.

The wolf appears like a shadow given form, his ember eyes blazing as he lunges for Kael. The blade at my throat drops as Kael scrambles back, his cocky grin twisting into something frantic and wild.

"Stay back!" Kael shouts, drawing his sword as Veylan circles him, his growl deep and unrelenting.

But Veylan doesn't stay back. He charges, and Kael barely manages to parry the attack, his blade glancing off Veylan's thick fur. The wolf's claws rake across Kael's chest, and he stumbles, blood blooming across his shirt.

I don't think. I move.

My hand wraps around the dagger strapped to my back, the weight of it grounding me as I step forward. Kael's eyes meet mine, wide with something I can't name.

"Stay out of this, Elira," Veylan says, his voice tight with panic.
"No," I say, my voice cold and sharp. "You don't get to do this."

Kael lunges for me, his blade swinging wildly, but I'm faster. The blade connects with his ribs, and he cries out, the sound twisting something inside me.

I swing again, and again, the fury driving every movement. My throat burning with each cries coming out of it. The world narrows to the clash of metal and the thud of my blows against his body.

Kael falls to his knees, blood dripping from his mouth as he looks up at me. "Elira," he whispers, his voice broken.

I raise my arm one last time, my hands trembling as I drive it into his chest. His body jerks, and then he collapses, lifeless, at my feet.

The silence that follows is deafening.

Lyric and Eryndor arrive moments later, their faces pale as they take in the scene.
"What the hell happened?" Lyric demands, her voice tight with shock.

I stare at Kael's lifeless body, my breath coming in sharp, ragged gasps. "He was going to sell me," I say, my voice hollow.

Lyric's expression crumples, and she drops to her knees beside Kael, her hand hovering over his bloodied chest. "Kael… you idiot."

Eryndor places a hand on her shoulder, his jaw clenched. "We don't have time for this. We need to move."

Veylan steps closer, his fur slick with blood as his ember eyes meet mine. *"You did what had to be done,"* he says, his voice steady but heavy with meaning.

But the weight of what I've done presses down on me, and for the first time, I feel like I might break.

Kael is dead.

And nothing will ever be the same.

Chains of Fate
Elira

The clearing is too quiet. The only sounds are my ragged breaths and the faint rustle of leaves as the night settles around us. Kael's body lies crumpled in the dirt, his blood staining the earth beneath him. My hands are trembling, still clutching the dagger slick with his blood.

I can't look away.

Lyric kneels beside him, her hands hovering uselessly, her golden eyes wide with shock. Eryndor stands a few feet away, his jaw tight, his fists clenched at his sides. No one speaks.

"I had to," I whisper, the words catching in my throat. "He was… he betrayed us."

Lyric's gaze snaps to mine, sharp and accusing. "He was one of us."

"No, he wasn't!" My voice breaks as the words tumble out, raw and desperate. "He was going to sell me—to Damien! He's the reason we're here. He was never one of us."

The weight of my own words crashes down on me, but before anyone can respond, a loud crack splits the air.
It's followed by another. And another.

The sound of boots on the forest floor.

Eryndor moves first, his hand going to the blade at his side, but it's too late. Figures emerge from the shadows, their armor glinting faintly in the dim light. Damien's soldiers, dozens of them, surround us, their weapons drawn.

"Drop it," one of them commands, gesturing toward my hands.

I glance at Lyric, who shakes her head slowly, tears streaking her face.

There's no way out of this.

The soldiers close in, binding our hands and forcing us to our knees. My mind is racing, but there's no time to think, no time to act.

"Where's Veylan?" I whisper, twisting my head to search for him.

The answer comes in the form of a low, agonized growl. My stomach drops as I spot him near the edge of the clearing, his massive form barely moving. Blood mats his dark fur, and his eyes are dim, flickering faintly in the darkness.

"No," I breathe, struggling against the soldier holding me. "Let me go!"

The man grips my arm tighter, shoving me back down.

And then he appears.

Damien steps into the clearing like a shadow given form.

Him. No.

His dark hair is slightly disheveled, his green eyes sharp and cutting as they sweep over us. The scars slashing across his face catch the faint light, adding to his brutal, commanding presence.

He stops a few feet away, his gaze lingering on Kael's lifeless body. "Well," he says, his voice low and smooth, "this is a surprise."

His attention shifts to me, and his lips curl into something resembling a smirk. "You've been busy."

"You're him," I say, my voice trembling with rage and something I can't name. "You're the man from the village."

"Ah, so you remember me," he replies, tilting his head slightly. "Good. That'll make this easier."

He turns to one of his soldiers. "What's the tally?"

"Four alive, including the girl," the soldier replies stiffly.

Damien hums thoughtfully, his gaze flicking back to Kael. "And this one?"

I grit my teeth, the anger rising again. "I killed him."

His green eyes narrow slightly, and for a moment, the smirk fades. "Did you?"

"He betrayed us," I spit, my voice breaking. "He was working for you."

Damien chuckles softly, shaking his head. "Working for me? No. Kael worked for himself. I gave him opportunities, and he took them. That's all."

His calm, almost amused tone grates on my nerves. "You're disgusting," I hiss.

He shrugs, unbothered. "I've been called worse."

He steps closer, towering over me. "Take them to the clearing," he orders, his voice snapping through the air like a whip.

The soldiers obey, dragging us farther into the forest despite our struggles. My mind races, my heart pounding as we're forced into a wide-open space, surrounded on all sides by Damien's men.

He surveys us for a moment before speaking. "Kill them, except the girl."

"No!" I shout, twisting against my bindings. "You can't—"

"I can," Damien interrupts, his voice icy and final.

"Take me instead!" The words spill out before I can think, desperation coloring every syllable.

The clearing falls silent.

Damien turns to me slowly, his green eyes narrowing. "What did you say?"

"I said take me," I repeat, forcing the fear out of my voice. "Kill me. Let them go."

Damien steps closer, his expression unreadable. "And why would I do that?"

"Because you don't need them," I say, holding his gaze. "You want me."

His lips twitch into a faint, humorless smile. "Bold assumption."

"It's not an assumption," I snap. "If you're going to kill someone, kill me. Let them go."

He studies me for a long moment, the silence stretching uncomfortably. Then, finally, he nods. "Release them. Take her."

Lyric cries out, lunging toward me, but the soldiers hold her back. "Don't do this!"

I meet her tearful gaze, my throat tight. "It's okay. Just… take care of Veylan."

She shakes her head, sobbing as the soldiers drag me away.

Damien's hand grips my arm, his touch firm and cold. "You've made your choice," he says softly, his green eyes flickering with something I can't place.

"And you've made yours," I reply, my voice trembling but defiant.

'You came here to kill me, didn't you?' 'What if I did?"

His smile widens, dark and taunting, and he leans in just enough that his breath brushes against my ear.

"Then I suggest you try harder," he murmur, his tone laced with a dangerous amusement that sends a shiver down my spine.

As they lead me away, I glance back one last time. Kael's lifeless body lies in the dirt, a haunting reminder of betrayal and sacrifice.

I don't look back again.

The Cage
Damien

The girl doesn't scream as the soldiers drag her to the carriage. Not once. Her head is high, her jaw set, and even in chains, she moves like she's got some kind of unearned power. I've seen it a hundred times before—no, a thousand.
Always the same.

A girl. Black hair, blue eyes. A look that's more curse than gift in this world. They always think they're special, that they're going to be the one to change it all. And they always end up the same way—broken, bleeding, forgotten.

But this one…

She's different. I don't know how or why, but she is. It's not just the way she stares me down, like she's daring me to blink first. It's not just her defiance, though that's part of it.

Hell, it's not even the way she moves, like she doesn't give a damn that she's one bad decision away from losing everything.

No, it's something else. Something under her skin, humming just out of reach, and it's pissing me off because I can't figure it out.

Standing in the clearing, I watch her for a moment longer, my gaze dragging over her like I'm trying to pin it down. Her hair's a mess, blood and dirt streaked across her face, and her eyes burn like two pieces of the fucking sky stole their way into her skull.

It's enough to make me hate her.

Not because she's beautiful—plenty of them were beautiful. No, it's because she shouldn't be. Not here, not now. She shouldn't have survived this long, shouldn't be standing there like she still has a goddamn choice in how this ends.

She smells like lavender. I caught it the first time I saw her, at the festival. It was faint then, mingling with the scent of fire and sweat and rebellion. But it's stronger now, darker, edged with something primal, something musky. It clings to her skin, a reminder of the moment I should have walked away.

But I didn't.

And here we are.

As I step into the carriage, the scent hits me again, threading its way through the stale air like it owns the place. She doesn't look at me, her focus locked on the barred window, but I can see the tension in her shoulders, the rigid set of her jaw and the tears in the corner of her eyes.

"You've made quite an impression," I say, my voice low and casual.

Her head snaps toward me, her eyes locking onto mine, and for a second, I feel the ground shift. "If you're trying to intimidate me, it's not working," she snaps, her tone biting.

I smirk, leaning back. "Good. Intimidation's boring."
She shifts, the chains clinking faintly as her shoulders stiffen. "You're a coward," she snaps. "Hiding behind your soldiers and your—whatever this is."

Her hand gestures vaguely to the carriage, and for a moment, amusement flickers through me.
"And what would you have me do? Fight you myself? Would that make you feel better about your situation?"

She glares, her lips pressing into a tight line.
The defiance in her gaze sends a strange thrill through
me, though I quickly shove the thought aside.
"You killed Kael," I say suddenly, the words
slicing through the air.

Her entire body tenses, and for the first time, I
see something flicker across her face—guilt, or maybe
regret.
"He betrayed us," she says after a moment, her
voice quieter now.

I hum thoughtfully, my gaze not leaving hers.
"Betrayal is a matter of perspective. Kael was useful.
Predictable. His greed made him easy to control."

"He was going to sell me to you," she spits, her
voice shaking.

"But you're still her," I counter, leaning forward
slightly. "What does that say about you?"

Her jaw clenches, and she looks away, her hair falling like a curtain between us. The scent of lavender drifts faintly through the air, mingling with the musk of blood and sweat. It pulls me back to the festival, to the moment I'd first caught her scent among the crowd.

Fuck. I want to touch her.

She'd smelled like warmth and defiance then, and now it's the same, though darker, heavier.
It's infuriating.

The carriage jerks to a stop, breaking the tense silence. I rise, my boots thudding softly against the wooden floor.

"Welcome to my world," I say, gesturing for the guards to open the door.

She steps out slowly, her gaze sweeping over the scene before her. My castle looms in the distance, its black towers piercing the gray sky like jagged fangs, a fortress that's swallowed its share of hope and spilled its weight in blood.

The fields surrounding it are barren, the crops long since withered, leaving nothing but dry, cracked earth.

She doesn't flinch, not the way most do. But her hands twitch at her sides, a tell she probably doesn't even realize she's giving away. That faint flicker of hesitation is enough to make me smirk.

"Not what you expected?" I ask, my voice laced with amusement.

She finally looks at me, her blue eyes locking onto mine with a heat that would make lesser men fold. "I've seen worse," she snaps, her tone sharp enough to draw blood.

I step closer, leaning in just enough to invade her space, watching as her shoulders stiffen and her jaw tightens. She doesn't back away, though. No, this one stands her ground, glaring at me like she'd slit my throat if her hands weren't bound.

"Worse than this?" I murmur, my voice dropping. "I doubt it."

Her gaze narrows, and for a split second, I swear she's daring me to get closer. The fire in her eyes is different now—less bravado, more rage. It makes her look alive in a way that grates against everything I've been taught about people like her.

I take another step, close enough that I catch the faint scent of lavender and musk lingering on her skin. It stirs something unwanted, something irritating, and I shove it down as quickly as it rises.

"You've got a lot to say for someone in chains," I say, my tone mocking as my gaze flicks down to the metal binding her wrists. "You think that fire of yours will keep you warm in there?"

Her lips curl into a snarl, and she takes a step forward, the chains rattling between us. "You think this—" she gestures at the castle with a flick of her bound hands, "—is supposed to scare me? It's just another pile of rock filled with another monster."

The words are meant to cut, and damn if they don't hit their mark.

I laugh, low and cold, stepping even closer until there's barely a breath of space between us. "Monster?" I murmur, tilting my head. "Little warrior, you have no idea."

Her breath catches for half a second—just long enough to tell me she's feeling the proximity too—but she recovers quickly, lifting her chin and fixing me with a glare that could cut stone.

"Don't worry about me," she snaps, her voice steady despite the tension thrumming between us. "Worry about yourself."

It's almost laughable, the way she throws her defiance around like a shield, as if it'll do a damn thing against what she's walked into. And yet…
I can't look away.

The guards move to pull her toward the gates, but I don't step back immediately. My eyes stay locked on hers, watching for any sign of weakness, any crack in the armor she's built around herself.

But there's nothing.

Not fear, not submission, not even regret. Just pure, unfiltered fury.

A Dark Bargain
Elira

The iron gates of the outside court creak apart, their hinges wailing in protest, as though even they knew better than to welcome anyone here. The bars, streaked with rust and mottled with patches of blackened metal, stand like jagged teeth waiting to snap shut.

I step through, the chains around my wrists biting into my skin, their weight forcing my shoulders back, stiff and defiant.

The courtyard stretches out before me, a sprawling expanse of lifeless stone and brittle earth. The walls rise on all sides, black and slick as if they'd been carved from shadows themselves, their jagged peaks clawing at the dismal sky. The air presses down, heavy with the scent of damp stone and something sour, metallic—like blood that had dried and never been washed away.

In the corners where the torchlight falters, the shadows twist like living things, curling and unfurling in ominous tendrils that seem to reach for the unwelcome. The air itself feels alive, heavy with the weight of whispers I can't quite hear, promising everything this place has devoured—and everything it still craves.

My boots crunch against the uneven stone, and the sound echoes unnaturally loud, each step a reminder that there's no going back. A soft drip, drip trails behind me, and I glance down to see dark streaks of red blooming along the gray stone.

My hands, bound and trembling, leave their mark—a trail of blood that feels more like an offering than a wound.

Ahead, the castle looms like something conjured from a nightmare. Its black walls gleam as though wet, the surface jagged and uneven, broken only by narrow windows that glow faintly with crimson light. The torches lining the courtyard cast everything in shades of blood and shadow, the flames crackling weakly as if even fire struggles to survive here.

Behind me, the forest is gone. Its towering trees and shifting canopy replaced by the oppressive presence of stone and the suffocating weight of silence. The place where my friends were left feels distant, a fading memory slipping through my grasp like sand.

Here, the air tastes different—thicker, metallic, and sharp. Every breath carries the weight of something ancient and unkind.

And Veylan…

A pang cuts through me at the thought of him, his ember eyes dimming as I was dragged away. He's out there somewhere. He has to be.

Damien walks ahead, his broad shoulders cutting a path through the sea of his soldiers. They part for him without a word, their heads bowing slightly as he passes. The sight sends a ripple of unease through me, but I swallow it down.

I won't give him the satisfaction of seeing me flinch.

"Move," one of the guards snaps, shoving me forward.

I glare at him but keep walking, my steps steady even as my knees threaten to buckle.

Damien moves ahead of me, his long strides confident and unhurried, the sound of his boots reverberating against the cold stone walls. The silence around him is a force of its own, heavier than the chains weighing down my wrists.

I keep my eyes on his broad back, the black fabric of his coat pulling taut over muscles that look carved from marble.

His hair, dark and slightly tousled, falls just past his collar, catching the faint glow of the crimson torchlight. He walks like he owns every inch of this cursed place—because he does.

And then he stops.

It's so sudden that I nearly stumble, the chains clinking loudly as I catch myself. I glare at him, but he doesn't move, his head tilting slightly as though he's caught the scent of something.

"Is there a problem?" I snap, the words harsher than I intended.

He turns slowly, his green eyes gleaming like polished emeralds under the flickering light. His gaze drops to the floor between us, where a single drop of red glistens against the gray stone.
My blood.

Without a word, he lowers himself, his massive frame folding gracefully as he crouches. Even kneeling, he exudes power, his broad shoulders and chiseled jawline dominating the small space.
His scarred face is shadowed, but the sharpness of his cheekbones catch the light, making him look both dangerous and breathtaking.
Damn him.

My throat tightens as he extends a hand, his long fingers brushing the ground where the drop of blood pools. He scoops it up with one finger, the motion slow and deliberate, and rises in a single fluid movement that leaves me rooted to the spot.

He doesn't stop there.

Damien raises his hand, the crimson drop gleaming like a jewel on the tip of his finger. His eyes lock onto mine, unblinking, as he brings it to his lips. His tongue flicks out, slow and deliberate, tasting it.

Humming.

My breath catches, and I can't look away, even as my chest tightens with equal parts fury and something I don't want to name.

"You taste like trouble," he murmurs, his voice low and smooth, the words sliding over me like silk dipped in venom.

I clench my fists, my nails digging into my

palms. "Get it out of your system?"

He smirks, his gaze still pinned to mine. "Not even close."

"You're disgusting," I spit, though the tremor in my voice betrays my unease.

"Disgusting," he repeats, his tone mocking as he takes a step closer, his towering frame casting me in shadow. "You don't even know what I am yet."

The air between us feels thick, charged, and I can feel the heat of him even with the chains separating us. I force myself to stand my ground, to meet his gaze without faltering.

"Whatever you are," I say, my voice low, "you don't scare me." His smirk deepens, and he leans in just enough that his breath brushes against my ear. "You should be."

Finally, he stops in front of a heavy wooden door, its surface scarred and weathered. He gestures for the guards to open it, and they do so without hesitation.

"Inside," he says, his voice low and firm.

The room is small, barely more than a cell. A single cot sits in the corner, and the walls are bare stone. "All this for me," I mutter, stepping inside.

Damien follows, his boots loud against the floor as the door slams shut behind him. The guards stay outside, leaving the two of us alone.

He leans against the wall, crossing his arms as his green eyes sweep over me. "You're... not what I expected."

"What do you want me to say?" I snap, turning to face him. "Thank you for not killing me yet?"

His smirk returns, sharp and infuriating. "You could start with why you're here."

I blink, caught off guard. "You tell me. You're the one who brought me here."

He pushes off the wall, stepping closer. The space between us shrinks, and I can feel the tension crackling in the air.

"You came into my world, my territory," he says, his voice dropping. "You think I wouldn't notice?"

I force myself to hold his gaze, even as my heart pounds in my chest. "I didn't have a choice."

"There's always a choice," he murmurs, his eyes

narrowing.

"And what about you?" I fire back, the words escaping before I can stop them. "Did you choose this? Your castle, your soldiers, your—" I gesture vaguely at him, "—whatever the hell you are?"

His smirk falters, just for a second, but it's enough.

He steps even closer, his presence overwhelming. "Careful, little warrior," he says softly, his tone laced with warning. "You're playing a dangerous game."

I lift my chin, refusing to back down. "Maybe I like dangerous games."
The silence between us stretches, thick and suffocating. His eyes search mine, and for a moment, I swear there's something other than anger in them.

But then he steps back, the mask sliding firmly into place.

"Rest," he says, his voice cold and detached. "You'll need it."

The door slams shut behind him, leaving me alone in the suffocating silence.

Barbs and Chains
Elira

For a moment, I stay frozen, my legs locked, my arms heavy with the weight of the chains.

I let out a slow breath, my gaze flicking to the cot in the corner. It's small, hard, and looks like it might crumble under the weight of a stiff breeze.

A shiver runs down my spine as I take in the bare stone walls, their damp surfaces gleaming faintly in the crimson torchlight spilling through the small, barred window.

This isn't a room. It's a cage.

I pace, my boots scraping against the uneven floor. My thoughts are a storm, spinning wildly between Kael's betrayal, Veylan's absence, and… him.

Damien.

The way he looked at me, like he was peeling back my skin to see what's underneath. The way he moved, controlled, predatory, every step calculated to make me feel small.

And then there was that damn moment. The blood. The smirk. The way his tongue slid over his finger like he wasn't just tasting blood but proving a point.

My chest tightens, my fingers curling into fists. "Bastard," I mutter, the word hissing through my teeth.

But no matter how much I curse him, it doesn't stop the heat crawling up my neck when I think about his eyes locking onto mine, the way his voice dipped when he whispered, 'You should be.'

I shake the thought away, dragging my fingers through my hair. "Focus, Elira," I whisper to myself. "You can't let him get in your head."

The sound of footsteps echoes outside, heavy and deliberate. My stomach clenches as I spin toward the door, my heart pounding in my chest.

When it swings open, it's not Damien—it's one of his guards. Tall, armored, and faceless behind a dark helmet, the man steps inside with a plate of food and a small pitcher of water. He sets them on the floor without a word, his movements efficient and uninterested.

I glare at him as he leaves, the door slamming shut again with a finality that makes my stomach twist.

The plate is nothing special—bread, a hunk of cheese, and what I think might be some kind of dried meat. The water smells faintly of metal, but I drink it anyway, my throat burning from thirst.

I sink onto the cot, my legs finally giving out beneath me. The weight of everything crashes down at once, pressing into my chest until I feel like I might shatter.

But I can't.

Not here. Not now.

I close my eyes, letting my head fall back against the stone wall. The cold seeps into my skin, grounding me. Somewhere out there, Lyric and Eryndor are free. Veylan is alive.

And me?

I'm still standing.

A soft creak breaks the silence, and my eyes snap open.

Damien stands in the doorway, his coat brushing the stone floor, his presence filling the small space like a shadow come to life. His green eyes flick to the untouched food before settling on me.
"You didn't eat much," he says, his voice almost casual.

"Wasn't hungry," I snap, sitting up straighter.

He steps inside, the door clicking shut behind him. His movements are slow, deliberate, as if he's giving me time to react—but to what, I don't know.

He stops just a few feet away, his gaze dragging over me like he's taking stock of every bruise, every scratch, every drop of blood left on my skin.

"You're going to have to keep your strength up," he says after a moment, his tone edged with something I can't place.

"For what?" I ask, my voice sharp. "Your amusement?"

His smirk returns, dark and unyielding. "For survival."

The air between us crackles with tension, heavy and suffocating. His presence is too much, pressing into every corner of the room, into every corner of me.
"I don't need your advice," I bite out, my chin lifting.

"No," he agrees, stepping closer, his shadow falling over me. "But you'll take it anyway."

I want to snap back, to tear him down with words that burn, but the heat in his gaze makes the words stick in my throat.
"Why am I here?" I ask instead, my voice quieter now, but no less fierce.

He tilts his head slightly, his eyes narrowing. "That's the question, isn't it?"

He steps closer, his boots brushing against the hem of my tattered clothes. I shrink back instinctively, the stone wall cold against my spine, but I refuse to look away.

"You think it's about you," he says, his voice low and dangerous. "That all of this—" he gestures around us, "—is because you're special. Different."

He leans down, his face inches from mine, his green eyes burning with something dark and unknowable.

"You're here because I let you be," he whispers, his voice cutting through the air like a blade. "And because something far worse than me wants you alive."

The words hit like a slap, and I can't stop the sharp intake of breath.

"What—what do you mean?" I stammer, hating the way my voice cracks.

His smirk is cruel, devoid of the faintest trace of humor. "Ask yourself, little warrior: if I wanted you dead, why are you still breathing?"

Before I can respond, he straightens, turning toward the door.
"Get some sleep," he says over his shoulder, his voice calm once more. "You'll need it for what's coming."

The door swings shut with a heavy thud, leaving me in the suffocating silence. My mind races, his words echoing in my head, refusing to settle.
Something worse than him?

The cold stone digs into my back, but I don't move. Sleep won't come tonight—not with the weight of whatever hell I've just walked into pressing down on my chest.

The Weight of Shadows
Damien

The hall stretches endlessly before me, the flickering torchlight casting long shadows against the stone walls. It's quieter now, the usual hum of my soldiers' movements replaced by the heavy stillness that follows one of its whispers.

I clench my fists, the leather of my now gloved hands creaking faintly, and keep walking.
It's there, in the back of my mind, like it always is. A shadow wrapped around my thoughts, its presence a constant ache behind my eyes. It doesn't speak in words—not exactly.

It's more a sensation, a pressure, an idea that twists and warps until it feels like my own.

Kill her.

The thought slithers through my mind like oil, dark and clinging.

She doesn't belong. She's dangerous. She's a threat.

My steps falter for a moment, my boots scuffing against the stone floor.

"No," I mutter under my breath, the word sharp and firm.

The presence doesn't recede. It never does. Instead, it shifts, the weight of it pressing harder, colder.

You can't save her. You can't save any of them.

The corridor narrows as I approach the council chamber, its iron door looming ahead. My hand trembles as I reach for the latch, the shadow inside me twisting, clawing at my resolve.

I push the door open and step inside. The room is dimly lit, the torches casting faint red hues across the walls. The air is thick here, suffocating, as though the very stones are imbued with the malevolence that has plagued me for years.

The force that saved my kingdom. And the force that will destroy it.

It came to me during the war, when we were losing. The enemy was relentless, their numbers vast, and my people were starving, broken. I made a choice— one that any king would have made.

Victory in exchange for a piece of myself. A small price, I thought. A noble sacrifice.

But it wasn't small. It wasn't noble.

It was a noose I tied around my own neck, and now, it tightens with every breath I take.

"You're weak," the shadow whispers, the sound not external but inside me, reverberating through my chest like the echoes of a scream.

"I'm still here," I say aloud, my voice steady. "That's more than you wanted."

It doesn't respond, but the weight in my head pulses, a reminder of its displeasure. It hates that I defy it. That I let her live.

Elira.

Her name stirs something in me, something I hate. I shouldn't care. I should've let her bleed out in the forest, left her to rot like the others before her.

But when I saw her at the festival, something shifted.

The force felt it too.

I close my eyes, leaning against the cool stone wall. Her scent lingers in my thoughts—lavender and musk, sharp and grounding in a way nothing else is. It should've made her easier to hate. Instead, it's like she's burrowed under my skin, clawing at parts of me I thought I'd buried long ago.

She's a threat.

The force presses harder, the thought crashing through me like a wave.

"She's mine to deal with," I snarl, my voice low and sharp, the sound bouncing off the empty walls.

The pressure ebbs slightly, but it doesn't fade. It never does.

I push off the wall, the anger simmering beneath my skin giving me the strength to move. The force may want her dead, but I'm not its pawn—not yet.

I can feel its rage simmering, its disappointment curdling into something colder, darker.

Let it be angry. Let it simmer.

Because as much as I hate her, as much as I want to tear her apart for the chaos she's brought into my world, I can't bring myself to do it.

Not yet.

Pieces in Motion
Elira

The cell is silent, but my mind is anything but. Damien's words swirl like smoke in my head, thick and choking, refusing to settle.

"You're here because I let you be. And because something far worse than me wants you alive."

Bastard.

The weight of his voice lingers, pressing into my chest like a stone. The way he said it—calm, deliberate, like he knew exactly how deeply it would cut.

Something worse than him?

I don't know what that means, but the thought

coils in my stomach like a snake. I stare at the torchlight outside the barred window, letting its faint glow chase away the shadows in the corners of the cell.

The door creaks open, and I jolt, my hands instinctively curling into fists.

It's not Damien this time. It's a woman.

Her steps are quiet, almost hesitant, as she enters the cell. She carries a tray of fresh bread and water, but it's her face that catches my attention—sharp cheekbones, dark eyes, and a cascade of auburn curls that spill over her shoulders.

She sets the tray down, her movements precise but not rushed.

"You're awake," she says, her voice soft but steady.

I blink, unsure how to respond. "And you are?"

She straightens, brushing her hands on the front of her worn tunic. "Amara. I keep things running around here."

"Lucky you," I mutter, sitting up straighter. My muscles ache, but I force myself to meet her gaze. "What do you want?"

Amara doesn't flinch at my tone. Instead, she tilts her head slightly, studying me like I'm some kind of puzzle she's trying to solve.

"You don't belong here," she says simply, her words a statement rather than a judgment.

I huff a bitter laugh. "Tell that to your king."

Her lips twitch, not quite a smile but close. "Damien is many things, but he doesn't keep people here without a reason."

"Is that supposed to comfort me?"

Amara shrugs, her dark eyes narrowing slightly. "It should scare you."

I glare at her, my jaw tightening. "If he's trying to scare me, he'll have to try harder."

For a moment, she says nothing, her gaze lingering on the chain binding my wrist to the wall. Finally, she speaks, her tone quieter now.

"Whatever you think of him, he's not your biggest problem."

The words send a chill through me, and I sit up straighter, my pulse quickening. "What does that mean?"

Amara's lips press into a thin line, and she shakes her head. "Eat," she says, nodding toward the tray. "You'll need your strength."

She turns to leave, her footsteps soft against the stone.

"Wait," I call after her, my voice sharper than I intended. "What's worse than him?"

Amara pauses in the doorway, her hand resting on the frame. She doesn't look back, but her words hang in the air like a curse.
"Ask him," she says, and the door closes behind her.

The silence swallows the room again, but it feels heavier now. The flickering light from the torches outside seems dimmer, the shadows thicker.

I sit back against the wall, my chest tight. Damien might be the devil in this castle, but it's becoming clear that he's not the only one pulling the strings.

And whatever's worse than him? It's closer than I'd like to believe.

A Guided Cage
Elira

The cold is the first thing I feel, a biting chill that creeps into my bones and drags me from restless sleep. The cot beneath me is hard, the blanket too thin to offer real warmth.

I groan, shifting slightly, and that's when the second thing hits me—a hand gripping my shoulder, firm and unrelenting.
"Up," Damien's voice cuts through the haze, sharp and commanding.

My eyes snap open, and for a moment, all I see is his face, too close and annoyingly perfect. His green eyes gleam with something bordering on impatience, and the scars slashing across his cheek and brow look deeper in the morning light.

"What the hell?" I mutter, pushing his hand away. "Ever heard of knocking?"

"This is me knocking," he replies dryly, stepping back. "You've had enough sleep."

I sit up slowly, glaring at him as I rub the sleep from my eyes. "Do you always wake people up like this, or am I just special?"

"You're special," he says, his tone mocking, "in all the worst ways."

The smirk tugging at the corner of his mouth makes my blood boil, and I force myself to stand, ignoring the ache in my muscles.

"What do you want now?" I snap, crossing m arms over my chest.

His gaze flicks over me briefly before he turns toward the door. "You wanted answers. Time to see the castle."

The promise of answers is enough to stir my curiosity, though I hate that he knows it. I follow him into the hallway, my boots clinking faintly against the stone floor.

The castle feels different in the daylight—or whatever version of daylight exists here. The gray light filtering through the narrow windows casts everything in pale, lifeless hues, making the blackened walls seem even more oppressive.

Damien walks ahead of me, his strides long and unhurried, his coat brushing the floor behind him. His hair is slightly tousled, the dark strands catching faint glints of red from the torches.

My fingers twitch against the chains at my wrists, and my mind wanders, tracing over the hundred ways I could kill him if I had the chance.

"You're predictable," he says suddenly, not bothering to look back.

I scowl. "How so, King?"

He finally stops, turning to face me with that infuriating smirk. "The way you look at me. Like you're sizing me up. Plotting."

"And if I am?" I challenge, my chin lifting.

His green eyes narrow slightly, and he steps closer, his presence overwhelming in the confined space. "Then I'd suggest you find a better plan. Because this—" he gestures to the chain dangling between us, "—won't get you far."

The tension between us crackles, and for a second, I consider taking the swing he's practically begging for.

Instead, I force a smile, sharp and biting. "Don't worry. When I do it, you won't see it coming."

His chuckle is low and mocking, and he leans in just enough that his breath brushes against my skin. "I'll look forward to it."

I shove past him, the chain rattling as I take the lead. "Are you going to show me the damn castle, or just waste my time?"
Damien's smirk softens into something almost amused as he falls into step beside me. "Impatient, aren't we?"

The halls stretch endlessly, their walls lined with faded tapestries that depict battles and horrors I'd rather not think about. The air is thick with the scent of damp stone and smoke, and every step echoes faintly, the sound swallowed by the oppressive silence.

"Why do you even live here?" I mutter, glancing at the crumbling ceiling above us. "It's like a tomb."

"It suits me," he replies, his tone light but edged with something darker.

I roll my eyes but don't press further. The castle is already giving me more answers than I'd wanted—none of them comforting.

We stop in front of a massive wooden door, its surface carved with intricate designs of twisting vines and jagged thorns. Damien pushes it open, revealing a room that takes my breath away.

The ceiling soars high above, disappearing into shadows. Long windows line the far wall, streaked with dirt and soot, but pale streams of light filter through, casting the room in an eerie glow.

A fire crackles in the hearth, its warmth barely reaching the edges of the room. The table in the center is covered in maps, books, and a half-finished meal.

"Sit," Damien says, his voice firm but not harsh.

I hesitate, my eyes narrowing as I take a step forward. "Why?"

"Because I said so," he replies, his smirk reappearing. I glare at him but sit, my chains clinking faintly as I settle into the chair. My gaze flicks to the food— bread, roasted meat, and a small pitcher of water.

"You eat like a king," I mutter.

He leans against the table, his green eyes watching me closely. "Maybe because I am one. And you eat like someone who hasn't in days."

He pours a small cup of water and slides it across the table.

"Don't mistake this for kindness," he says, his voice low. "You're more useful alive."

I grab the cup, my fingers tightening around it as I glare at him. "Comforting," I say, taking a sip.

"You'll need your strength," he adds, his tone dropping slightly. "This place isn't kind to the weak."
I meet his gaze, the tension between us thick and unrelenting.

"You act like you care," I snap, setting the cup down with more force than necessary.

"Care?" He chuckles softly, shaking his head. "No, little warrior. I don't care. But I've learned that dead pawns don't win games."

His words hit harder than they should, but I refuse to let him see it.

Instead, I glare at him, my jaw tight. "I'm not a pawn."

His smirk widens, his voice dropping to a near whisper. "You're whatever I need you to be."

I don't respond. Instead, my gaze drops to the food, my stomach twisting with hunger so sharp it's painful. I hesitate for only a moment before reaching for the bread, tearing off a piece with shaky hands.

The first bite is a revelation. It's stale, but it doesn't matter. The moment it hits my tongue, I'm ravenous. I reach for the meat next, barely chewing before swallowing, the hunger driving away any shred of decorum.

Damien leans back against the table, crossing his arms as he watches me. His green eyes narrow slightly, his smirk gone.
"Starving, are we?" he drawls, but there's no malice in his tone.

I glare at him between bites, crumbs clinging to the corners of my mouth. "What did you expect?" I snap, my words muffled by the food.

His lips twitch, not quite a smile but close. "Not this, admittedly."

"Well, sorry if I'm not dainty enough for your royal standards," I bite back, tearing into another piece of bread.

His gaze lingers on me, something flickering behind his eyes that I can't quite place. "No," he says softly, almost to himself. "This is better."

I pause mid-bite, my eyes narrowing. "What's that supposed to mean?"

He tilts his head, his expression unreadable. "You're not what I expected."

"And what did you expect?" I challenge, my
voice sharper now.

He wait a long time before answering, his gaze
dragging over me as though weighing his response.
"Someone softer," he says finally, his tone almost
amused. "Easier to break. Like all the others before
you."

The words sting more than they should, and I sit
up straighter, fixing him with a glare. "Sorry to
disappoint."
His smirk returns, faint but infuriating. "Oh, I wouldn't
say that."
The tension between us thickens, the air
crackling with unspoken words. I shove another bite of
bread into my mouth, more out of spite than hunger at
this point.
"Anything else you want to criticize?" I ask, my voice
dripping with sarcasm.

He chuckles softly, shaking his head. "Not at the moment."

I finish the bread and reach for the meat, chewing with deliberate intensity as I stare him down.

He doesn't look away, his gaze steady and unnervingly calm.

For a moment, it feels like we're locked in some kind of battle—one I refuse to lose.

Finally, he straightens, brushing a speck of dust from his coat. "Get some rest when you're done," he says, his voice smooth but distant. "We'll continue this tomorrow."

I snort, wiping my mouth with the back of my hand. "Looking forward to it." His laughter rings out, sharp and genuine, and it grates on my nerves.

His smirk widens just slightly, and without another word, he turns and strides toward the door.

"Wait." My voice cuts through the silence before I can stop myself.

He pauses, his hand resting on the heavy wooden door. Turning slightly, he raises an eyebrow, his green eyes glinting with faint amusement. "Something to add, little warrior?"

"You're just… leaving me here?" I ask, gesturing vaguely to the vast, empty room.

He chuckles, low and mocking, stepping back toward me. "Would you prefer I stay and keep you company?"

I narrow my eyes, ignoring the heat that rises at his tone. "That's not what I meant. What if I—" I hesitate, the words feeling foolish even as they form. "What if I escape?"

"Escape?" he repeats, as if the word itself is ridiculous.

"Yes," I snap, my chin lifting defiantly. "What's stopping me?"

"Oh, I don't know," he says, his voice dripping with sarcasm. "The guards. The walls. The fact that you'd barely make it past the courtyard before this place swallows you whole."

I glare at him, my jaw tightening. "You seem awfully confident for someone who's leaving their prisoner unshackled."

He tilts his head slightly, his smirk softening into something more thoughtful. "Fair point."

Without warning, he steps closer, reaching for the chain binding my wrists. I tense, instinctively pulling back, but his grip is firm, his fingers brushing against mine as he works the lock.

The shackles fall away with a faint clink, and I stare at him, my arms feeling oddly weightless.

"There," he says, his voice quieter now. "Consider it a challenge."

I frown, flexing my hands as I glare up at him. "You're not worried?"

His smirk returns, sharp and infuriating. "Not in the slightest."

He leans in slightly, his voice dropping to a near whisper. "But by all means, try. It might be the most fun I've had in years."

I clench my fists, fighting the urge to throw something at him. "You're insufferable."

"And you're predictable," he counters, his tone light but edged with something darker.

He steps back, his presence lingering in the space between us like a shadow. "Enjoy the castle, little warrior. It'll enjoy you."

Before I can respond, he turns on his heel, the door creaking shut behind him, leaving me alone with the silence—and the unsettling weight of his confidence.

The Maze of Shadows
Elira

The silence after Damien's departure is suffocating, pressing into the room like a physical weight. My wrists ache where the shackles had been, the skin raw and bruised, but the absence of the chains feels heavier than their presence.

He let me go.

He actually let me go.

The thought gnaws at me as I pace the room, my eyes flicking to the door every few seconds. His confidence, his smug assurance that I couldn't escape—it's like a dare.

I grab a knife from the table and tucked it into my waistband, its dull edge gleaming faintly in the torchlight.

"Let's see how confident you are when I'm gone," I mutter under my breath.

The corridor outside is quiet, the flickering torches casting faint pools of light on the stone walls. I move quickly but carefully, my footsteps soft against the uneven floor.

The first guard is stationed near a narrow staircase, his back to me. He's tall and broad, the black of his armor blending with the shadows.

My grip tightens on the knife as I approach, the cold metal reassuring against my palm.

I strike fast, driving the blade toward the gap in his armor at the back of his neck. But he's quicker than I expect, spinning around and catching my wrist before the blade can find its mark.

"You bitch," he growls, his grip like iron.

I snarl, twisting my body and slamming my knee into his side. The armor absorbs most of the impact, but it's enough to make him loosen his hold.

The knife slips from my fingers, clattering to the floor as he lunges for me.

I duck under his outstretched arm, grabbing the knife and spinning on my heel. The blade slices across his exposed hand, and he lets out a sharp curse, stumbling back.

I don't wait. I dart past him, my boots pounding against the floor as I sprint down the corridor.

The castle seems to shift around me, the twisting hallways and narrow staircases all blending together in a disorienting blur.

Another guard appears at the end of the hall, his sword already drawn. My chest tightens as I skid to a stop, my mind racing.

The first guard is behind me, his heavy footsteps closing in fast.

I dart into the nearest doorway, slamming it shut behind me and bolting it with trembling hands.

The room is different—softer, warmer. The sharp, damp smell of the rest of the castle is replaced by something subtler, faintly spiced.

I glance around, my breath catching.

The walls are lined with bookshelves, their dark wood polished to a dull sheen. Thick rugs cover the stone floor, their intricate patterns rich with deep reds and blacks. A massive bed dominates the center of the room, its dark sheets perfectly made, the edges tucked with military precision.

The air is warmer here, less oppressive, but no less dangerous.

Because this isn't just any room.

This is Damien's.

The door behind me rattles, the guard pounding against it with enough force to make the hinges groan. My heart races as I scan the room, my eyes landing on a second door to the left.

I dart toward it, but I barely make it three steps before the main door bursts open.

The guard lunges, his armored hand grabbing my arm and yanking me back.

I twist, the knife in my hand slicing across his shoulder. The blade glances off the metal, but the force of it is enough to make him stumble.

I yank my arm free and bolt for the second door, slamming it behind me.

This room is smaller, but just as richly decorated. A desk sits near the window, its surface cluttered with papers and a single, flickering candle.

The guards' shouts grow louder, and I know I don't have much time.

I grab the nearest object—a heavy, silver candlestick—and brace myself.

The door flies open, and the first guard storms in, his sword raised.

I swing the candlestick with all my strength, the weight of it connecting with his helmet with a sickening clang.

Skull cracking.

He stumbles, body falling on the floor, but the second guard is already behind him, his blade slicing through the air.

I duck, the sword narrowly missing my head, and shove the desk into his path. Papers scatter as he trips, crashing into the wooden frame with a curse.

Before I can make another move, a voice cuts through the chaos, low and sharp.

"Enough."

The guards freeze, their heads snapping toward the doorway.

Damien stands there, his green eyes glinting like polished emeralds in the dim light. His coat is unbuttoned, revealing the broad expanse of his chest, and his scars catch the faint glow of the candlelight.

I tighten my grip on the candlestick, my breath coming in short, sharp bursts.

"Leave us," Damien says, his voice calm but unyielding.

The guards hesitate for only a moment before backing away, their gazes lingering on me with thinly veiled contempt.
The door clicks shut, and the silence that follows is deafening.

Damien steps closer, his gaze dragging over me like a weight. "You've been busy," he murmurs, his tone almost amused.

I glare at him, the candlestick still clutched in my hand. "Go to hell."

He smirks, his head tilting slightly. "Darling, you're already there."

Fire and Steel
Elira

The air between us thickens, the faint scent of smoke and spiced leather curling in the back of my throat. Damien doesn't move, but his gaze is enough to pin me in place, green and cutting, like he's already stripping me apart.

I clench the candlestick tighter, my fingers aching from the grip. He notices, of course he does, and the corner of his scarred mouth quirks up in that maddening way.
"Are you going to try it?" His voice is low, almost lazy, but there's a sharpness beneath it. "Or do you just like holding phallic objects for fun?"

Heat floods my cheeks, and I take a step forward, raising the makeshift weapon. "Keep talking, and I'll show you exactly how fun this can be."

His laughter is quiet, dark, like the rumble of distant thunder. He doesn't back away. If anything, he steps closer, the weight of him crashing into my senses. "I'd love to see you try, little warrior."

I swing before I can think, the candlestick slicing through the air. He sidesteps easily, his hand snapping out to catch my wrist. His fingers clamp down, not hard enough to hurt, but enough to hold me in place.

The candlestick clangs to the floor between us, the sound echoing like a scream.

"Cute," he murmurs, his green eyes gleaming with amusement. "But predictable."

I twist, slamming my free hand into his chest. It's like hitting a wall. His grip tightens, and he pulls me forward, the movement so quick it knocks the breath from my lungs.

"Let me go," I snarl, my voice raw and venomous. "Make me," he counters, his tone infuriatingly calm.

The heat of him is unbearable, his body too close, his grip unrelenting. I slam my knee toward his stomach, but he shifts just enough to avoid it, his smirk widening.

"Is this how you thank someone for saving your life?" "Saving me?" I bark out a laugh, twisting again. "You dragged me here in chains, you arrogant bastard!"

His grip loosens for a fraction of a second—just enough for me to twist free. I shove him back with both hands, but he doesn't stumble. He just watches me, his expression shifting into something darker.

"Feel better?" he asks, his voice dropping an octave.

I grab the knife from my waistband, the blade flashing in the dim light. His gaze flicks to it briefly before returning to mine, utterly unbothered.

"You really think that's going to work?"

"Keep talking," I snap, lunging toward him.

He moves faster than I expect, his hand catching mine mid-swing. The knife clatters to the floor, and before I can react, his other hand wraps around my waist, pulling me flush against him.

The breath punches out of me, and suddenly, it's too much. The heat, the weight, the sharp scent of him filling every inch of the space between us.

"Stop," I hiss, my voice trembling.

"Make me," he repeats, his voice a whisper against my ear.

I shove at his chest, my nails digging into the fabric of his coat. He doesn't budge. Instead, his fingers flex against my waist, firm and unyielding, as if he's anchoring me in place.

"You hate me," he murmurs, his tone almost thoughtful. "I can feel it in every twitch of your body."

"Good," I spit, tilting my head back to glare at him.

His green eyes narrow, his smirk fading into something sharper, hungrier. "But hate isn't enough, is it?"

The words hit like a slap, and I react without thinking. My hand flies up, aiming for his face, but he catches it easily, his fingers wrapping around my wrist.

"You're quick," he says, his voice low and rough. "But not quick enough."

"Let me go," I snap, struggling against his hold.

"And miss this?" His grip tightens just enough to keep me still. "Not a chance."

The tension crackles between us, sharp and electric. My heart pounds against my ribs, and every breath feels like a fight.

His gaze flicks to my mouth, lingering for half a second before snapping back to my eyes. The intensity in his expression sends a shiver racing down my spine, but I shove it aside, replacing it with fury.

"You're disgusting," I say, my voice trembling with rage.

"And you're fascinating," he counters, his voice soft but cutting. "Isn't that funny?"

"Not really."

His lips twitch, a hint of a smirk returning. "It's not supposed to be."

He finally releases me, stepping back just enough to give me space, though his presence still looms like a storm cloud.

His gaze lingers, sharp and unyielding, before he finally takes a step back.

"You're not as clever as you think," he says, his tone low, almost taunting.

I glare at him, the knife still clenched in my hand. "And you're not as invincible as you think."

His smirk sharpens, but there's no humor in it this time. "We'll see, little warrior."

Without another word, he turns and strides toward the door, his coat flaring slightly behind him. The heavy wood creaks as he pulls it open, and the sound reverberates through the room as it shuts behind him with a resounding thud.

The silence feels heavier now, pressing down on my chest. My legs give out, and I drop to the floor, the cold stone biting into my skin.

The knife clatters from my grasp, spinning once before coming to rest at my feet.

My heart pounds, the echo of his words still ringing in my ears.

Not clever enough.

I grit my teeth, the weight of his smugness digging under my skin like splinters. He's wrong. He has to be.

But the truth sits heavy in my chest. Charging in, fighting him on impulse—it's gotten me nowhere. Every move I've made has played right into his hands. My gaze drifts to the knife, and my fingers twitch against the stone.

Next time will be different.

He expects fire from me—rage, chaos, desperation.

I'll give him none of it.

Beneath the Surface
Elira

I take a shaky breath, my wrist aching from where he'd grabbed me. The knife feels heavier in my hand now, like it's mocking my failure.

But then, faintly, I hear it—low, guttural, and angry.

A voice.

I freeze, straining to listen. It's coming from the other side of the door.

I inch closer, careful not to make a sound. The voice grows louder, sharper, and my breath catches as I realize—it's

Damien.

But he's not speaking to anyone.

His words are clipped, punctuated by the sound of something crashing. A heavy thud follows, like a fist hitting stone.

"No," he growls, his voice raw. "I've given enough. You're not taking her!"

The silence that follows is deafening, broken only by his ragged breathing.

I press my ear against the door, my pulse hammering in my chest.

"You don't control me," he snarls, the venom in his tone sending a shiver down my spine. "Not anymore."

Another crash—this time louder, like a table or chair splintering under force.

His breathing grows heavier, each inhale sounding like it's ripped from his lungs.

"Enough!" he roars, and for a moment, the walls around me seem to tremble.

I pull back, my mind racing. Who is he talking to? There was no one else in the corridor.

A muffled groan reaches me, low and pained. Against my better judgment, I crack the door open just enough to see.

Damien is on his knees, his hands gripping his head as though trying to claw something out. His coat is discarded on the floor, his shirt half-untucked, and the flickering candle lights dances across the scars on his face, making him look more stunning than ever.

"You think I don't know what you're doing?" he spits, his voice quieter now but no less venomous. "You think I haven't seen this before?"

He slams his fist into the stone floor, the impact leaving his knuckles bloodied.

"Not her," he growls, his head snapping up as if looking at something I can't see. His green eyes burn with fury, but there's something else there—something raw and desperate.

"You want me," he says, his voice trembling with barely restrained rage. "Then take me. I'm so fucking tired of all this."

The silence that follows is thick, suffocating. He sags slightly, his head bowing, and for a moment, he looks utterly defeated.

I step back, the door creaking faintly, and his head snaps toward the sound.

My breath catches as our eyes meet, his green gaze sharp and unyielding despite the pain etched across his face.

"What the hell are you doing?" he snarls, his voice a low rumble that sends a chill down my spine.

I grip the edge of the door, my mind scrambling for an excuse. "I heard something," I say, my voice quieter than I intended. His expression hardens, the vulnerability vanishing like it was never there. "Get out."

"Damien—"

He stiffens, his head turning sharply toward me. His green eyes lock onto mine, and for a heartbeat, the air between us crackles like a storm about to break.

"What did you just say?" His voice is low now, dangerous, but there's something else beneath it— something almost... hungry.

I swallow hard, every instinct screaming at me to run, but I stand my ground, my chest heaving.

"Damien," I repeat, louder this time, the weight of his name heavy on my tongue.

He steps closer, the space between us shrinking until his presence is overwhelming. The faint scent of leather and smoke curls around me, intoxicating despite the warning bells ringing in my head.

"Say it again," he murmurs, his voice dropping to a rough whisper. His hand brushes the edge of the doorframe, the movement casual, but his eyes burn with intensity.

The words catch in my throat, my pulse hammering as his gaze drags over me, slow and deliberate. My name feels like a weapon now, poised on the edge of my lips, but I can't force it out again.

His lips curl into a smirk, sharp and knowing, and he leans in slightly, his breath warm against my cheek. "Not so bold now, are you?"

My fists clench at my sides, the tremor in my hands betraying the defiance I'm desperately clinging to.

"I—"

The sound of a horn blaring outside cuts me off, sharp and jarring.

Damien's expression darkens in an instant, the predatory edge fading as his head snaps toward the window.

"Don't move," he growls, the command laced with urgency.

But before I can respond, he's gone, his coat flaring behind him as he strides down the corridor.

The horn sounds again, longer this time, followed by the faint but unmistakable clang of weapons being drawn.

My heart pounds as I step toward the window, my fingers brushing the cold stone. Outside, in the flickering torchlight, I see shadows moving—figures scaling the outer walls, their weapons glinting like teeth.

"I'm here."

A Beast at the Gates
Damien

The blare of the horn cuts through the air like a blade, the sound reverberating through the stone walls of the castle. My boots hit the cold floor in rapid strides, the echo of each step swallowed by the roar building in my chest. The attack isn't a surprise. Not really. But the timing is infuriating.

And then there's her.

Elira.

Her voice saying my name—just once—has lodged itself in my head like a splinter I can't shake. Low, defiant, dripping with challenge.

"Damien."

The way her lips moved around it, the slight hitch in her breath—I can't stop hearing it.

Now all I can think of is her saying it again, but not in defiance. No, I imagine it drawn out, husky, her voice trembling with my cock inside her.

My jaw tightens as I push the thought aside.
Not now.

The second blast of the horn is longer, its urgency undeniable.

The guards at the doors hesitate, their expressions pale as they murmur among themselves. Useless cowards. I don't need to see the carnage to know what's happening out there.

A predator has made its way to my gates. "Open it," I bark, my voice sharp enough to snap them out of their stupor.

One of them swallows hard, his hand trembling as it reaches for the latch. "My lord, it's—"

"I don't care what it is," I snarl, cutting him off. "Open the damn door."

Behind me, the sound of footsteps reaches my ears, lighter but quick, and my temper flares hotter.

I don't have to turn around to know who it is.

"Did I not tell you to stay put?" I growl, whipping around to find Elira jogging to catch up, her expression set in that infuriating mix of determination and defiance.

She doesn't answer, of course. She doesn't listen either, her boots falling into step alongside mine like she belongs here. Like she's untouchable.

Her hair is wild, her cheeks flushed. It shouldn't affect me, but it does.

I've never hated a voice so much in my life—or wanted to hear it again. Her saying my name, the bite in her tone... it's maddening.

I glance at her as we approach the door, and for a second, my mind betrays me. I see her lips parted for an entirely different reason, her breath catching as she moans my name instead of snarling it.

Heat rushes through my already growing buldge in my pants, primal and unwelcome, and I clench my fists, willing the thought away.

"Turn back," I snap, my tone harsher than intended.

She glances at me, her blue eyes blazing. "Not a chance."

"Stubborn little—" The words die on my tongue as the doors creak open.

The sight beyond them is chaos.

Bodies litter the courtyard, broken and bloodied, their armor torn like paper. The air reeks of death, the metallic tang of blood mingling with the cool night air.

And in the center of it all, the beast stands.

Massive and black as midnight, its ember eyes glowing like hellfire. Blood drips from its jaws, staining the cracked stone beneath its paws.

The guards falter, their weapons trembling in their hands.
"Kill it," I command, my voice cutting through their hesitation like a whip.

But no one moves.
The beast lets out a low, guttural growl, the sound vibrating through the ground. It takes a step forward, its claws clicking against the stone, and the guards step back.

Cowards.

I grip the hilt of my sword, my mind racing. "It's him," Elira whispers beside me, her voice barely audible.

I glance at her, my brow furrowing. "What?"

Her gaze doesn't leave the wolf. "Veylan. It's him."

I pause, the weight of her words sinking in.

She's connected to this thing. Of course she is. I roll my eyes and pinch the bridge of my nose.

The wolf's eyes flick to her, and something in its stance shifts. The tension in its massive shoulders eases, its growl softening into something almost... protective.

For a moment, no one moves.

"Stay here," I command, my voice low and dangerous as I step forward.

Elira grabs my arm, her fingers digging into the fabric of my coat.

"Don't," she says, her tone more pleading than I've ever heard it. 'He says he's not gonna hurt you, if you let him in." She add.

Then, she swear under her breath. 'I asked him to rip you fucking heart out, but he doesn't want to."

I glance down at her hand, the warmth of her touch seeping through the layers of fabric, and I hate how much I feel it.

"Let go," I snap, but she doesn't.

"Just fucking listen for once," she spits, her blue eyes blazing with frustration. "He says he's not gonna hurt you, if you let him in."

I blink, momentarily thrown by the absurdity of her words. "Let him in? Are you out of your goddamn mind?"

She swears under her breath, shaking her head like she's having an argument with herself. "I told him to rip your fucking heart out, but he doesn't want to. Something about 'the fates' and not being allowed to."

Her words hit like a punch to the gut. The fates. The cursed fucking fates.

Of course, they'd have a hand in this.

The wolf takes another step forward, its massive form illuminated by the scrotching sunlight. Blood mats its dark fur, the coppery scent sharp in the air.

I glance between it and Elira, my jaw tightening. "You're serious," I say, my voice low and incredulous.

She lets out a harsh laugh, the sound devoid of humor. "Dead serious. And if you don't let him in, I think he's gonna stop asking nicely."

The wolf's growl rumbles through the ground, vibrating in my chest.

I grit my teeth, my gaze locking with the beast's glowing eyes. "Fine," I bite out, the word tasting like ash.

The guards flinch as I step aside, their fear radiating in waves. The wolf moves slowly, each step deliberate as it crosses the threshold.

It stops in front of me, its head lowering slightly, and for a moment, I swear there's something in its eyes— something ancient and knowing.

"Elira," I snap, my voice sharper than intended.

She steps closer, her presence grounding me in a way I don't want to admit.

"Tell your... puppy to behave," I say, gesturing toward the wolf.

She crosses her arms, her expression unimpressed. "You're the one who needs to behave. He's not here to kill you, remember? Unfortunately."

I let out a short, humorless laugh, my hands flexing at my sides. "We'll see about that."

The Devil's Claim

Elira

The wolf's claws scrape against the stone floor as he strides into the castle, leaving streaks of blood in his wake. Veylan moves with the kind of confidence that makes men think twice before breathing too loudly.

I envy him.

I glance at Damien, his expression carved from stone. His green eyes burn with something dark, unrelenting, as they track every step the wolf takes. He doesn't flinch, doesn't falter. But the tension in his body is palpable, like he's coiled and ready to strike.

"This isn't happening," Damien says, his voice low and dangerous, pushing his hair back.

"It is," I snap, crossing my arms as I meet his glare.

His gaze shifts to me, sharp and cutting. "You don't get a say."

"I don't need one," I retort. "Veylan stays."

The wolf growls softly, a sound that vibrates through the floor. Damien's lip curls, and he takes a step closer to me, his towering frame casting a shadow that feels like it might swallow me whole.

"You think you can dictate terms in my castle?" he murmurs, his voice a low, lethal whisper. "You're nothing here."

I stiffen, my pulse hammering in my ears, but I don't back down. "You might think you own this place," I say, my voice steady despite the heat of his glare, "but Veylan doesn't answer to you. And neither do I."

His hand moves so quickly I don't see it coming, his fingers wrapping around my wrist in a grip that's firm but not painful. My heart leaps into my throat as he pulls me closer, the scent of blood and steel clinging to him like a second skin.
"You think you're untouchable?" he asks, his voice low and rough. "You think this mutt makes you invincible?"

The heat of his breath brushes against my skin, and I hate the way my body reacts, every nerve on high alert. My lips part, a sharp retort on the tip of my tongue, but his grip tightens ever so slightly, silencing me.

"I could break you," he says, his tone so soft it's almost a whisper. "Right here, right now."

My chest heaves, anger and something else swirling in a dangerous mix. "Then why don't you?" I snap, my voice shaking with the weight of my defiance.

His green eyes blaze, and for a moment, I think he might. But then he lets go, the loss of his touch as jarring as the intensity of it.

"Because I don't have to," he says, his smirk dark and infuriating. "You'll break yourself before I ever get the chance."

The wolf growls again, louder this time, and Damien's gaze flicks to him. "Call him off," he commands, his voice snapping like a whip.

I laugh, short and humorless. "You don't get it, do you? Veylan doesn't take orders. And he's not going anywhere."

Damien's jaw tightens, his fists clenching at his sides. "One wrong move," he says, his tone low and menacing, "and I'll put him down myself."

"You'd die trying," I reply, my voice steady.

He steps even closer, his presence overwhelming, his green eyes locking onto mine. "I don't die easy," he murmurs, his voice dripping with challenge.

The guards shift nervously, their fear radiating in waves. Damien finally tears his gaze away from me, his focus snapping to them.

"Get out," he barks, his tone making me flinch.

They scatter like rats, the door slamming shut behind them. The silence that follows is thick, oppressive, and filled with the weight of everything unsaid.

Veylan huffs, his ember eyes watching Damien like he's sizing up a rival. Damien doesn't back down, his shoulders squared, his hand twitching at his side as though he's debating reaching for his blade.

"You're not the first person to think you can walk in here and change the rules," Damien says, his

voice low and cutting. "But let me be clear—this is my kingdom. My castle. And you are nothing but a pawn."

"Funny," I say, tilting my head. "You look more like the pawn to me."

His expression darkens, the shadows of the room seeming to cling to him as he steps forward. My pulse spikes, but I don't move, refusing to let him see the crack in my armor.

"Careful," he says, his voice a warning and a promise. "You're playing with fire."

I force a smirk, even as my chest tightens. "Maybe I like the burn."

His hand twitches again, his jaw tight as he stares me down. The air between us feels electric, like it might ignite at any moment. And then, just as quickly as it came, the moment breaks.

Damien takes a step back, his lips curling into a humorless smile. "You'll regret those words," he says, his tone calm but laced with steel. He turns toward the door, his coat flaring behind him as he strides away.

"Damien," I call after him, my voice sharper than I intended.

He stops, his shoulders stiffening, but he doesn't turn around.
"Veylan isn't leaving," I say, my tone firm.

His laugh is low, almost mocking, as he glances over his shoulder, his gaze burning trough me with anger.

And then he's gone, the door slamming shut behind him.

Veylan nudges my side, his warmth grounding me as I let out a breath I didn't realize I was holding.
"You're a real piece of work," I mutter, sinking to the floor beside him.

The wolf's rumble of laughter vibrates through my chest, and I don't mind the sound.

Veylan's massive head nudges my arm, his ember eyes flickering with something ancient. I let out a shaky breath, my fingers threading through his thick, blood-matted fur. His warmth grounds me, but it's not enough to stop the storm building in my chest.

"Kill them," I whisper, my voice trembling with suppressed rage. "Kill all of them, and we'll leave."

His growl is low, almost disapproving, as his ember eyes meet mine.

No.

I stiffen, pulling back to glare at him. "What do you mean, no? You're supposed to protect me! Get me out of here!"

This is where you're meant to be, he says, his voice calm but unyielding, brushing through my mind like smoke. *You're not lost. You're where you need to be.*

The words hit like a punch, and I shove away from him, my fists clenching. "That's bullshit. I don't belong here. None of this makes any sense!"

Veylan tilts his massive head, his gaze steady and enigmatic. *Not yet. But it will.*

"Cryptic as always," I mutter, dropping back against the cold stone wall. My chest heaves, my frustration boiling over as my voice rises. "What do you expect me to do? Just sit here and wait for whatever fate has planned for me? For him?"

The wolf's rumble is low, almost amused. *You're not the waiting type. That's why you'll figure it out.*

He shifts, settling beside me, his massive body a barrier against the oppressive cold of the room. *But not tonight. Rest.*

"Rest," I echo bitterly, my voice dripping with sarcasm. "Right. Because everything's just peachy."

Beneath the Skin
Elira

In my room, or should I say cell, Veylan is sleeping on the bed. Taking all the little space we had and I'm sitting at the edge of the cot.

Thinking.

My life's such a mess since that damn day where Kael kidnaped me.

"You've made yourself comfortable," Damien says, leaning in the door frame, one arm stretched all the way up on the wall, flexing his muscular arm. His voice sharp as a blade, his green eyes locked on Veylan.

The wolf lets out a rumble that sounds suspiciously like a laugh.

"Comfortable enough. It's better than out there."

Damien's jaw tightens, his scarred face hardening, looking directly at Veylan. "I could throw you out right now."

"You could try," I cut in, crossing my arms.

His gaze snaps to me, sharp and unrelenting. "And you'd what? Watch?"

"No," I say, my voice steady despite the fire in his eyes. "I'd stop you."

His smirk twists into something darker. "Bold words, little warrior."

The tension between us crackles like a live wire, and I hate the way my pulse races. The way my body seems to react to his presence before my mind can catch up.

"You don't scare me," I snap, stepping closer.

"Good," he murmurs, his tone low and infuriating. "I'd hate for this to be easy."

Fuck him.

The knife is in my hand before I know it, the blade flashing as I swing it toward him. He moves faster than I expect, catching my wrist in a grip that sends a jolt through my arm.

"Still trying to kill me?" he asks, his voice calm, almost amused.

I snarl, twisting in his grasp, but he doesn't let go. His other hand grabs my shoulder, pulling me off balance, and before I know it, we're falling.

The world tilts, and then the cold stone floor slams into my back. The air rushes out of my lungs, and the knife clatters from my hand, spinning uselessly across the floor.

Damien is on top of me, his weight pinning me down, his knees bracketing my hips. His hands grip my wrists, pressing them against the floor on either side of my head.

I struggle, twisting and bucking, but he doesn't budge. And that damn scary wolf do absolutely nothing to help me.

"Stop squirming," he growls, his voice rough and low.

"Get off me," I snap, glaring up at him, my chest heaving.

His smirk returns, sharp and infuriating. "No."

The heat of him is unbearable, searing through the thin fabric of my tunic where his chest presses against mine. I can feel every hard line of him, every inch of his strength, and it sends a shiver down my spine that I can't suppress.

And then I feel it.

My breath catches as his hips shift, the unmistakable press of his arousal against my core. My body betrays me, a flush spreading through my skin as a strange, unwelcome heat pools low in my stomach.

Damien notices. Of course, he does. His smirk deepens, his green eyes glinting with dark amusement.

"You're ugly mouth is quiet all of a sudden," he murmurs, his
voice dropping to a whisper.

"Go to hell," I spit, my voice trembling with anger and something else I refuse to name.

He leans in closer, his breath brushing my ear. Sending shivers directly to my needing traitor of a cunt. "Hell isn't far, darling. Stick with me—I'll take you there myself."

I twist again, trying to break free, but it only presses us closer. His grip tightens, his fingers firm around my wrists, and I feel the low rumble of his laugh against my chest.

"Still think you can win?" he asks, his tone mocking.

"You're disgusting," I snap, refusing to look away even as my cheeks burn.

His lips curve into a slow, wicked smile. "And you can't seem to get enough of it, can you?"

For a moment, the air between us feels charged, electric. I can hear the blood pounding in my ears, feel the weight of his body pressing me into the stone, and it's unbearable—because it's not entirely unwelcome.

Veylan's low growl cuts through the moment, sharp and commanding.

Damien glances over his shoulder, his

expression hardening. "What?"

"*You're both idiots,*" the wolf says dryly. "*Get up before someone does something they'll regret.*"

Damien turns back to me, his smirk returning. "Looks like your pet's trying to save you."

I glare at him, my chest heaving. "I don't need saving."

His green eyes darken, his smirk fading as his gaze searches mine. "No," he says quietly, his voice almost soft. "You don't."

And then, just like that, he lets go.

The loss of his touch is jarring, and I scramble to my feet, my heart pounding as I put as much distance between us as the room allows.

Damien watches me for a long moment, his expression unreadable. Then he turns, striding toward the door without another word.

"You'll regret this," I call after him, my voice sharper than I intended.

He glances back, his green eyes glinting. "Not as much as you will."

Lines in Blood
Elira

Two days.

Two days of silence, of endless waiting, of pacing the room like a caged animal.

I haven't seen him. Haven't heard his sharp, mocking tone or felt his suffocating presence hovering just behind me. The absence of him should be a relief, but it isn't.

Veylan stays close, his massive form a constant, grounding presence. He doesn't speak much, just watches me with those ember eyes like he's waiting for me to break.

I only leave the room to eat. The dining hall is just as cold and unwelcoming as the rest of the castle, the black stone walls absorbing the meager torchlight and reflecting nothing back. Even the wolf, despite his size, feels small in the vast space.

Back in my room, the hours blur into one long stretch of restless pacing and unanswered questions. I've scoured every corner, every crack in the stone walls, looking for something—anything—that might tell me what's going on.

By the second evening, I can't take it anymore. Sitting on the edge of the bed, I stare at Veylan, my fingers drumming against my thigh.
"Where is he?" I snap, my voice comes out sharper than I meant.

The wolf doesn't answer immediately. When he does, his voice brushes against my mind, calm and steady. He's occupied.

"Occupied with what?" I demand, standing to pace the room again. "Plotting my demise? Torturing some poor soul in another wing of this godforsaken place?"

Veylan's rumble is low, almost amused. *You miss him.*

"I don't! He's a monster. My enemy." I bark, spinning to glare at him. "I just want to know what the hell is going on."

He tilts his head, his ember eyes glinting in the dim light. *You're impatient. That's why you struggle.*

I groan, dragging my hands through my hair. "You're as bad as he is.Insufferable men."

The wolf lets out a low chuckle, his massive head resting on his paws. *Be patient. The answers will come.*

The silence in the room stretches, heavy and uncomfortable, as I sit stiffly on the edge of the chair, my fingers curling into the fabric of my pants. Veylan is sprawled near the doorway, his massive form quiet but alert, his ember eyes flicking between me and the door.

The faint sound of footsteps in the hallway catches my attention. They stop just outside the door, and a shadow falls under the crack. My chest tightens. The door creaks open, and a guard steps inside, his boots loud against the stone floor.

His gaze sweeps the room and lands on me, lingering too long. A sneer curls his lips, and my stomach churns. Veylan growls softly from his place by the door, the low sound reverberating through the room like a warning.

I open my mouth to speak, but before I can, a familiar presence presses into the room. Damien steps in, his movements smooth, unhurried, like he has all the time in the world.

I hadn't even heard him enter, and now he's here, filling the space with his overwhelming presence.

His jade eyes flick to the guard, narrowing slightly as he surveys the scene. His coat sways as he moves, the dark fabric and intriguing black and red details at the bottom brushing the stone floor like the sweeping of a blade.

The guard stiffens, his posture shifting awkwardly under Damien's scrutiny. "My lord," he stammers, the sneer vanishing from his face as he inclines his head.

Damien leans against the wall, crossing his arms as his gaze sharpens. "You're late," he says, his tone flat but lethal.

"My lord," the guard says, his voice dripping with disdain. "You called?"

Damien's jaw tightens, his green eyes narrowing at the man. "What do you want?"

The guard doesn't answer immediately. Instead, his gaze slides back to me, and his lips curl into a sneer. "She doesn't look like much. Not worth the trouble you're keeping her for."

My stomach twists, the weight of his words settling like a stone.

He's right.

His eyes rake over me, slow and deliberate, and I grip the edge of the table to stop my hands from trembling.

"You should watch your mouth," Damien says, his voice quiet and laced with warning.

The guard snorts, taking a step closer. "What for? She's just another bitch you've dragged in here. Maybe you should let me show her what she's good for. Like the others."

The world narrows, everything outside of this moment fading to black.

Damien moves like a storm, his long coat sweeping behind him as he closes the distance in two strides. His hand clamps around the guard's throat with terrifying speed, lifting the man clean off the ground and slamming him into the wall with enough force to crack the stone.

The sound echoes through the room—flesh meeting stone, the muffled crunch of bone—and the guard's helmet clatters to the floor. His eyes bulge, his hands clawing at Damien's grip, but it's useless. Damien doesn't just hold him—he owns him.

"You looked what's mine," Damien says, his voice low and eerily calm, the kind of calm that makes the hairs on the back of my neck stand on end.

The guard gasps, his boots kicking uselessly as Damien's fingers tighten, the sound of his wind pipe crushing sickening me. His lips turn purple, and a wheezing sound escapes his throat, like a bellows struggling to draw air.

Damien doesn't speak at first. His expression is cold, calculated, and terrifyingly calm. His free hand moves with deliberate precision, sliding into the sheath at his hip and drawing a blade. The dagger is a thing of beauty—sleek and sharp, the edge catching the dim red light and gleaming like liquid silver.

Without a word, Damien tilts his head slightly, as if considering the guard's fate. Then, with one smooth motion, he levels the dagger at the man's chest and drives it in.

The blade sinks in effortlessly, the sound wet and nauseating. Blood spurts from the wound, dark and vivid, spraying across Damien's chest and cold face and spattering onto the floor. The guard chokes, his body jerking as Damien twists the blade, the metal scraping against bone.

But he's not done.

Damien smiles then, slow and menacing, his emerald iris glowing with a terrifying mix of amusement and rage. He pulls the dagger free, letting it clatter to the floor, and replaces it with his bare hand. His fingers press into the wound, digging deeper, the sickening crunch of ribs shattering under his grip filling the room.

I choked on vomit.

The guard's screams turn to gurgles as Damien tears into his chest cavity, his other hand still pinning the man against the wall like a rag doll. Blood pours freely now, pooling at their feet in thick, viscous waves.

Damien's hand disappears into the man's chest, and with a sharp jerk, he rips it back out, clutching a still- beating heart in his fist.

The sound is grotesque—flesh tearing, bones cracking—and the guard's body slumps lifelessly in Damien's grip.

Damien turns, holding the heart aloft as blood drips from his fingers. He takes a step forward, the crimson organ pulsing weakly in his hand, and tosses it to Veylan.

The wolf doesn't hesitate. His jaws snap shut around the heart with a sickening crunch, blood staining his black fur as he swallows it whole.

I'm speechless, and murmur to Veylan, "What the fuck?" He simply shrugs in my mind.

Damien wipes his bloodied hand on the guard's tunic, his smirk widening as he looks down at the crumpled corpse.
"You threatened what's mine," he says, his voice low and deadly.

He nudges the body with the toe of his boot, disdain dripping from every movement. "Your heart had the audacity to make a place for her, so I fucking destroyed it."

The words hit like a punch, stealing the air from my lungs. My hands shake, my pulse pounding in my ears, but I can't look away. Damien toward me, his blood-streaked hand reaching for my chin, tilting my face up to meet his gaze.

Blood smears across his face, streaked over the sharp line of his jaw and the scars that cut through his cheek. His lips, stained crimson, part slightly as his tongue flicks out, slow and deliberate, licking the blood clean.

I don't realize I'm holding my breath until the sound of my own shaky exhale fills my ears. His gaze never wavers, never falters, pinning me in place with an intensity that makes my chest tighten.

Damien stops his face just inches from me, his towering frame casting me in shadow. His hand rises, long fingers slick with blood, and he holds one up between us, the crimson liquid dripping lazily down his palm. My stomach clenches, but I don't move.

"Open," he murmurs, his voice low, dark, and impossibly commanding.

I don't even think—my lips part automatically, the heat in his gaze searing through me like fire. He presses the pad of his bloodied finger against my bottom lip, the metallic tang flooding my senses.

My tongue brushes against his skin, tentative at first, tasting the sharp, bitter flavor of iron and something else—something darker. I should feel disgusted. I should feel horrified. But I don't. Instead, there's a strange, unwelcome heat unfurling in my chest, a shiver running down my spine that has nothing to do with fear.

"Good girl," he breathes, his voice a rough whisper that slides over me like smoke. His eyes glint with something dangerous as he presses his finger deeper into my mouth. "Taste it."

My tongue curls around his finger instinctively, my cheeks flushing as I suck gently. The movement feels foreign, wrong, and yet... strangely natural. My eyes flutter shut for a moment, my senses overwhelmed by the heat of his touch, the sharp taste of blood, and the weight of his presence.

When I open them again, his face is closer, his lips curling into a wicked smile. "Fuck…" He hums in approval.

"It tastes like enemy," he murmurs, his voice sending a shiver straight through me.

My throat tightens, but I don't pull away, even as he slides his finger free, the blood smeared across my lips now. He lifts his other hand, brushing a thumb over my cheek, and I flinch slightly, the touch too soft for the sharpness of the moment.

"You should be horrified," he says, his tone almost conversational as his thumb skims over my lips, smearing the blood further. "But you're not, are you?" I glare at him, my defiance cracking under the weight of his gaze. "You don't scare me," I manage, though my voice trembles.

"Liar," he murmurs, leaning in just enough that his breath brushes against my skin. "You're terrified."

"Of you?" I snap, my voice sharp despite the heat coiling low in my stomach. "Not a chance."

His smirk widens, dangerous and infuriating. "Little warrior with a broken heart," he says softly, stepping back and leaving me breathless and burning.

"Remember this," he murmurs, his voice soft but laced with steel. "You don't belong to yourself anymore. You're mine."

"Damien," I whisper, my voice trembling.

He just gets his blade, gracefully bending to pick it up and leave my room yelling. "Someone will clean that."

I don't know how to respond, so I don't. Instead, I sink into the nearest chair, my body trembling.

Veylan moves closer, his side pressing against my side. *I love his style.*

"He's insane," I murmur, my voice barely a whisper.

The wolf's growl is low, almost amused. *And yet you'll stay.*

When Loyalties Burn
Elira

I'm yanked out of sleep by Veylan's growl, low and vibrating with urgency. His ember eyes lock onto mine, and without a word, he nudges me toward the door.

The clash of steel wake me through the night, accompanied by the shouts of the rebels and the sharp cries of soldiers falling to their blades.

The castle courtyard is a battlefield, illuminated by the eerie red glow of torches and the moonlight spilling over the jagged walls. Chaos reigns, and the air smells of blood and smoke.

"What's happening?" I whisper, already pulling on my boots.

"They're here," he says simply, his voice brushing against my mind like smoke. *"The rebels."*

My heart stutters. Lyric, Eryndor—they're here. My friends, my allies. For a fleeting second, hope rises in my chest. But then Veylan's growl deepens, and I realize the weight of what this means. Damien.

I rush down the corridor, Veylan at my side, his massive frame moving silently despite the urgency in his steps. The sounds of battle grow louder as we approach the courtyard, and when I step into the open air, the sight before me makes my blood run cold.

Rebels swarm the castle grounds, their weapons flashing as they cut through Damien's soldiers with brutal efficiency. But the soldiers fight back just as fiercely, their black armor glinting in the firelight as they push against the onslaught. Bodies litter the ground, both rebel and soldier, their blood staining the cracked stone.

And in the middle of it all, Damien stands.

His coat is gone, his shirt torn and soaked with blood. His eyes burn with fury as he cuts through the chaos, his blade a blur of silver and crimson. He's a force of nature, a god of war carved in shadow and steel, but even gods can fall.

A rebel catches him off guard, the tip of their blade slicing across his side.

And I yell.

He stumbles, blood dripping from the wound, but his expression doesn't falter. He twists, his own sword finding its mark in the rebel's chest, but another attacker takes their place.

"Damien!" The word rips from my throat before I can stop it, and his head snaps toward me.

And I don't fucking know why I care.

For a moment, everything else fades—the clash of steel, the screams, the roar of the battle. Veylan slashing in the crowd not looking if it's the royal guard or the rebels. The foe, or the friends.

But do I even know at this point?

Damien's eyes meet mine, and I see it: the raw, unyielding determination, the defiance that refuses to bow even in the face of death.

And then another rebel strikes.

The blade sinks into his shoulder, the force of it driving him to one knee. My heart lurches, and before I can think, I'm running toward him.

"Elira, no!" Lyric's voice roars in the ashes, but I don't stop.

Another rebel raises their sword, their intent clear in the deadly arc of their blade. They're going to kill him. Damien, the man who's caused me nothing but

pain and confusion, the man I hate and can't look away from, the man that destroys both world.

My hands burn.

It's sudden and overwhelming, like fire crawling under my skin. The air around me thickens, humming with a power I've never felt before, and when I raise my hands, the world tilts.

A wall of shimmering energy explodes from my fingertips, slamming into the rebels like a tidal wave. They're thrown back, their bodies hitting the ground with bone-crunching force.

The light fades as quickly as it came, leaving me breathless and trembling, my hands still glowing faintly.

I fall to my knees beside Damien, my chest heaving as I try to make sense of what just happened. His jade eyes flicker open, pain and something else swirling in their depths as they lock onto mine.

"You're… insane," he rasps, his voice weak but laced with that infuriating smirk.

"You're welcome," I snap, pressing my hands against his wound to stop the bleeding. The heat in my palms surges again, and I flinch as the glow intensifies, the wound beneath my hands slowly knitting itself back together.

"What the—" Damien starts, but I cut him off.

"Shut up and let me help you," I say, my voice shaking. "For once in your life, just shut up."

His laughter is quiet, but it sends a shiver down my spine. "You saved me," he murmurs, his gaze heavy on mine. "Why?"

"I don't know," I whisper, my voice barely audible over the chaos around us. "I just… couldn't let you die."

His hand moves, bloodied fingers brushing against my cheek. "You're going to regret that," he says, his voice soft but laced with something dangerous.

Before I can respond, a roar cuts through the air, and I look up to see Veylan tearing through the remaining rebels with a ferocity I've never seen. Lyric and Eryndor stand at the edge of the courtyard, their faces a mix of shock and betrayal as they take in the scene before them.

"Elira!" Lyric's voice is sharp, cutting through the noise. "What the hell are you doing?"

I can't answer. I don't have one.

"It all fell down," Damien murmurs, his voice heavy with something I can't name.

I look around—the blood, the bodies, the fire consuming the edges of the courtyard—I realize he's right. Everything is falling apart.

Marked by Fate
Damien

The world tilts.

Not from the blood loss—I've dealt with worse—but from the weight of what just happened. My legs refuse to obey me.
"Kill her!"

I flinch at the voice cutting in my fucking head.

Every attempt to push myself off the blood-soaked ground ends in failure, my muscles locking under the strain.

Elira stands above me, her hands trembling as she hovers over my collapsed form. Her hair's a tangled mess, her face pale and streaked with dirt and blood, but those goddamned blue eyes… they burn. There's a crackling energy beneath her skin, raw and pulsing, like it's trying to escape.

"What did you do?" My voice comes out as a low rasp, thick with the taste of iron. The effort of speaking makes my vision blur.

Her lips part, but words fail her. She looks at her hands like they belong to someone else, her fingers trembling, slick with my blood. "I-I didn't mean to…" she whispers, her voice thin and fragile, and I can tell she's barely holding it together.

Fuck.

I want to make it better.

Something's changed. Something inside her. And inside me.

I can still feel her power coursing through my veins, filling the hollow ache left by the wound she just closed. It's not natural—it's invasive, primal, as though she's branded me from the inside out. My shoulder,

once torn open and gushing, is now whole, though the searing heat lingers like an aftershock.

"Fuck…" I manage, dragging in a ragged breath. "You healed me."

"I didn't…" Her voice falters, breaking on the words. "I don't know how."

She opens her mouth, but before she can answer, there's movement. My gaze shifts, heavy-lidded but sharp, to see Lyric stalking toward us. The bloodied blade in her hand reflects the faint light, and her expression is a storm of grief and fury.

"Elira." Lyric's voice cracks like a whip, but there's a tremor beneath it. "Move."

Elira stiffens, stepping back instinctively before planting her feet. "Wait," she pleads, her voice trembling. "Lyric, I—"

"You chose him," Lyric spits, the words slicing through the air like a blade. Her golden eyes flick to me, and the rage there is pure, unrelenting. "After everything, you chose him."

"No!" Elira shakes her head, her movements frantic. "It wasn't like that—he—"

"Move," Lyric interrupts, her tone cold and final. "Don't make me do this."

I try to push myself up, but my body fails me. The throbbing heat in my shoulder has dulled, but the rest of me feels like lead. It's almost laughable—Damien, the terror of kingdoms, laid out like a fucking cripple. If Lyric wants me dead, she'll get no fight from me.

But Elira doesn't move.

She steps in front of me, her arms outstretched, shielding me. Her entire body shakes, her chest heaving as she faces down Lyric's blade.
"What are you doing?" I growl, my voice rough. "Get out of the way."

"Shut up," she snaps without looking at me. Her focus is locked on Lyric, her blue eyes wide and desperate glowing in the light of chaos, fire surrounding us. "Don't do this," she begs. "Please, Lyric. Don't."

Lyric hesitates, the blade in her hand wavering for a moment before her jaw tightens. "You don't get it, do you? You're protecting the man who killed innocent, who will destroy this world and yours. He deserves to die."

"Kael betrayed us!" Elira shouts, her voice raw. "I didn't have a choice!"

Lyric's laugh is sharp and bitter. "There's always a choice. And you chose him."

The tension between them is unbearable, the kind that makes the air feel too thick to breathe. Lyric's grip tightens on her sword, and I see the decision harden in her eyes.

The ground trembles.

It's subtle at first, a faint vibration beneath my palms, but it grows stronger, shaking the bloodied earth. A low growl ripples through the clearing, sending a chill down my spine. The air shifts, thickening with something primal, something ancient.

Veylan steps out of the shadows.

The giant wolf's moves like liquid muscle, his black fur matted, his ember eyes brighter than the flames of hell. His presence dominates the clearing, his growl reverberating through the ground like a thunderclap.

Lyric freezes, her blade lowering slightly. "What the hell…"

Elira's shoulders sag with relief. "Veylan," she whispers.

The wolf's gaze snaps to me, and I swear I see something smug in those fiery eyes. He moves closer, his claws clicking against the earth. His growl softens as he stops beside Elira, towering over her.

"Get on," he says, his voice brushing against my mind like smoke.

Elira hesitates. "What about—"

"They've made their choice," Veylan interrupts, his tone unyielding. "And you've made yours."

The words hit her like a blow. She looks back at Lyric, her face crumpling with guilt, before turning to me. "Can you…?"
"No," I grit out. My legs are useless, my arms barely holding me up.

Veylan huffs, crouching low enough for her to hoist me onto his back. The movement is jarring, and pain lances through me as she adjusts my weight. She climbs on behind me, her arms wrapping around my chest to steady us.

"Hold on," Veylan says, his growl deepening.

The wolf takes off, the world blurring around us as his massive paws pound against the ground. The wind tears at my face, and for the first time in what feels like an eternity, the suffocating weight of the castle is gone.

Bound by Pain
Damien

The forest presses in around us, its shadows thick and suffocating. The moon above offers little light, its pale glow obscured by the jagged canopy of branches. Veylan's massive paws strike the ground in a relentless rhythm, his breath steady despite the weight he carries.

Elira clings to me from behind, her arms firm around my chest. Her touch burns, though the pain in my body keeps me from focusing on it too long.
"Weak," it hisses, sharp and grating, like glass dragged across stone. *"You let her use that power. You let her save you. Fool."*

The malevolent force digs into my skull, each word a hot spike driven deeper into my mind. My teeth clench as I try to push it out, to silence the agonizing pull it has on me, but the effort sends fresh waves of pain searing through my body.

I should have known it wouldn't stay quiet for long.

Elira leans closer, her breath brushing against my neck as she whispers, "Damien, are you—"

"Fine," I snap, harsh. Her arms loosen slightly, and guilt worms its way through me even as the voice roars again. *"She is a threat. Kill her. Kill her now!"*

My head pounds, the pain spreading down my spine. I grind my teeth, ignoring the metallic tang of blood in my mouth. The connection between us burns hot and raw, tethering me to this damn thing I can't escape.

"We're close," Veylan's deep voice rumbles, breaking through the torment. His pace slows as the forest gives way to a rocky clearing overlooking a dark, endless valley. The wolf crouches low, and Elira slides off his back with ease, her boots crunching against the gravel.

She turns to me immediately, her hands reaching to steady me. I shrug her off, forcing my feet to the ground despite the sharp, twisting pain radiating through my chest.

"Don't," I growl, keeping my voice low. "I don't need your help."

Her blue eyes blaze with anger, but she steps back, crossing her arms over her chest. "Fine. Bleed out, then."

I lean against a jagged rock, my breaths shallow and uneven as I fight to keep upright. The malevolent force howls in my mind, louder now, its rage a relentless drumbeat that drowns out everything else.

"You let her live!" it screeches. *"You let her grow stronger! She will destroy you, and you will deserve it!"*

"Shut up," I mutter under my breath, pressing the heel of my hand against my temple. The voice doesn't listen. It never does.

Elira's gaze flicks to me, her brows furrowed. "What's wrong with you?"

"Nothing you can fix," I snap, my tone cutting, though my vision blurs slightly at the edges. The force's laughter scrapes through my skull, and I double over, gripping the rock as bile rises in my throat.

Her hands are on me again, steadying me despite my protests. "You're not fine," she says, her voice softer now. "What's happening to you?"

"Not your concern," I rasp, though her touch sends a jolt through me that's impossible to ignore.

Veylan's ember eyes glow faintly in the darkness as he steps closer. "You won't last long like this," he says, his tone calm but firm. "The bond has been activated. You're resisting it, and it's tearing you apart."

I force myself upright, glaring at the wolf despite the black spots dancing in my vision. "What bond?"
"The mate bond," he replies simply, like it's the most natural thing in the world.

Elira freezes, her head snapping toward the wolf. "Mate bond? What the hell are you talking about?"

Veylan's gaze shifts to her, his massive form radiating calm. "Your lives are entwined. Always has been. Your powers awakened to protect him because the bond demanded it. His survival is tied to yours now."

"Bullshit," she snaps, taking a step back. "I don't believe in any of this."

The wolf tilts his head, his expression unreadable. "Believe or not, it changes nothing. The mark on your wrist is proof enough."

Elira lifts her arm hesitantly, pushing up her sleeve. The faint glow of the swirling pattern etched into her skin catches the moonlight, golden and red like molten fire. She stares at it, her breathing shallow, before turning to me.

"You knew," she accuses, her voice trembling.

I bark out a laugh, the sound bitter and broken. "Do I look like someone who has a fucking clue what's going on?"

The malevolent force snarls again, louder this time, the sound nearly bringing me to my knees. *"Kill her! Before she kills you!"*

"Get out of my head," I hiss, my voice strained.

Elira stares at me, her anger fading into something that looks like concern. "Damien... who are you talking to?"

"None of your business," I snap, my hand gripping the hilt of my sword to ground myself. "Just... keep your distance."
Her expression hardens, but she doesn't press further. Instead, she turns back to Veylan, her voice quieter now. "What does this mark mean?"

"It's a connection," the wolf replies. "A bond forged by fate. It grants power, but at a price. Your paths are no longer your own. Like long time ago."

"I didn't ask for this," she says, her voice shaking.

Veylan's gaze softens slightly. "No one does. But it's yours all the same."

Elira's eyes meet mine, and for a moment, everything else falls away. The pain, the anger, the noise—it all fades under the weight of her gaze.

But then the malevolent force screams again, its fury a physical force that sends me to my knees.

"You can't run from it forever," Veylan says, his voice low but steady. "The bond will demand more. Be ready."

I glare at the wolf, though my vision swims with pain. "I'm ready for nothing," I mutter, but the truth lingers in the air between us, unspoken and undeniable.

She's mine. But I'm not what she needs.

Threads of Fate
Elira

The fire crackles softly, its warm glow dancing over Damien's face, casting shadows that accentuate the sharp angles of his jaw and the curve of his cheekbones.

His eyes are closed, his long lashes resting against his scarred skin. His dark hair is tousled, and strands fall haphazardly over his forehead, softening the harshness of his features.

His shirt—or what's left of it—is torn, revealing a broad chest marred with scars. The muscles of his shoulders shift slightly as he breathes, the steady rise and fall of his chest mesmerizing in its calm. The firelight plays tricks on his skin, turning it golden in some places, red in others. His lips, full and chapped, part slightly as he exhales.

I can't stop staring.

I hate it. I hate how beautiful he is, even in the chaos, even in the silence. Hate how my gaze keeps drifting to the hollow of his throat, the way his skin gleams where the firelight touches it.

Hate how the memory of his bloodied hands lingers, yet I still can't bring myself to look away.

"Stop staring," Veylan's voice rumbles through my mind, the deep timbre tinged with faint amusement.

"I'm not," I whisper sharply, dragging my gaze back to the pile of branches in my hands.

I am.

The wolf huffs, his ember eyes glowing faintly in the firelight. *"You are."*

I focus on weaving the branches together, the makeshift hut starting to take shape. It's crude and lopsided, but it'll do for the night. The chill in the air bites at my skin, and I shiver slightly as I secure another branch.

Veylan stands a few feet away, his massive form blending with the shadows of the forest. His fur, dark and sleek, gleams faintly as he watches me. He hasn't moved much since we stopped here, his sharp eyes scanning the treeline for threats.

I glance at Damien again. He hasn't stirred, his body resting against the trunk of a large tree. His arms lie loosely at his sides, one hand curled slightly, the other resting on the hilt of his sword even in sleep.

"Why did you help us?" I ask Veylan quietly, my hands stilling against the branches.

His gaze flicks to me, the faintest glimmer of something ancient and knowing in his eyes. *"Because it's what I'm meant to do."*

I roll my eyes. "That's not an answer."

I sigh, sitting back on my heels and brushing dirt from my hands. "You're always so mysterious. It's getting on my damn nerves. Why can't you just tell me the truth?"

Veylan tilts his head, his ears twitching slightly. *"The truth is not mine to give. It's yours to uncover. The truth is sometimes hard to hear. Painfull to digest."*

I glare at him, my frustration mounting. "You're impossible."

My gaze drifts back to Damien, the firelight painting his scars in vivid detail. I wonder what they mean, where they came from. Wonder what he's dreamed about in his restless sleep, his brows furrowing every so often as if haunted by something I can't see.

"Is he connected to you?" I ask, my voice barely above a whisper. "To me?"

Veylan's silence stretches for a moment, the crackling fire the only sound between us. When he finally speaks, his tone is heavy, like he's carrying the weight of countless years. *"He is tied to you. As I am. As we all are."*

I frowned, leaning back against the pile of branches. "I need something more clear please."

Veylan steps closer, his big body towering over me. *"You have always been connected. Across lifetimes, across worlds. Always finding each other. Always losing each other."*

The words send a chill down my spine, and I shake my head. "That's impossible."

"Is it?" Veylan asks, his tone soft but unyielding. *"You feel it, don't you? The pull? The familiarity?"*

I swallow hard, my gaze darting back to Damien. "Even if that's true, it doesn't explain anything. Why now? Why us?"

Veylan's gaze shifts to the sky, his voice quieter now. *"Because the fates are not kind. They do not give without taking. They have chosen this time, this life, for a purpose. To end the force that has destroyed so much."*

"And if we fail?" I ask, my voice trembling.

"Then everything falls," Veylan replies simply, his gaze meeting mine. *"But you will not fail."*

The weight of his words settles over me, heavy and unrelenting. I glance back at Damien, his face serene despite the tension I know is lurking beneath the surface.

"I don't know how to do this," I admit softly.

Veylan's gaze softens, and he steps closer, his massive head brushing against my arm. *"You'll learn. You always do."*

I let out a shaky breath, my fingers curling into the soft fur at Veylan's neck. I glance down at him, his head level with my chest. His eyes glow softly, their ancient wisdom a stark contrast to the fierce form he inhabits.

"You knew me," I whisper, my voice tentative. "Before all of this… you knew me, didn't you?"

Veylan doesn't answer immediately, his gaze fixed on the flickering flames. When he finally speaks, his voice brushes against my mind like a soft hum, ancient and unyielding. *"I have always known you."* The admission sends a shock wave through me. "How? How is that possible?"

He shifts closer, his head pressing gently against my leg. The weight is comforting and instinctively, my hand moves to stroke his fur. It's coarse yet warm beneath my fingers, and the rhythmic motion calms my trembling hands.
"You have lived many lives, Elira," he says, his voice low and steady. *"And in each of them, I have been there. Watching. Guiding. Protecting."*

"Protecting me from what?" My voice cracks, the question breaking through the knot in my throat.

"From the force that seeks to consume you. The same force that threatens everything now." His ember eyes flick up to meet mine, unwavering and full of something that feels like sorrow. "You are tied to it, just as you are tied to him."

"And Damien?" I ask, my fingers pausing in their rhythm. "He's… part of this?"

Veylan tilts his head slightly, his gaze softening. "He has always been part of it. But the fates have taken you from him, over and over." This time he doesn't bother responding to me in my head. He speaks softly, with his gravelly voice.

My chest tightens, the weight of his words pressing down like a physical thing. "Taken me how?"

"By death. By betrayal. By forces beyond your control." His voice grows quieter, heavier. "But always, he find you again. And always, you he lose you."

His words hangs in the air, a bitter truth that settles in my chest like a stone. I stroke Veylan's fur absently. "What makes this time different?" I ask, my voice
trembling.

Veylan's head rises slightly, his gaze fixing on mine. "Because this time, the fates have given you a chance to end it. To break the cycle. To destroy the force that has plagued you both."

The silence stretches, broken only by the soft crackle of the fire and Damien's steady breathing. Veylan shifts slightly, his frame rising as he steps toward Damien. I watch in silence as he lowers his head, his powerful jaws parting with surprising gentleness.

Before I can say anything, Veylan grips Damien by the collar of his torn shirt, his movements slow and careful. With a strength that seems effortless, he lifts him, carrying him toward the makeshift hut I've built.

My breath catches as I watch, a strange mix of awe and unease knotting in my chest.

Veylan ducks his head to enter the hut, carefully lowering Damien onto the soft patch of moss and branches. Damien stirs slightly, a faint groan escaping his lips, but he doesn't wake.

The wolf turns back to me, his ember eyes glowing in the dim light. "*Go to him,*" he says, his voice brushing against my mind with a command that feels like an embrace. "*He needs you as much as you need him.*"

I hesitate, my gaze flicking between Damien and Veylan. "And you?"

Veylan moves to the entrance of the hut, his massive body settling across the opening like a living barrier. His eyes flick to mine, a faint glimmer of amusement in their depths. "I will guard you both. Sleep. No one will pass me."

Worlds collide
Elira

My head rests on something firm and warm, and for a moment, the haze of sleep makes me think it's Veylan. But then the steady rise and fall beneath my cheek sharpens in my awareness, and I freeze.

It's not the wolf. It's Damien.

The realization hits me like a bucket of cold water, but I don't move. His heartbeat thunders in my ear, steady and maddening. His scent—woodsmoke, leather, and something darker—wraps around me, invasive and intoxicating all at once.

"You're awake." His voice is low, rough, like gravel sliding against stone.

I stiffen, my fingers curling against his chest, brushing against the torn fabric of his shirt and the hard muscle beneath. I don't answer, my breath hitching as the moment stretches, taut and unbearable.

"Didn't think you'd be so comfortable," he drawls, his tone edged with amusement. "Considering you spend most of your time threatening to kill me."

"Shut up," I mutter, pushing myself up onto my elbows. But the movement only brings me closer, my face hovering just inches from his.

The moonlight entering between the branches casts his features in sharp subtle relief—the harsh angles of his jaw, the faint shadow of stubble, the scars that cut across his cheek and brow. His green eyes catch the light, glinting like emeralds.

Beautiful. It's the only word that comes to mind, and I hate it.

"Don't look at me like that," he murmurs, his voice softer now, but no less dangerous.

"Like what?" I snap, though the heat in my cheeks betrays me.

"Like you're thinking about something you shouldn't be," he says, his lips curling into a wicked smirk. His hand lifts, brushing a strand of hair from my face. The touch is featherlight, but it sears like a brand.

My stomach twists, a mixture of anger and something darker coiling low. "You're annoying, I don't even know you, I don't know what's going on and…"

"And you're lying," he replies, his smirk widening. "You want this. Admit it. Even if you don't know why."

I shove at his chest, but he doesn't budge. His hand moves to my wrist, holding it against him, his grip firm but not painful. "Admit it," he repeats, his voice dropping, the challenge in his tone unmistakable. The need.

"I hate you," I whisper, but the words lack conviction. My pulse hammers in my throat, my body betraying me as heat pools low in my belly and wetness between my legs.

His gaze drops to my lips, and the air between us becomes suffocating. "No, you don't," he murmurs, his voice a low growl. "Not enough to stop this."

Before I can argue, his lips crash against mine, stealing the breath from my lungs. The kiss is hard, demanding, a battle of wills that I lose the moment his tongue brushes against mine. My hands tangle in his hair, pulling him closer as a soft, involuntary moan escapes me.

"Fuck," he mutters against my lips, his voice thick with desire. "You taste like my end."

I bite hard on his lower lips, and he hum in appreciation. His hands move to my waist, lifting me effortlessly as he flips us. The world tilts, and suddenly, I'm on my back, his weight pressing me into the soft cold ground.

His hardness grinding hard between my legs making me see stars behind closed eyelids.

His lips trail down my jaw, his teeth grazing my neck as his hands tug at the hem of my shirt.

"Wait," I protest, but it's weak, half-hearted.

He pauses, his green eyes meeting mine. "What?"

"I haven't bathed," I admit, my cheeks flushing with embarrassment.

He smirks dangerously, leaning down to press a kiss to the hollow of my throat. "Good," he says, his voice rough. "I want all of you, just like this."

Before I can respond, his mouth is on me again, trailing down my body as he undresses me with infuriating precision. His lips find the curve of my hip, then lower, his tongue teasing against the sensitive skin of my inner thigh.

"Damien," I gasp, my hands fisting in his hair as he drags his tongue over me, his mouth claiming me with a hunger that leaves me trembling. His name falls from my lips like a prayer, each syllable laced with desperation.

"Say it again," he growls, his voice muffled against my skin. "Say my name."

"Damien," I breathe, my back arching as his tongue flicks against me, his fingers digging into my thighs to hold me in place.

"Good girl," he murmurs, his tone dripping with satisfaction. "You'll be screaming it soon."

I shiver, a flush crawling up my skin as his hands push my thighs apart, his movements deliberate, commanding. I try to press them closed again, instinct and embarrassment taking over, but he grabs my wrists, pinning them above my head with one hand.

"You're not hiding from me," he says, his jade eyes locking onto mine, the sharpness of his scars only making his intensity more overwhelming. "I want all of you."

The heat of his words sends a jolt straight to my core, and before I can argue, his mouth descends lower, pressing firm, open-mouthed kisses along my stomach. He's relentless, his hands gripping my thighs and holding me in place as he slides down my body, his lips and tongue tracing a burning path across my skin.

When his head lowers between my legs, I stiffen. "Damien," I whisper, my voice trembling. "I—"

"You think I care?" he murmurs, his voice muffled but no less commanding. "I don't give a damn how long it's been. You're mine, and I want to taste what's mine."

Before I can respond, his tongue flicks over my clit, hot and slick, sending a shockwave of sensation through my body. I gasp. The roughness of his stubble scrapes against my vulva, the sensation mingling with the unbearable heat of his tongue as he licks me slowly, deliberately, sucking and biting on the sensitive flesh of my core.

"You taste like fucking sin," he growls against my skin, his voice dark and satisfied.

I arch against him, my breaths coming in ragged gasps as his tongue delves deeper, exploring every inch of me with a hunger that feels almost unholy.

The wet sounds of his mouth on me fill the air, intimate and obscene, and I bite my lip to stifle a moan.

"Don't you dare hold back," he growls, releasing my wrists to grab my hips and pull me closer to his mouth. "I want to hear you."

His tongue moves with deliberate skill, circling and flicking, his lips sealing around the most sensitive part of me and sucking gently before moving again.

He's relentless, devouring me like I'm the only thing keeping him alive. My hands tangle in his dark hair, my thighs trembling as he pulls me closer and closer to the edge.

"Damien," I gasp, his name falling from my lips like a prayer and a curse all at once.

He hums against me, the vibration sending a fresh wave of heat through my body. "That's it," he murmurs, his voice rough and dark, muffled by the way his mouth presses against me. "Say my name again."

"Damien," I whisper, close to an orgasm, my voice trembling as his tongue delves deeper, teasing and tasting, relentless in its pursuit of my pleasure. My back arches, my hands gripping his shoulders as his name tumbles from my lips again and again, my body shaking.

When I finally shatter, it's with a cry that echoes through the small space, my body arching off the ground as he pulls every last tremor from me, his mouth never stopping, never easing up until I'm nothing more than a trembling mess beneath him.

He pulls back slightly, his lips glistening, his green eyes dark with satisfaction as he looks up at me. "You're fucking perfect," he murmurs, his voice rough and filled with an edge of pride.

Before I can respond, he leans over me, his mouth crashing into mine, and I taste myself on his lips—sharp, salty, and intoxicating. His hands explore every inch of me, rough and reverent, his touch igniting fires I didn't know existed.

"You're mine," he growls against my lips as he pushes into me, the stretch and burn of him a delicious agony. His forehead rests against mine, his green eyes dark with desire as he moves, each thrust a declaration.

"Mine," he repeats, his voice rough and raw. His hands grip my hips, pulling me closer as he claims me completely, his body pressing into mine like he can't get close enough.

And then, as the haze clears, I see it—a mark on his forearm, glowing faintly in the dim light. The same mark that appeared on me when my power first emerged.

"What is that?" I whisper, my fingers brushing against it.

"Fate," he replies, his voice soft but unyielding. "It's always been fate."

The Edge of Everything
Damien

Her body is sprawled beneath me, her skin flushed and glistening, her breath uneven and ragged. The taste of her still lingers on my tongue—salt and sin, addictive in a way that makes my chest tighten. Her hair fans out around her head, dark against the tone of her skin, constellation of freckles framing her soft face, her lips parted as she struggles to catch her breath.

She's the most beautiful fucking thing I've ever seen.

Her blue eyes lock onto mine, burning with something that matches the heat roaring in my veins. She doesn't say a word, but she doesn't need to. The mark on my arm pulses, faint but insistent, a constant reminder that we're bound together, whether we like it or not.

 "Damien," she whispers, my name rolling off her lips like a challenge and a plea all at once.

It's the last shred of my restraint gone.

I reach for her, my hands rough as they slide up her thighs, parting them further. Her breathing hitches as I press my palm against her slick heat, teasing her with just enough pressure to make her squirm.

"Goddess," I murmur, my voice low and rough. "Every fucking inch of you."

Her hands come up, gripping my shoulders, her nails digging into my skin, breaking my flesh and I can't get enough. She could skin me alive, and I would say thank you.

I move between her legs. My cock brushes against her entrance, and her hips tilt instinctively, seeking more.

"You want this?" I ask, my voice sharp, demanding. I won't move until I hear her say it.

"Yes," she breathes, her voice trembling with desperation. "I want you."

That's all it takes.

I push into her slowly, savoring the way her body stretches to take me, the way her breath catches and her back arches. She's tight, so fucking tight, and I grit my teeth, forcing myself to go slow even as every part of me screams to take her harder, faster.

"Fuck, Elira," I growl, my hands gripping her hips as I sink deeper. "You feel—fuck."

Her nails rake down my back, her moan spilling into the air between us as I bottom out. I hold still for a moment, my jaw tight, my forehead pressed against hers as I fight to stay in control.

"Move," she whispers, her voice shaking with need. "Please."

I pull back, almost all the way, before slamming into her again. She cries out, her body arching beneath me, her nails digging into my arms as I set a brutal, relentless rhythm. The sounds she makes are fucking perfect—soft, breathless moans that turn into gasps and cries with every thrust.

"You take me so well," I murmur, my voice rough and low. "Look at you, little warrior. Falling apart for me."

She glares up at me, her cheeks flushed, her eyes blazing even as her lips tremble. "You're so—" The words die in a gasp as

I angle my hips, hitting that spot that makes her body tense and her nails bite into my skin.
"So what?" I taunt, my lips brushing against her ear. "So good? So deep? So big? Say it."
"Infuriating," she snaps, but the tremor in her voice betrays her.

I chuckle, the sound dark and satisfied, and lean down to press a kiss to the curve of her neck. My teeth scrape against her skin, and she shivers, her legs tightening around me as her body clamps down on my cock.
"Makes two of us then," I growl.

"Fuck, Elira," My thrusts growing sharper, harder.
"You're fucking perfect."

Her hands move to my hair, pulling me closer, and I capture her lips in a kiss that's all teeth and tongue and desperation. The taste of her, the feel of her—it's all-consuming, overwhelming, like she's burned herself into my soul.

Her cries grow louder, her body trembling beneath me as she teeters on the edge. I shift my weight, grabbing her thigh and hooking it over my arm to open her up even more. The angle makes her scream, her head falling back as her nails rake down my chest.
"Say my name," I demand, my voice rough and raw. "Say it when you come."

"Damien," she gasps, her voice breaking as her body tightens around me, her orgasm crashing over her like a tidal wave. The sight of her, the feel of her—it undoes me.

I follow her over the edge, my release tearing through me with a force that leaves me shaking. My hips jerk against hers, my grip on her thigh tightening as I spill into her, my breaths coming in ragged gasps.

For a moment, neither of us moves. The only sounds are our breathing, rough and uneven, and the crackle of the fire. My hand moving to cup her face as I struggle to catch my breath.

Her head rests on my chest, her breath warm and soft against my skin. The weight of her feels impossibly light, her body curled against mine like it belongs there.
I don't move. Not yet. The first rays of sunlight creep through the cracks in the hut's walls, casting her in a glow that only sharpens the raw beauty of her face.

She stirs, her lashes fluttering against her cheeks before those damned blue eyes open. For a moment, she doesn't move either, her gaze fixed on where her fingers lie against my chest, just above the mark. The mark that fucking burns now.
Her voice breaks the silence, low and hesitant.
"Hello." She timidly murmurs. "Already awake again?"

I tilt my head, my lips curving into a lazy smirk. "Hard to sleep with someone draped over me." My tone is rough, but my hand lifts to brush a strand of dark hair from her face. The action is automatic, thoughtless.

She tenses, but she doesn't pull away. Her hand stays where it is, resting on my chest, her fingers twitching slightly. I can feel her pulse there, rapid and unsteady, betraying her defiance.

"You could've moved me," she says, her voice sharper now, the edge I've come to expect creeping back in.

I chuckle low in my throat, the sound rumbling between us. "I could've done a lot of things."

She glares at me, but her cheeks flush, and it only makes me want to push her further. My hand slides down to her waist, my fingers brushing against the curve of her hip.

Her breath hitches, and I feel it like a goddamn victory.

"You're impossible," she mutters, but I see her smiling and it's my new favortie view. Better than the North mountain. Better than the sun. Better than anything.

She shift swiftly, the motion only brings her closer, her hair tumbling over her shoulders, her bare skin catching the golden light.

I catch a glimpse of the mark on her forearm, faint but unmistakable, and my stomach tightens.

"We match now," I say, my tone lighter than it should be. My hand lifts to trace the mark on my own arm, the glow dimming as I move. "Fate, apparently."

Her gaze flicks to it, and I see the questions brewing in her eyes. "Why does it look like that?" she asks, her voice quieter now. "Like it's alive."

I sit up, the motion fluid despite the dull ache still lingering in my body. The movement exposing the faint scars and fresh marks that litter my skin. I don't miss the way her eyes linger there, the way her lips part just slightly as she takes me in.
"Magic," I say simply. "Old magic. The kind that doesn't give a damn what you want."
Her eyes narrow, and she crosses her arms over her chest.
"It's a bond," I admit. "It's... permanent."
"They've been fucking with me for years, but this—" I glance back at her, my jaw tightening. "This is their masterpiece." I mutter, the bitterness in my tone sharp enough to cut. I lean back against the rough wall of the hut.

Elira doesn't say anything, but I can feel her eyes on me, searching, probing. She's waiting for me to continue, to lay it all out for her. I'm not sure why I do.

"They've made me deal with evil. It's been inside my head for years," I say finally, my voice low, almost guttural. "Whispering, screaming, demanding. It don't stop, Elira. Ever. It's like a swarm of locusts, gnawing at my thoughts, twisting them until I can't tell where they end and I begin."

Her lips part, but no words come out. She looks stunned, her blue eyes wide, the firelight catching the curve of her cheekbones, the soft line of her jaw.
"It doesn't care about me," I continue, the words spilling out now, jagged and raw. "Not you, not me, not anyone. All they want is chaos. It thrive on it—feed on it. And this bond?" I gesture between us, the faint mark on my forearm catching the light.

Her arms drop to her sides, and she steps closer,

her voice low and steady. "But why? Why you?"

I let out a harsh laugh, raking a hand through my hair. "Because I was stupid enough to make a deal with it."

Her breath catches, and I feel her recoil, even though she doesn't move.

"It was during the war," I say, my gaze fixed on the fire. "My kingdom was falling apart. I was desperate. I thought I was strong enough, smart enough, to outmaneuver our enemy. To use it's power without paying the price." My jaw tightens, the memory like acid on my tongue. "I was wrong."

Her silence is deafening, pressing against me like a physical weight.
"It gave me what I asked for," I continue, my voice bitter. "Strength. Strategy. Victory. But it didn't just take my soul, Elira. It took everything. My people. My land. My fucking humanity. They turned me into this."

My hand clenches into a fist, the mark on my face and chest burning faintly. I glance at her then, my jade eyes locking onto her blue ones.

Her hand lifts hesitantly, hovering near my arm before settling on the mark. Her touch is light, tentative, but it sends a shockwave through me that I can't ignore. "He won't let us win. And my people now rebel against me. People hate me. The monster." I admit.

She lifts her chin, her blue eyes blazing with that infuriating defiance that's both maddening and magnetic. "Because they don't know. I didn't."

My breath catches, and for a moment, the room is unbearably still.

For the first time in years, a flicker of something other than despair stirs in my chest.

Hope.

Steam Meets Secrets
Elira

I keep falling on and off of sleep. But the first rays of sunlight stream through the gaps in the wooden walls, casting soft golden lines over the hut's rustic interior. The warmth of the light contrasts sharply with the weight of the night before, still pressing against my skin like an invisible chain.

I shift, the ache in my body a delicious reminder of what happened. My cheek is pressed against Damien's chest, his heartbeat a steady rhythm in my ear. His arm is draped over my waist, heavy and possessive, and his scent—woodsmoke, leather, and the faint tang of blood—lingers like a claim.

And then I hear it: a soft, rumbling chuckle that breaks through the quiet.

Veylan.

"Oh, don't stop on my account," his voice brushes through my mind, smooth and entirely too pleased. *"It was quite the show."*

Heat rushes to my face, and I freeze, my breath catching. "You were awake?" I hiss, barely above a whisper, my eyes darting toward the massive wolf curled near the doorway.

Veylan stretches lazily, his ember eyes gleaming with amusement. *"Awake? Darling, I was attentive. You made it hard not to be."*

I groan, burying my face against Damien's chest to avoid meeting the wolf's gaze. "Oh, gods."

Damien stirs beneath me, his deep, gravelly voice cutting through my mortification. "What's the mutt barking about now?"

Veylan's tail thumps once against the floor, the sound smug. "Just complimenting the lady on her… stamina. Truly impressive for her first time with you." His eyes glint wickedly. "I mean, who wouldn't be shy after a performance like that?"

My cheeks burn hotter, and I sit up, pulling the blanket around me like armor. "Hey!"

Damien chuckles, his hand sliding up to rest on my hip, his grip firm but teasing. "He's not wrong, though. You did scream my name. A lot."

"Shut up," I snap, glaring at him as I smack his shoulder.

"Careful," he murmurs, his lips curling into a smirk. "I might take it as an invitation for round two."

Veylan lets out a low, rumbling laugh, his massive head tilting. "Spare me. I'm already scarred for life."

"You're like 5,000 years old," Damien retorts, his tone dry. "I think you can handle it."

The wolf huffs, his tail swishing in amusement. "5,012 years. But I never expected to play chaperone for such enthusiastic fated lovers."

What the hell. This is old. Before I can annoy him with questions he speaks loud.

"While you were sucking each other's faces," Veylan's voice rumbles, laced with dry amusement, "I caught a smell. A hot spring nearby. Perhaps we could go look for it. You both stink."

I snap my head toward him, my cheeks instantly flushing. Damien chuckles low in his throat, a sound that's both infuriating and entirely too beautiful.

"The puppy has a point," Damien says, running a hand through his hair. His sharp green eyes flick to me, amusement dancing in their depths.

"You're worse," I snap, crossing my arms. "You reek of blood and smoke."

"Then we'd better find this spring," Damien replies smoothly, his smirk growing. "Wouldn't want you passing out from the stench."

Veylan huffs a laugh. "The bickering is endless. You both stink. Let's fix it."
"I don't stink," I snap, crossing my arms over my chest as I glare at both of them.

"You do," Veylan replies flatly, his ember eyes glinting with mischief. "Not as much as him, but still. It's unbearable."

"Fine," I mutter, throwing my hands up in defeat. "Let's go to your magical hot spring, then. I could use a bath anyway."

Damien smirks, his lips twitching upward as he rises to his feet. His presence looms as he steps closer, his tone mocking. "Guess we're going for a little walk, little warrior. Try to keep up."

I roll my eyes but don't argue, my heart still racing from the wolf's comment. Veylan pads ahead, his massive form cutting through the underbrush with ease, leaving Damien and me trailing behind. I can feel his gaze on me as we walk, and it's enough to make my skin prickle with heat.

The trees part as we enter the clearing, and the sight of the hot spring steals my breath. Steam curls off the water, turning the air hazy and golden as the early morning light filters through the trees. The mineral scent is sharp but clean, blending with the earthy aroma of the forest.

Wildflowers dot the edges of the spring, their vibrant colors breaking up the muted greens and browns. Smooth rocks frame the bubbling water, glistening with moisture in the soft light.

"Well," I mutter, my voice quieter now. "It's...
beautiful."

"Yes," Veylan says smugly, settling near a cluster of
rocks. "Now go. Wash the filth off."

I shoot him a glare, but he just rests his massive
head on his paws, utterly unbothered. Damien steps past
me, his broad shoulders brushing mine as he surveys the
spring. The faint glow of his mark catches the light, the
jagged lines stretching over his forearm like a brand.

My brand.

The wolf points his head toward something near
the spring. "You'll need this," he says, motioning to a
cluster of plants with thick, waxy leaves.

I crouch beside them, pulling a knife from my
belt to cut the leaves. The stems ooze a thick, soapy
liquid smelling like mint as I slice through them.

Gathering the leaves, I crush them in my hands, the lather forming quickly. I find a smooth rock in the stream and use it to grind the pulp into a paste. Mixing it with some of the clear water, I fashion a crude soap that's liquid but effective.

Damien watches me with a raised brow, leaning against a tree with his arms crossed. "Not bad," he says, his tone skeptical but impressed. "Where'd you learn to do that?"

I glance up at him, my hands still working the soap into shape. "Survival," I reply curtly. "You learn fast when you don't have a choice."

"Survival," he repeats, his voice soft but edged with something I can't place. "Must've been a hell of a life."

"You have no idea," I mutter, standing and wiping my hands on my pants. "Now can we go?"

Damien steps up beside me, his gaze sweeping over the scene before settling on me. "Go on, wildflower," he says, his tone mockingly sweet. "Make use of your little creation."

I scowl at him but don't argue, wanting to ask about the new pet name, but I don't. I want a bath more than I want answers right now.

"Fine. Just don't watch."

"No promises," he replies, his smirk widening.

Veylan huffs a laugh. *"You humans and your modesty. Always so uptight."*

Ignoring them both, I step to the edge of the spring and strip down, my cheeks burning as I slip into the water. The heat is immediate, soothing the tension in my muscles as it envelops me.

I glance back, catching Damien's gaze before quickly looking away.

The water laps against my skin, and for the first time in days, I feel something close to peace. But that peace is short-lived when Damien crouches by the edge, his green eyes sharp and probing.

"Tell me more about how you knew how to make the soap?" he asks suddenly, his tone skeptical.

I shrug, focusing on the task of scrubbing my arms. "It's not that hard. You just need the right materials."

"That's not what I mean," he says, his gaze never leaving me. "How do you know? Where'd you learn?"

The question hits a nerve I didn't expect, and I pause, my hands stilling in the water. "Where do you think?" I reply, my voice clipped. "From my world. The one you dragged me out of."

His brows furrow slightly, but he doesn't press. "And what was it like? Your world."

I hesitate, the memories flooding back in a wave of bitterness and pain. "Not like this," I say finally, gesturing to the spring, the wildflowers, the forest. "There's no magic. No wolves who talk. No..." I glance at him, my jaw tightening. "You."

"Sounds dull," Damien says, but there's no bite in his voice.

I let out a bitter laugh, scrubbing harder at my skin. "It's broken. The air is poisoned. The water's undrinkable unless you're rich enough to afford filters. People live stacked on top of each other, fighting for scraps. My mom worked herself to death trying to keep me alive. And my dad? He left before I could even remember his face."

Damien's expression softens, but only slightly. He leans back, his gaze fixed on me like he's trying to unravel something. "And now you're here."

"Lucky me," I mutter, dunking my head under the water to rinse the soap from my hair.

Veylan lets out a soft chuckle in my mind, his ember eyes flicking between Damien and me. *"For all your anger, you seem oddly at ease with him,"* he says.

"I'm not," I snap, glaring at the wolf.

He tilts his head, amusement glinting in his eyes. *"You keep telling yourself that."*

Echoes of the Damned
Elira

The forest's dense canopy filtered the midday sun into scattered beams, illuminating our path with an eerie glow. Veylan led the way, his paws silent on the forest floor, while Damien and I followed closely behind. The air grew cooler as we ventured deeper, the scent of damp earth and decaying leaves intensifying with each step.

The world changed from the beauty of greenery to the silent rot of dying plants.

"There's something ahead," Veylan's voice resonated in our minds, tinged with unease. *"An old structure. It reeks of ancient magic."*

Damien's jaw tightened, his eyes narrowing. "Stay alert," he muttered, his hand instinctively resting on the hilt of his sword.

As we pushed through the underbrush, the silhouette of a dilapidated old gothic church emerged, its spires clawing at the sky like skeletal fingers. Black vines choked the stone walls, and shattered stained-glass windows cast fragmented colors onto the ground.

"This place feels wrong," I whispered, a shiver running down my arms.

"It's a remnant of the old world," Damien replied, his voice low. "A time when power was sought through any means necessary."

As we crossed the threshold, the church's oppressive atmosphere enveloped us. The air hung heavy with the cloying scent of mildew, mingling with the sharp tang of iron from blood long since dried but never forgotten.

Each breath felt like inhaling the very essence of decay.

The nave stretched out before us, a desolate expanse where time had ravaged once-sacred adornments. Pews, now reduced to splintered remnants, lay scattered like the bones of forgotten penitents. The altar, draped in tattered cloth, stood as a forlorn sentinel to rituals lost to history. Above, the vaulted ceiling loomed, its arches festooned with cobwebs that swayed gently in the stagnant air, whispering secrets of the past.

Faded murals clung to the walls, their pigments dulled yet their grotesque imagery unmistakable. Once-devout faces contorted into expressions of agony, their eyes wide with terror, mouths frozen in silent screams. The scenes depicted a descent from pious worship into macabre rituals, each brushstroke narrating a tale of sanctity corrupted by an insatiable hunger for power.

The floor, once a mosaic of intricate red tiles, was now a fractured tapestry. Cracks snaked across the surface, some yawning wide to reveal the cold, damp earth beneath. With each cautious step, the ground seemed to groan in protest, as if resenting our intrusion into this sanctum of despair.

The very atmosphere seemed to pulse with malevolent energy, a tangible force that pressed against our senses. Shadows pooled in the corners, defying the feeble shafts of light that pierced the stained-glass windows, their once-vibrant hues now muted and sorrowful.

The oppressive silence was broken only by the distant drip of water, each drop echoing like a mournful lament through the cavernous space.

Nature itself recoiled from this place. The encroaching vines that had overtaken the exterior walls halted abruptly at the entrance, their tendrils curling away as if in fear.

No chirping of insects or rustling of small creatures disturbed the stillness; even the air felt devoid of the usual life that permeated the forest beyond.

A shiver coursed through me, not merely from the chill but from the overwhelming sense of dread that permeated the very stones of this forsaken church. It was as if the building itself mourned the atrocities it had witnessed, its gothic grandeur now a decaying monument to the darkness that had consumed it.

"Look here," Veylan's mental voice guided us to a corner where the floor had collapsed, revealing a hidden chamber below. Bones littered the space—tiny skeletons of infants intertwined with larger, adult remains. The walls bore inscriptions, their meanings obscured by time and grime.

"Human sacrifices," I breathed, horror settling in my chest. "They offered their own to the malevolent force."

Damien's face was a mask of controlled fury, his eyes darkening. "This is where it all began," he said through gritted teeth. "The pacts, the bloodshed—all in the name of power."

A sudden, sharp pain shot through Damien's face, causing him to stagger. He pressed a hand to his temple.

"SHUT UP!" Damien yelled, his voice raw with defiance, reverberating through the empty space.

"Damien!" I rushed to his side, concern etching my features. "What's wrong?"

He shook his head, trying to clear the invasive thoughts. "It's the force," he managed to say, his voice strained. "It's... restless."

Veylan's eyes narrowed, his fur bristling. "We need to leave this place. Its darkness feeds the entity."

As we turned to exit, a glint caught my eye—a hidden compartment beneath the altar. Inside lay an ancient tome, its pages brittle and ink faded. I carefully opened it.
"When two souls, bound by fate and love unyielding, unite, their bond shall be the key to vanquishing the darkness."

"Damien," I called softly, showing him the passage. "Our bond—it says it's the only thing capable of destroying the force."

He studied the text, his expression unreadable. "Then we have a chance," he said quietly, determination hardening his features.

Veylan's voice is solemn. "Love is a powerful weapon, but it requires sacrifice. Are you both prepared for what lies ahead?"

I met Damien's gaze, the weight of our shared destiny settling between us. "Together," I affirmed, my voice steady.

A smirk tugged at the corner of his lips, mischief dancing in his eyes. "Think you can keep up, wildflower?" he teased, his voice a low rumble.

I arched an eyebrow, matching his challenge. "Try me."

In a swift motion, Damien closed the distance between us, his hand gripping the back of my neck with a possessive roughness that sent a thrill through me. His lips crashed against mine, fierce and demanding, as if staking his claim. I responded with my fingers tangling in his hair, pulling him closer, deepening the kiss with a fervor that matched his own.

When we finally broke apart, breathless and flushed, he rested his forehead against mine, his eyes dark with desire. "You're mine," he growled, the words both a declaration and a vow.

I met his gaze, unflinching. "And you're mine," I replied, my voice unwavering.

A low chuckle escaped him, his thumb brushing over my lower lip. "Gods help anyone who stands in our way."

Obsession's Shadow
Damien

The trek back through the forest was silent, save for the crunch of leaves beneath our boots. Each step feel heavier than the last, the weight of the prophecy settling into my bones.

Veylan padded ahead, his sharp gaze scanning the shadows that crept between the trees. He had said nothing since we left the church, but his tense gait spoke volumes.

Elira walked beside me, her expression unreadable, though I could feel her occasional glances. Everything about her was maddening—the way she walked, the faint scent of her, even the memory of her body pressed against mine in the dark. Her perfect tits bouncing in the shadows.

The silence stretched, oppressive and thick, until finally, I couldn't stand it any longer.

"Say it," I muttered, my voice sharper than intended.

She blinked, startled, before narrowing her vivid blue eyes at me. "Say what?"

"Whatever it is you're dying to get off your chest," I snapped, my irritation bubbling over. "You've been looking at me like I'm about to sprout horns."

Her lips thinned into a line, and for a moment, I thought she'd let it go. But Elira wasn't the type to back down.

"Fine," she said, crossing her arms. "You keep shutting me out. One minute, you're snarling at me; the next, you're kissing me like your life depends on it. Do you even know what you want, Damien?"

Her words hit harder than I cared to admit. I stopped walking, the distance between us closing as she turned to face me.

"You think this is easy?" I growled, stepping closer. "That I don't know what's at stake? I—"

The words faltered, images flashing unbidden in my mind: her bare skin glowing in the firelight, her nails digging into my back, the soft, breathless moan that escaped her lips as I claimed her.

It had been reckless, a moment where the need for her had eclipsed reason. And now, it was seared into me, a memory I could neither erase nor escape.

She deserves so much better than me. But I'm a selfish bastard, so I'll never let her go.

A sharp, cold wind whipped through the trees, cutting through my thoughts like a blade. It carried with it a faint, bone-chilling whisper.

They're coming.

Veylan's ears twitched, and his deep growl echoed in our minds. "We're not alone."

My hand instinctively went to my sword, the cold hilt grounding me. Elira mirrored my movement, her grip steady on her dagger.

Her bravery is captivating. My little warrior.

I caught her gaze, and in that fleeting moment, it hit me again: she wasn't just my salvation. She was my obsession. The thought of losing her—to the force, to anyone—festered in the darkest corners of my mind.

From the shadows, the forest seemed to shudder, its usual stillness disrupted. Figures emerged, their forms draped in tattered cloaks that clung to them like shadows given flesh. Their eyes gleamed unnaturally, pale orbs that held no humanity.

"Shades," Veylan snarled, his fur bristling as he crouched into a defensive stance. "Bound to the force's will."

The shades moved unnaturally, their limbs jerking as though pulled by invisible strings. One by one, they closed the distance, their movements eerily silent.

"Stay close," I ordered, stepping in front of Elira. Her indignant huff told me she didn't appreciate being shielded, but I didn't care. This wasn't a battle she could fight alone.

The first shade lunged, its claw-like fingers reaching for her throat. I sidestepped, my blade slicing cleanly through its form. Instead of collapsing, the creature dissolved into ash, its remnants scattering into the air.

"They're not endless," Elira called out, her dagger finding its mark in another shade's chest. It too disintegrated, leaving only silence in its wake. "But they're fast."

Another surged forward, and Veylan intercepted, his massive form colliding with the shade in a blur of teeth and claws. Elira and I moved in tandem, our strikes precise and deliberate, but for every shade we felled, another seemed to emerge from the shadows.

"We can't hold them off forever," I said through gritted teeth, cutting down another. The force's influence pulsed in the air, feeding the shades' numbers.

"Then we make a run for it!" Elira shouted, her voice resolute.

Veylan snarled, his gaze locking onto mine.

"There's a clearing ahead. We can—"

A shade slammed into me, its weight throwing me to the ground. Its claws raked across my front, tearing into the flesh beneath. Pain seared through my side, but before it could strike again, Elira is there.

Her dagger plunged into its back, and the creature let out an unearthly wail before collapsing into ash.

Fucking perfect.

"Get up!" she snapped, grabbing my arm and hauling me to my feet. Her strength startled me, and for a moment, all I could do was stare at her.

Mine. The word pounded in my skull, primal and unrelenting. She was mine to protect, mine to fight for. The force itself could tear me apart, but it would never have her.

"Move!" she barked, breaking my trance.

Together, we sprinted toward the clearing, Veylan leading the way. The shades gave chase, their inhuman cries echoing through the forest. My vision blurred from blood loss, but I kept going, driven by the fire in Elira's eyes and the determination etched into every line of her face.

The clearing came into view, bathed in pale moonlight. Veylan skidded to a halt, planting himself firmly to face the oncoming shades with a ferocity that radiated primal dominance.

"Keep going!" he growled. "I'll hold them off."

"No!" Elira shouted, her voice breaking. She stepped toward him, but I caught her wrist, stopping her.

"He's right," I said, my voice rough. "We can't stay here."

Her eyes met mine, wide and filled with something I couldn't name. Anger? Fear? Grief?

"You'd better come back," she hissed at Veylan, her voice trembling.

Veylan didn't reply, his focus already on the advancing horde. Elira and I turned and ran, the shadows of the binding at our heels.

But even as I ran, my thoughts remained chained to her—to the fierce, wild fire in her spirit and the maddening hold she had over me. Whatever sacrifice lay ahead, I would face it. Because she is mine, and I would destroy anything that tried to take her from me.

A Flicker in the Dark
Elira

The wind whipped past us as we ran, the sounds of snarling and the clash of steel fading behind. My breath came in sharp bursts, my chest tight with the effort, but I couldn't stop. Not with Damien's blood staining the air around us.   Not with the lingering echo of Veylan's last growl.

"Damien," I called, my voice hoarse as I glanced at him. He was pale, his usual defiance softened by the shadows of pain etching his features.

His hand clutched his side, blood seeping through his fingers and dripping to the forest floor. "You're bleeding too much. We have to stop."

"No," he ground out, his green eyes blazing despite his staggered steps. "We keep going."

"You'll die if we don't—"

"Better me than you," he snapped, cutting me off. His words struck with the force of a blade, silencing my protest.

The shadows thickened, and the trees seemed to close in around us. Every rustle, every flicker of movement from the corners of my vision, felt like another shade about to pounce.

My dagger trembled in my grip.

We stumbled into a small hollow, a dip in the forest floor shielded by a ring of gnarled roots and dense undergrowth. Damien nearly collapsed, his back hitting the bark of a tree as he slid down. His breathing was shallow, his hands shaking as he tried to hold pressure against his side.

"Take it off," I ordered, dropping to my knees beside him.

He raised an eyebrow, the ghost of a smirk twitching at his lips. "Elira, I'm flattered, but—"

"Your shirt, idiot," I hissed, yanking at the clasps. "You're bleeding out."

His smirk vanished, and he shifted to help me, wincing as the motion pulled at his wound. As I peeled back the ruined leather, the gash beneath is deep and angry, blood pouring in a steady stream. I pressed my hands against it instinctively, the warmth of his blood seeping into my skin.

"You're not allowed to die," I whispered, the words trembling as they left me.

His hand covered mine, the strength in his grip surprising. "I'm not planning on it, wildflower."

I scowled at the nickname but didn't pull away. "I'm going to try something. It might hurt."

He grunted, the shadow of amusement flickering across his face. "Everything hurts already. Do your worst."

Closing my eyes, I focused on the flicker of warmth inside me. The same energy that had erupted unbidden when the shades first attacked. I didn't know how it worked, but I reached for it, imagining it flowing into Damien, knitting his torn flesh back together.

The air grew heavy, a faint hum filling the hollow. My hands tingled, and beneath them, Damien's wound began to close. His breath hitched, his muscles tensing, but he didn't cry out. When I opened my eyes, the gash was gone, leaving only a faint scar in its place.

Damien stared at me, his green eyes wide and searching. "How did you—?"

"I don't know," I admitted, pulling my hands back. They were clean, the blood gone as if it had been absorbed by the strange power within me. "It just…
happened."

He reached out, his fingers brushing against my cheek. "You're full of surprises."

Before I could respond, the sound of distant snarls cut through the air. My stomach tightened. The shades were still hunting us.
"We can't stay here," I said, standing and offering him my hand.

Damien took it, his grip firm as he rose. He looked steadier, his color returning, but his eyes still burned with something darker. "They'll come for you. They always will."
"Let them try," I replied, gripping my dagger and meeting his gaze.

For a moment, the tension between us was palpable, his lips parting as if to say something more.

But he only nodded, the corners of his mouth tugging upward in a grim smile.
"Then we'll make them regret it."

The journey through the dense forest continued, the shadows stretching longer as the sun dipped below the horizon. Damien moved with renewed strength, though his gaze frequently flickered back to me, as if to ensure I was still there. The air around us felt heavier, the oppressive presence of the shades lingering even as we pressed onward.

"Do you think Veylan will be okay?" I asked, my voice quieter than I intended.

Damien's jaw tightened. "He's survived worse. He'll find us."

I huff a breath and stop walking, incapable of holding it anymore.

When he turns to face me, I let it out. "I don't know why we feel this close to each other. But I want to tell you that…I wish…I wish we could have all the time to go on dates, learn each other to the bones. I'm tired of running."

He closes the distance between us, his beautiful soft smile making my heart melt. Even with his stature, his scars, when he smiles at me. The only thing I see is softness.

He grab my chin, pulling my face up and drop a featherlight kiss on my chapped lips. "We will."

I nodded, but doubt crept into my mind. The thought of losing

The trees began to thin, revealing a small clearing bathed in moonlight. At its center stood a crumbling stone structure, its walls entwined with thick vines. It looked ancient, forgotten by time, yet it seemed to pulse with a faint energy.

"What is that?" I asked, my steps slowing.

Damien's expression darkened. "A ruin from the old world. We shouldn't stay long."

Despite his warning, I felt an inexplicable pull toward the structure. As we approached, I noticed symbols etched into the stones—patterns that seemed to shift and twist when I tried to focus on them.

The moment I touched it, a jolt shot through me, and I stumbled back, my heart racing.

Damien was at my side instantly, his hands steadying me. "What happened?"

"I don't know," I said, staring at my hand. "It's like the ruin pushed back."

His gaze shifted to the structure, his eyes narrowing. "We shouldn't linger. Whatever power this place holds, it's not meant for us."

Reluctantly, I nodded, but as we turned to leave, the faint hum of the ruin grew louder. The ground beneath us trembled, and a cold wind swept through the clearing, carrying with it a whisper that sent chills down my spine.

Damien's grip on his sword tightened, his posture tense. "We need to move. Now."

Without another word, we plunged back into the forest, the presence of the ruin fading but the unease it left behind lingering. The path ahead seems darker, the shadows deeper, and for a moment, I wondered if we are running toward safety or further into danger.

Fierce and Fragile
Damien

The forest seemed to breathe around us as we ran, the damp air heavy with tension. Whatever force lay dormant in that ruin was no longer content to stay forgotten. It had marked us—marked her.

Elira's breathing was steady, though she darted glances over her shoulder as we pressed onward. She was scared; I could feel it radiating off her in waves. And yet, her grip on her dagger never faltered. She was ready to fight, even when outmatched.

My foolish, stubborn wildflower.

I winced as my side throbbed, the newly sealed wound still raw beneath the scar. Her power had healed me, but it wasn't enough to restore me entirely. I needed time to recover.

Time we didn't have.

"Do you feel that?" Elira asked, her voice low. Her eyes flitted to the trees, searching the oppressive shadows pressing in around us.

"The air," I replied, keeping my voice low. "It feels alive, watching us."

The forest thinned again, and ahead of us, a stream cut through the underbrush, its surface glittering with moonlight. The sound of the water was a reprieve, though the unease in my chest didn't abate.

"We'll rest here," I said, nodding toward the stream. "Just long enough to gather our strength."

Elira hesitated, scanning the area before giving a reluctant nod. She crouched by the water, dipping her hands in and splashing it over her face. Her dark hair tumbled over her shoulders, strands clinging to the curve of her neck as droplets glistened on her pale skin. The moonlight kissed her features, highlighting the sharp cut of her jaw, the fullness of her lips, and the intensity of her vivid blue eyes that seemed to catch every ounce of light.

Her slender frame looked deceptively delicate, but her movements told a different story. The slight flex of her muscles beneath the torn fabric of her sleeves, the graceful arch of her back as she straightened, all spoke of a strength forged by survival.

"You're staring," she said without looking at me, her voice breaking the quiet.

I smirked, crouching beside her. "You're easy to look at."

She rolled her eyes but didn't push me away.

Instead, she asked, "What was that place? The ruin?"

I exhaled, staring at the rippling water. "A remnant of the old world. A place of power that was meant to be forgotten. Whoever built it sought strength, but they paid for it with their souls."

"And now it wants ours," she said bitterly.
"It wants yours," I corrected, my voice rough. "It felt your power."

Her hand stilled in the water, her eyes lifting to meet mine. "Why do you call me that?" she asked suddenly, her voice quiet but steady. "Wildflower. Little warrior." Her gaze locked with mine, the vivid blue a stark contrast against the dark forest, holding both challenge and curiosity.

Her lips parted slightly, her breath catching as if my words had struck something deeper within her. "And what about you? You've made a deal with the force. You're tied to it. Doesn't it want you too?"

So much questions.

It's annoying. But she's cute.

My jaw tightened, and for a moment, I considered lying. "It already has me," I said, my voice low and dark. "But you... you're different. You're fierce, like a warrior, and fragile in ways you don't even understand. Like a wildflower growing in a wasteland. Beautiful. Resilient."

Her expression softened, her gaze searching mine as though trying to piece together the truth behind my words. Her lips pressed together, trembling slightly, but she didn't look away.

The air between us was heavy with things unsaid, truths we weren't ready to confront. I moved closer, instinctively drawn to her despite the danger around us. The moonlight caught in her eyes, their vivid blue a sharp contrast to the dark world closing in.

"You're too close," she murmured, her voice low but not quite steady.

I smirked, my hand brushing against her cheek, my thumb trailing down to her jaw. Her skin was soft beneath my touch, a sharp contrast to the grit and tension of the forest around us. "And yet you're not moving away."

Her lips parted, a faint tremble betraying the tension between us. Her chest rose and fell in shallow breaths, and I felt the heat radiating from her skin.

My gaze dropped to her mouth, and I leaned in, the scent of her intoxicating, grounding me more than anything else in this cursed forest.

"Damien," she whispered, her voice catching.
"Say the word," I said, my voice rough. "Tell me to stop."

Her hands gripped my shirt, not pulling me closer but not pushing me away either. Her head tilted

slightly, her lips brushing against mine as she spoke. "I… can't."

It was all the permission I needed. My lips crashed against hers, fierce and unyielding, claiming what I had wanted for far too long. She responded instantly, her fingers tangling in my shirt, pulling me closer. The kiss was frantic, desperate—a collision of two souls caught in the chaos around them.

Her back hit the rough bark of a tree, and I pressed against her, my hands framing her face as I deepened the kiss. She gasped softly, her body arching into mine, and the sound sent a surge of raw need coursing through me. Everything about her, from the way she tasted to the way she clung to me, threatened to undo me.

A sharp, distant growl shattered the moment, and we broke apart, our breaths ragged. Her eyes were wide, her lips swollen from the kiss, and I saw the same mix of desire and regret mirrored in her expression.

"We can't…" she started, her voice shaky.
"I know," I said, my forehead resting against hers. "But that doesn't mean I'll stop wanting to."

The growl came again, closer this time, and I pulled back reluctantly, my hand still lingering on her cheek. "We need to move. Now."

She nodded, her dagger already in her hand as she stepped away from the tree. The tension between us hadn't faded, but the danger pressing in demanded our focus. Without another word, we turned and ran, the forest swallowing us once more.

The Hunt
Elira

The night suffocates with its stillness, the kind that burrows into the chest and refuses to let go. Every step feels heavier. My lungs ache, and my thoughts spiral, darting to the faces of those I've left behind—Lyric's steady determination, Veylan's unwavering loyalty. Are they safe? Are they even alive? The weight of not knowing presses harder than the pursuit itself.

But I push forward because stopping isn't an option.

Damien's presence looms ahead, a shadow that moves with deadly precision. His shoulders are tense, each step deliberate, as if he's holding back something feral.

We didn't talked much and I start to feel have an eerie sensation prickling in my mind.

The moonlight catches the hard lines of his face, but it's his silence that unsettles me the most. He's like a predator in waiting, coiled tight and ready to strike. Even now, with the danger surrounding us, he commands the space around him, a force I can't look away from.

"We need a plan," I say, my voice cutting through the eerie stillness.

He glances over his shoulder, his green eyes stark against the dark. "The plan is to survive."

"That's not a plan," I snap, frustration bubbling, tired. So tired.

He halts suddenly, and the shift is so sharp that I nearly stumble into him. He turns, and for a heartbeat, I see concern, or maybe frustration. But then his expression hardens, and it's gone, replaced by something darker.

His gaze feels like a blade, cutting through the air between us. I can't tell if he's protecting me or trying to keep himself from unraveling. "I can't. I won't!" he says, the words low but laced with an edge I can't ignore and clearly not directed to me.

My power hums beneath my skin, desperate to be unleashed. I know I could end this—end him—with a single burst.

But I can't. The thought of hurting him shatters me more than the blade ever could.

The snarl that escapes his lips isn't human. His hand moves to his sword, and the way he grips it— slow, calculated—sends a shiver down my spine. "Run," he says, his voice layered with something deeper, darker. "Make it fun."

"No," I breathe, my hand tightening around my sword. "This isn't you. Fight it!"

His response is a cruel smile, one that twists his features into something unrecognizable. He lunges without warning, his blade cutting through the space where I had been standing just a heartbeat before. I dive to the side, my feet scrambling for purchase on the uneven ground.

"Damien, stop!" I scream, the desperation in my voice tearing at my throat.

He doesn't stop. His movements are precise, relentless, like a predator toying with its prey. I barely manage to block his next strike with my blade. Tears blur my vision, but I can't afford to falter.

Not now.

My power asking to get out, asking for blood.

"You're better than this!" I plead, my voice cracking as I parry another blow. "You're stronger than it!"

"You don't know me," he snarls, his voice guttural, inhuman. "You never have."

The words cut deep. He slams his sword against my dagger, the impact sending the smaller weapon flying from my hand. I stumble back, tripping over a root and falling hard onto the forest floor.

Pain shoots through my side, and I look up to see him standing over me, his sword raised.

"Damien, please," I sob, my voice barely a whisper. "Don't do this."

His eyes flicker, just for a moment, but it's enough. I see him, the man beneath the darkness, fighting to break through.

But the malevolent tightens its grip, and he presses the blade to my throat. Sensations of tick hot blood dripping from the wound filled my sense and I grith my teeth in pain.

My power surges, hot and volatile, begging to be unleashed. I could stop him. I could end this. But the thought of hurting him is unbearable.

So I resign. Because love makes you weak. "Do it," I whisper, tears streaming down my face. "If this is who you are now, end it."

His hand trembles, and as if something snaps inside him, he stumbles back, the sword falling from his grasp. His knees hit the ground, and he lets out a guttural cry, his hands clawing at his head.

"Elira," he chokes out, his voice raw. "Gods, Elira... I... I didn't..."

I push myself up, my body shaking. The sight of him—broken, vulnerable—shatters me in a way I didn't think possible. This muscular, large, six-foot four soldier, king, broken.

I throw myself at him, my arms wrapping around his shoulders as sobs wrack my body.

"It's okay," I say, though it's a lie. Nothing about this is okay. "You're here. You're with me."

His arms tighten around me, his hold desperate, like he's afraid I might disappear. "I'm sorry," he whispers, his voice cracking. "I didn't mean to—"

I cut him off with a kiss, my lips crashing against his. It's messy, frantic, a collision of desperation and need. His hands move to my face, his touch rough but grounding, as if he's trying to convince himself that I'm real.

That I'm still here.

The forest around us fades, the danger momentarily forgotten as we lose ourselves in each other. He presses me back onto the ground, his weight a comforting presence, and I pull him closer, needing to feel him, to remind myself that he's here. Still mine.

His arms tighten around me, his hold desperate, like he's afraid I might disappear. "I'm sorry," he whispers, his voice cracking. "It wasn't me. The force... it took control. It's like a fire, burning away everything I am. I tried to fight it, Elira, I swear, but it used my darkest thoughts, my fears, my anger."

I pull back just enough to look into his eyes, green and full of anguish now. "And you stopped," I say softly, brushing his hair from his face. "You fought it off."

His forehead presses against mine, his breath warm and uneven. "Because it's you," he says, his voice trembling. "You're the only thing that matters. I can't lose you."

Tears spill down my cheeks, but I lean into him, capturing his lips with mine. The kiss is desperate, a collision of fear, relief, and unspoken promises. His hands find my waist, pulling me closer, and I let myself melt into him, into the safety of his arms.

His hand drifts to my cheek, his thumb tracing the line of my jaw, erasing the last visible trace of my tears. "You're too good for me," he says, his lips twitching in a faint, bitter smile.

"Good," I whisper, leaning into his touch. "Because I'm not going anywhere."

His lips crash against mine again, rough and hungry. I respond with equal fervor, my fingers tangling in his hair, pulling him closer until there's no space left between us.

His hands roam my body, not gentle, but reverent, as if he's memorizing every inch. "You're mine," he growls, the words vibrating against my skin. "Say it, Elira. Say you're mine."

"I'm yours," I breathe, arching into him, my own hands exploring the hard lines of his back, his shoulders. "But you're mine too, Damien. Don't forget that."

A low chuckle escapes him, dark and full of promise. "Never." He kisses me again, slower this time, the heat between us simmering but no less intense. His hand moves to my thigh, hitching it over his hip as he shifts against me, drawing a gasp from my lips.

He stares at me for a long moment, his breathing uneven, his expression torn between relief and something darker. Then, with a sudden movement, I push him back gently, guiding his back to the forest floor.

His body yields beneath me, the tension in his shoulders slowly unraveling as he watches me with a mix of curiosity and reverence.

"Elira," he murmurs, his voice low, a warning and a plea all at once.

I silence him with a finger pressed to his lips. "You're always in control," I say softly, my eyes locking with his. "But not this time. Let me."

His chest rises and falls sharply as I lean over him, my hands moving to the buttons of his shirt. The fabric clings to his skin, damp with sweat and the remnants of the fight.

Slowly, deliberately, I undo each button, exposing the hard planes of his chest beneath. My fingers trail along the ridges of muscle, the scars etched into his skin telling stories I don't yet know.

The moonlight filters through the trees, casting shadows that dance across his body, and I take a moment to marvel at him—the strength, the vulnerability he so rarely shows.

"You're beautiful," I whisper, my voice trembling slightly. "All of you."

A low growl escapes him, his hands moving to my hips, gripping them firmly. "Elira," he says again, his tone darker now, need threading through every syllable. "Do you know what you're doing to me?"

I smirk, shifting slightly so that I'm straddling him.

Oh, I can feel it just fine.

His breath hitches as I grind against him, the hardness of his arousal pressing against me through the fabric of his pants. My own desire pools low in my belly, igniting a fire that threatens to consume us both.
"Show me," I challenge, leaning down so that my lips hover just above his. "Tell me."

His hands tighten on my hips, his control fraying at the edges. "You drive me mad," he growls, his voice rough and unrestrained. "The way you move, the way you look at me... Gods, Elira, I can't think when you're like this. Don't you feel how hard you make me?"

I capture his lips in a fierce kiss, swallowing his words as my hands move lower, undoing the fastenings of his pants. He lifts his hips slightly, helping me push them down, and I pause, my gaze drifting over him. He's everything—powerful, vulnerable, mine.

I make quick work of my own clothes, the cool air brushing against my heated skin as I return to him. His hands roam over me, rough and unforgiven, and I gasp as he pulls me down, aligning his huge dick with my bare and glistening cunt perfectly. For a moment, we stay like that, the tension between us crackling like a live wire.

"Elira," he murmurs, his hands steadying me. "Take what's yours."

And I do. Slowly, deliberately, I lower myself onto him, a soft moan escaping my lips as he fills me completely. His head falls back, a guttural sound tearing from his throat, and his hands grip my thighs, guiding me as I begin to move. It's slow at first, a rhythm that builds with every thrust, every breath.

"Look at me," he says, his voice a command and a plea. I do, my gaze locking with his as his hand moves between us. He gathers the evidence of my pleasure on his fingers, stroking the pad of it on his base and my vulva lips, then bring them to his lips and humming softly as he tastes us. The raw intimacy of the gesture steals my breath.

"You're perfect," he says, his voice thick with emotion. "Every inch of you. Mine."

I lean forward, my hands bracing on his chest as I quicken my pace. His hands grip my hips, helping me find a rhythm that's both rough and tender, and I let myself get lost in the intensity of it—the way his body responds to mine, the way his name falls from my lips like a prayer.

His hand moves to my throat, not constricting, just resting there, and I meet his gaze, daring him silently to push further. Instead, he groans, his control slipping as I reach up, wrapping my fingers lightly around his neck.

His reaction is immediate, his hips surging up to meet mine, and I can feel his pulse racing beneath my fingertips.
"You like this," I whisper, my voice trembling with power and desire. "You love it when I take control."
His lips curve into a wicked grin, his voice rough as he replies, "Only you, Elira. Always you.""

The Betrayal
Elira

The path is steep and rocky, winding higher into the mountains with every step. I stop to catch my breath, my boots crunching against loose gravel as I take in the view around me.

The wind bites at my face, carrying the scent of pine and frost, and for a moment, I'm struck by the silence. It's a fragile kind of peace, broken only by the distant howl of the wind. I press a hand to my chest, as if that will keep the storm of emotions inside me from spilling over.

Mountains stretch out before me, their snow-covered peaks glistening in the soft light of dawn. The expanse is vast, the sheer magnitude of it making me feel impossibly small.

It's unreal.

The snow reflects a faint blue hue, casting a serene glow that contrasts sharply with the chaos and bloodshed of the past days. For a moment, I forget the weight on my shoulders, the dangers lurking behind us, and simply stare. It's nothing like I've ever seen before.

I feel Damien come up behind me, his presence steady and grounding. He doesn't say anything at first, letting the silence stretch as I take in the view. My chest tightens, and an unexpected ache blooms in my heart.

"I wish my mother could have seen this," I whisper, my voice trembling. The words escape before I can stop them. "She would have loved it. She always talked about seeing the world, the places beyond the ruins. But she never got the chance."

Damien's hand brushes against mine, a silent offering of comfort. "She would have been proud of you," he says quietly. "For surviving. For fighting."

I don't look at him, my eyes fixed on the horizon. "I don't know if that's true. I've done things—terrible things. Things she would have hated."

Damien's hand brushes against mine, his fingers rough and warm. "She would have understood. Survival isn't clean, Elira. But you've fought for more than just yourself. That's something she would have admired."

I swallow hard, forcing back the tears that sting my eyes. "Sometimes I don't know who I am anymore."

He doesn't answer immediately, but when he does, his voice is steady, carrying a weight that makes my breath hitch. "You are Elira Veyastra, the one who defies the darkness. You are fire and ash, born of ruin but unbroken. You are sacrifice and strength. You are the giant wolf beholder. That's who you are." "And mine." He add, shrugging and smiling proudly before putting one knees on the ground.

I want to cry. No. I cry.

Tears falling from my eyes I look at him bowing before me. He's eyes on mine solemnly.

"Queen." He spoke before looking at the ground.
"What are you talking about?" I ask with a
shaky voice.
"After everything, I'll make you my official wife. And I'll give you the crown. As Queen."

The moment stretches, heavy with unspoken words, until the sound of footsteps crunching against the gravel draws our attention. I turn to see Lyric and Eryndor catching up, their figures dark against the pale morning light. Lyric's golden eyes flick to the mountains, her expression softening for a rare moment before sharpening once more.

"It's beautiful," she says, her voice quiet but firm. "A reminder of what's worth saving."

Eryndor stops beside her, his posture tense, his braided hair catching the light. "Or what we've already lost," he adds, his gaze shifting to Damien. His eyes are sharp, cutting, filled with something I can only describe as hatred.

The tension crackles between them, thick and oppressive. Damien doesn't flinch under Eryndor's stare, his own expression hardening into something unreadable.

Lyric steps forward, her golden eyes narrowing as she grips the hilt of her sword. "You think we've forgotten? What you've done? What he's done?" Her voice is sharp, each word cutting deeper than the mountain air.

"Lyric," I begin, holding my hands up in a placating gesture. "Please, just give me a minute to explain."

Her blade flashes as she draws it, the sound of steel slicing through the air sending a jolt of fear through me. "I don't want your excuses, Elira," she snaps. "You chose him. You betrayed us. And now you expect us to listen?"

Eryndor moves to stand beside her, his expression cold and unyielding. "You're no different from him," he says, his voice low but venomous. "You've sided with the enemy."

Damien takes a step forward, his own sword half-drawn. "Say that again," he growls, his voice dangerous.

"Stop!" I shout, my voice breaking with desperation. The surge of power within me flares to life, hot and untamed, and before I can control it, fire erupts around me.

The flames roar, a blinding wall of heat and light that forces Lyric and Eryndor to stumble back. The ground beneath us cracks, scorched and blackened, as the fire subsides just as quickly as it appeared.

The silence that follows is deafening. My chest heaves, the remnants of the fire still crackling in the air around me. Lyric's sword hangs loosely at her side, her golden eyes wide with shock. Eryndor's expression is unreadable, but I can see the tension in his posture, the way his hand tightens around his weapon.

"I don't want to fight you," I say, my voice trembling but firm. "But I will if I have to."

A low growl rumbles through the clearing, and the hairs on the back of my neck rise as Veylan steps from the shadows. His imposing figure is a silhouette against the faint morning light, his ember-colored eyes burning with intensity. He moves with a predator's grace, each step deliberate and commanding.

"Enough," he snarls, his voice resonating in our minds like a physical force. "You will listen, or I will rip your throats out in a single bite."

Lyric stiffens, her grip tightening on her sword, but she doesn't move. Eryndor's gaze shifts to Veylan, his jaw clenched, but even he doesn't dare to challenge the wolf.

Veylan's gaze sweeps over the group, his eyes settling on me. "Speak, Elira," he commands. "And make them understand, or I will."

Reckoning of Fate
Elira

The fire dies down, but its memory lingers in the scorch marks on the earth and the blistering heat that clings to the air. My heart pounds as I look at Lyric and Eryndor, their faces shadows of doubt and defiance. Veylan's words hang heavily between us, unchallenged yet bristling with unspoken emotions.

I step forward, my hands still tingling with the remnants of power. "You're right to hate me," I begin, my voice steady but low. "You've lost people. We've all lost people. And I've made choices I can't take back. But every single one of those choices was made to stop something greater than any of us. If we keep fighting each other, we're doing exactly what the force wants."

Lyric's gaze burns into mine, golden and sharp, but she doesn't speak. Eryndor's jaw tightens, his knuckles whitening around the hilt of his weapon. The silence is heavy, thick with tension and the ghosts of unspoken words.

Damien steps beside me, his presence like a shield. His voice is calm but unyielding. "We don't have time for this. You think your anger will bring them back? The ones you lost? It won't. But standing here, tearing each other apart, only ensures we lose more."

Eryndor finally speaks, his voice a low rumble of barely contained fury. "And what guarantees do we have that you won't destroy us next, Damien? That you won't turn against us the moment it suits you?"

Damien's gaze hardens, his green eyes cold and unrelenting, but the bastard smiles. "None. I can't promise you anything. You don't have to trust me."

The wind picks up, carrying the scent of frost and ash. Lyric's fingers flex on her sword, the tension in her posture betraying the war raging inside her. "You talk about trust," she says, her voice breaking the quiet like a blade slicing through fabric. "But you ask too much. You expect us to forget—to forgive."

I step closer to her, my voice softer but no less fierce. "I'm not asking you to forgive. I'm asking you to fight. Fight with me, for what's left of this world, for the chance to build something better. For my world. Even if I don't get everything that implies right now. If we fail here, there won't be anything left to forgive."

Lyric's eyes search mine, the fire in her gaze wavering for the first time. She doesn't lower her sword, but she doesn't raise it again either. Eryndor shifts beside her, his face a mask of conflict, and the silence stretches once more, a taut thread threatening to snap.

Veylan breaks it with a growl, low and menacing, his eyes fixed on both of them. "Decide now," he says, his voice a rumble that shakes the very ground. "Elira speaks the truth. If you doubt her, then leave. But know this: if you walk away, you're no longer fighting for the world you claim to protect. You're only fighting your own bitterness."

Lyric's lips press into a thin line, and she sheaths her sword with a sharp click. "I'll fight," she says, her voice quieter now. "But don't expect me to forget."

Eryndor hesitates, his hand still on his weapon. His eyes flicker between Damien and me, and finally, he exhales heavily, letting his grip loosen. "For now," he says, his tone cold but resigned. "But one wrong step, and I'll finish what we started here."

Relief floods through me, though I don't let it show. The tension eases, but the air remains thick with unease.

Damien glances at the group. He exhales, the weight of his words heavy even before he speaks. "There's something you need to know," he begins, his voice low but steady. "About why I've done what I've done."

Lyric stiffens, her golden eyes narrowing. "You mean the slaughter? The betrayals? The atrocities you've carried out in the name of the crown?"

Damien nods, unflinching under her sharp gaze. "Yes. All of it. You think I wanted to kill, to destroy? I didn't. I made a deal—a deal with the force itself."

Eryndor's breath catches, and even Lyric's anger falters, replaced by a flicker of confusion. "For fame?" Eryndor asks, his voice cold but edged with curiosity.

Damien's jaw tightens, and he takes a step forward, his presence commanding. "For all of you. Years ago, during the war, our kingdom was on the brink of collapse. Our enemies outnumbered us, and the people were starving. I thought I could save them—if I had more power, more strength. The force came to me, whispering promises of victory, of salvation. All it wanted in return was a part of me."

"Your humanity," I whisper, the words settling like a stone in my chest.

He nods, his gaze locking with mine. "It gave me everything I needed to win. But the price... the price was higher than I could've imagined. Every time I fought, every decision I made, it twisted me. It fed on my anger, my fears, until there was nothing left but the beast it wanted me to be."

Lyric's hand hovers near her sword, her expression unreadable. "And you didn't think to tell us this before? To warn us about what we were truly fighting?"

Damien's voice sharpens, frustration bleeding into his tone. "And what would you have done? Run? Turned on me sooner? Defend me?" He huffs a laugh.

"You don't know that," Lyric snaps, her voice trembling. "You don't get to decide what we can handle."

Eryndor steps forward, his eyes hard as flint. "So what now? You've made your choices, sealed your fate. Why should we trust anything you say?"

Damien's gaze hardens, but there's a flicker of vulnerability beneath the surface. "Because I'm still fighting. The force doesn't own me yet. And with Elira's power, with all of us together, we might actually have a chance to end this."

The silence stretches, thick with tension. Lyric looks to me, her eyes searching. "And you knew this?"

I shake my head.

Lyric exhales sharply, her fingers curling into fists. "You've made a mess of everything," she says, her voice low. "But if you're lying, Damien... I'll make sure you pay for every life you've taken."

Eryndor says nothing, his expression grim, but he finally nods. "Let's get to Relvaris. There's a library Maybe we'll find something that can stop this. Fast. All the village to the Est are dying of starvation, the ground's rotting, the trees burnings by themselves."

Veylan's gaze meets mine, a flicker of approval in his ember eyes before he turns to the others.

"Then we move," he says, his voice brooking no argument. "The force won't wait for us to mend our wounds."

Damien nods.

Lyric raises an eyebrow, skepticism laced in her tone. "And how exactly do you plan to get us into a city that's likely crawling with sentries and rebels with them decapitating you?"

A smirk tugs at Damien's lips, cold and calculated. "I have my ways."

I glance between them, my pulse quickening at the thought of entering a city teeming with potential dangers. But the promise of answers, of something that could finally give us an edge, is too tempting to ignore.

"Relvaris it is," I say, my voice firmer than I feel. "We'll figure out the rest when we get there."

Without a second thought, I run to Veylan, now that I know I won't start a war by moving.

"Veylan!" I cry out, the relief in my voice tearing through the stillness.

His ember eyes meet mine, and for a moment, the wolf's usually sharp demeanor softens. I throw my arms around his thick neck, burying my face into his fur. His warmth steadies me, grounding me in the chaos.

"You're alive," I whisper, my voice trembling.

Veylan lets out a low rumble, a sound almost like a chuckle, and nudges me gently with his massive head. "*You doubted me?*" his voice echoes in my mind, tinged with humor.

I pull back just enough to look at him, my hands still buried in his fur. "Never," I say, a shaky smile breaking through. "But it's good to see you anyway."

The moment is broken by Lyric's sharp intake of breath. "What the fuck?" she yells, her voice cutting through the air like a blade.

I blink, confused, until I see her pointing at my wrist. The mark—a vivid, fiery sigil—glows faintly against my skin, pulsing in time with my heartbeat.

Eryndor steps closer, his expression darkening as he stares at it.
"Care to explain?" Lyric demands, her golden eyes blazing.

I open my mouth to respond, but the words catch in my throat. The mark feels alive, burning with a power I barely understand, and the weight of their eyes on me is suffocating. Veylan steps forward, positioning himself protectively between me and the others.

"Enough," he growls, his voice a command that silences even Lyric's anger. "The mark is hers. She will explain when she is ready. Until then, no harm will come to her."

Lyric's jaw tightens, her hands balling into fists, but she doesn't argue. Eryndor says nothing, his gaze lingering on the mark before turning away. The tension is palpable, but no one dares to challenge Veylan's authority.

Whispers of Ash
Elira

The journey to Relvaris is swallowed by the night, the darkness wrapping around us like a suffocating shroud. The stars are hidden, the moon's light barely piercing through the oppressive black. Each step feels heavier, the silence of the night pressing down, thick and unrelenting.

Damien walks beside me, his presence a storm—volatile and dark. His hand brushes mine as we climb over gnarled roots, and though it's unintentional, the heat of his touch lingers longer than it should.

I see him battle the force every wake moment. It's saddening to me. I see the way he closes his eyes, in pain and murmur to himself.

It's getting worse.

"Your breathing's loud," he says, his tone teasing but low, barely cutting through the tension around us.

I glance at him, narrowing my eyes. "And your face is annoying."

He chuckles, the sound rough and rich, sending a ripple of warmth down my spine. "Good. Keeps you on edge. But wait, wanna sit on it?"

"Maybe," I mutter, smiling to myself.

Behind us, Lyric and Eryndor exchange wary glances. Lyric's golden eyes are sharp, distrust carving lines into her expression. Eryndor's posture is stiff, his hand never straying far from his weapon. Veylan moves ahead, his hulking form cutting through the mist like a shadow given life.

He pauses occasionally to sniff the air, his movements deliberate and predatory.

Damien's voice breaks the silence again. "We'll reach the outskirts by nightfall. The city's under tight control, so we'll need to be careful."

"Careful," Lyric scoffs, her voice like a blade. "Coming from you."

Veylan's growl rumbles through the air, cutting off any retort Damien might've had. "Both of you shut up. We're being watched."

I stiffen, my fingers curling around the hilt of the sword on my back. Damien steps closer, his body brushing against mine as he places himself slightly in front. The gesture isn't lost on me, nor is the way my pulse quickens at the proximity. He smells like leather and smoke, and the heat of him seeps into my skin.

The tree stills, and the tension coils tighter. My power hums beneath my skin, eager and wild, but I force it down, focusing instead on the shadows shifting in the distance.

"Move quietly," Veylan commands, his voice resonating in our minds. "We're not alone."

As we press on, the oppressive air thickens, and the faint sound of whispers tickles the edge of my hearing. I glance at Damien, whose jaw tightens, his green eyes scanning the path ahead.

The Shadows of Relvaris
Elira

The city rises ahead like something out of a dream—gothic and enchanting, with tall spires that pierce the sky and cobblestone streets that glint softly under the moonlight. The iron gates stand open, their ornate designs curling like vines, and faint lantern light spills from windows, casting warm glows onto the stone facades.

Relvaris looks untouched by the corruption plaguing the rest of the world, its charm almost disarming. In the distance, the snow-capped mountains frame the scene, their peaks glowing faintly in the pale moonlight.

"This place seems so calm," I whisper, my voice catching as I take in the strange blend of beauty and unease.

Damien's gaze flickers to mine, the hardness in his green eyes softening for just a moment. "It hasn't been touched yet, but that doesn't mean it's safe. Looks can be deceiving. And I'm here, so is he."

The faint hum of life echoes around us. People move in the distance, their laughter light and carefree, as though they have no idea of the creeping darkness waiting beyond their city's borders.

A child runs across the street, her giggle carrying through the air, and for a heartbeat, the scene feels so normal that my chest tightens with longing.

Lyric's voice pulls me back. "It's beautiful," she says, her golden eyes narrowed. "Too beautiful."

Eryndor's expression is sharp as he takes in the towering architecture and the calm faces of the passersby. "They don't know what's coming."

Veylan stays close, his massive form blending into the shadows as his ember eyes scan the surroundings with a predator's precision. "*Stay alert,*" he growls in our minds. "*This peace is fragile.*"

We move carefully through the gates, our footsteps echoing softly against the cobblestones. The streets feel alive, the warm glow of lanterns and the faint hum of life contrasting sharply with the harshness of the world we've left behind.

Damien walks close to me, his hard arms brushing mine as we navigate the narrow alleys. My pulse quickens at the proximity, though I keep my eyes forward, hyper-aware of his presence.

I slow my steps as a group of children dash by, their laughter ringing through the street. One little girl pauses to wave at me before disappearing into the shadows, and for a brief, heart-stopping moment, I imagine a life where this peace could be real.

Where this city wouldn't be consumed by the darkness creeping closer.

"You're looking at me again, little warrior," Damien murmurs beside me, his voice low and rough. The nickname pulls my attention back to him, and I catch the faint smirk tugging at his lips.

"I'm not," I lie, turning my gaze forward again. "I'm observing."

His chuckle vibrates in the space between us, his hand brushing against mine as he leans closer. "Call it what you like. But you look like you're imagining something impossible."

I glance at him, my breath hitching at the way his green eyes burn into mine. "What if it's not? What if there's still something here worth saving?"

Damien's smirk fades, his gaze softening in a way that's almost disarming. "Then we'll fight for it.

But don't let the beauty fool you, wildflower. This city has its shadows too."

Heat rises to my cheeks, but before I can respond, Lyric clears her throat sharply. "Save your flirting for later. We're here for a reason."

Damien straightens, his playful smirk returning as he throws a glance over his shoulder. "Jealous, Lyric?"

She glares, her golden eyes sparking. "Not in the slightest."

The tension eases slightly, but my chest still feels tight. We make our way deeper into the city, and the air shifts subtly. The vibrant life of the outer streets gives way to quieter alleys, the light dimming as the towering spires loom closer. The library rises before us, its grand doors carved with intricate symbols that pulse faintly with light, their glow casting eerie patterns on the cobblestones.

Damien pauses, his gaze narrowing as he studies the markings. "These wards… they're still active. This place is more than just a library."

Lyric and Eryndor exchange wary glances, their hands instinctively moving to their weapons. Veylan's low growl rumbles through our minds, a reminder of the fragility of the peace around us.

"Be ready," I say, my voice steady despite the unease coiling in my gut. Damien steps closer, his presence a steady heat at my side, and for a fleeting moment, I feel a spark of courage. "Whatever answers we need, they're in there."

Beneath the Shelves
Damien

The library stretches out before us, a cavernous expanse of shadows and secrets. The air is thick here, laced with the scent of ancient parchment and damp stone. It's cold enough to seep into my bones, but I welcome it—the discomfort keeps my mind sharp. Relvaris may look untouched by the rot outside its gates, but no place is truly safe.

Elira walks ahead of me, her steps cautious but steady. The faint glow of the wards etched into the archways casts shifting patterns of light over her and her perfect ass.

Her black hair gleams like polished obsidian, and the curve of her waist draws my eyes like a magnet. I don't bother to hide it. If she notices, she doesn't call me out this time. A shame, really. Her fire when she's angry is something I've come to crave.

"Walk with me," I say, my voice a low growl that echoes faintly in the vaulted space. "I don't trust this place." She spares me a glance over her shoulder, her vivid blue eyes sharp with defiance. "I'm not a child, Damien. I can handle myself."

"I know you can, wildflower," I reply, smirking as her eyes narrow. "But humor me."

Her muttered response is lost in the shuffle of footsteps as Lyric and Eryndor move deeper into the stacks. Veylan remains near the entrance, his ember eyes scanning the shadows. The wolf doesn't need words to make his distrust of this place clear.

I'm used to the silence, the weight of the unsaid. But here, in this library, it feels different. The stillness presses against me, crawling under my skin. The air itself feels alive, charged with a magic that's both ancient and hostile. It's watching us. Waiting.

Elira's fingers brush against the spines of books as we walk, her touch light and reverent. I can't look away from her, the way her lips part slightly when she stumbles upon something that catches her interest. She doesn't realize what she does to me, and I'm too much of a bastard to tell her.

"Find anything useful?" I ask, letting my voice dip just enough to make her glance back at me.

"Not yet," she says, her tone clipped. "Unless you count dust and bad lighting."

"Careful," I murmur, stepping closer. "You're starting to sound like me."

She snorts, but the sound is softer than her usual scorn. Progress.

We stop in front of a shelf lined with tomes so old their titles have faded to illegibility. Elira reaches for one, her hand hovering over the cracked leather binding. My fingers close around her wrist before she can touch it.

"Don't," I say, my voice sharp. Her gaze snaps to mine, startled but unyielding.

"Why not?" she demands, her chin lifting in challenge. "It's just a book."

"Books like these aren't 'just' anything," I reply, letting my grip linger a moment longer than necessary. Her pulse flutters under my thumb, and I release her before I forget myself. "They're traps. Curses. If you're lucky, they'll kill you quickly."

Her lips press into a thin line, and I can see the argument building behind her eyes. Instead of fueling it, I step closer, crowding her against the shelf.

"You're too valuable to risk, wildflower," I say, my voice dropping to a low rumble. "Not to this place. Not to anything."

Her breath catches, and for a moment, the tension between us shifts, crackling with something more potent than magic. Her defiance softens, and she doesn't push me away.

"You can't keep protecting me from everything," she says, her voice quieter now. "You're not invincible, Damien."

"Maybe not," I admit, my hand brushing against hers as I lean closer. "But I'm damn near close when it comes to you."

Her cheeks flush, and she looks away, breaking the spell. But she doesn't move, and that's enough to keep the fire burning low in my chest, and make my dick hard again.

Before I can push further, a sharp sound breaks the moment. A creak, faint but deliberate, echoes through the stacks. Elira stiffens, her hand instinctively reaching for her dagger.

"We're not alone you pervert," she whispers, her voice barely audible.

"Fuck," I agree, drawing my sword in one smooth motion. "We're not."

Lyric and Eryndor appear from the shadows, their expressions tense.
"Just me," Lyric says, her golden eyes scanning the darkness.

"Good," I mutter, rolling my eyes and adjusting the bulge in my pants.

"But we need to move. If this library holds the answers we're looking for, we won't be alone for long." The rebel leader add.

We find a table near the center of the library, its surface covered in layers of dust that swirl with each step. Elira sits first, brushing away the grime before opening one of the books she'd chosen.

I take the seat beside her, close enough that our knees brush. She glances at me but doesn't say anything, the corner of her mouth twitching slightly before she returns to the page.

I'd tear this entire city apart for her if she asked, and I think she knows it.

Lyric and Eryndor sit across from us, their weapons resting within easy reach. Veylan circles the perimeter. For now, the big puppy is content to guard.

"We're looking for anything on the malevolent force," I say, my voice cutting through the quiet. "History, weaknesses, how to kill the bastard. And perhaps, mated bound, and Elira."

"You're awfully bossy for someone with no plan," Lyric mutters, flipping open a tome with a sharp movement.

I smirk. "You love it."

She glares at me but says nothing more. The silence that follows is heavy but productive, the sound of pages turning and quiet murmurs filling the space.

Elira leans closer to me at one point, her shoulder brushing mine as she points to a passage.

"This mentions something about ancient bloodlines," she whispers, her voice sending a shiver down my spine. "It's vague, but it's something."

"Keep digging," I reply, my eyes fixed on her as she reads. A moment later, Lyric's voice cuts through the silence. "Here! Listen to this."

Her finger trails over a page as she reads aloud, "'The force thrives on connection. It is bound to its hosts, feeding on their fears and ambitions. Sever the host, and the force weakens. But beware—the death of one may strengthen its ties to another.'"

Eryndor frowns. "So killing Damien would just make it latch onto someone else?"

Lyric shakes her head. "Not necessarily. It says here that if the force is isolated, its power can be contained. Bound."

"Bound how?" Elira asks, her voice tight.

Lyric flips to the next page, her brow furrowing. "It doesn't say. But it mentions a relic— something called the Bloodstone. It's supposed to sever connections completely, but there's a price."

I lean forward, my jaw tightening. "What price?"

Lyric hesitates, her golden eyes meeting mine. "The host's life. Whoever the force is tied to... they die."

The room falls into silence, the weight of the revelation pressing down on all of us. I glance at Elira, and the pain in her eyes is like a blade to my chest. She knows what this means.

So do I.

"That's not an option," Elira says, her voice shaking but resolute. "There has to be another way."

"There might be," Lyric says cautiously, her gaze shifting to another passage. "The Bloodstone doesn't destroy the force. It... transfers it. If all the host died, I think… the force will too."

Before anyone can respond, Veylan pads closer, his massive form looming over the table. He clears his throat—or the wolf equivalent—a gruff noise that commands attention. "I have informations," he growls, his voice rumbling like thunder in our minds.

All heads snap to him. Lyric's golden eyes narrow. "And you're just now mentioning this?"

Veylan's ember gaze doesn't waver. "It wasn't time."

Damn Puppy
Elira

My pulse pounds in my ears, a deafening rhythm that drowns out the world around me. The mark on my wrist feels like it's burning, its faint glow mocking me with every heartbeat.

"What did you just say?" My voice trembles, a mixture of disbelief and fury.

Veylan's ember eyes meet mine, steady and unflinching. "You and Damien have lived this story before. Many times."

Damien steps closer, his presence a wall of heat and fury. "Start talking, puppy. No riddles."

Veylan exhales heavily, his massive form seeming to fill the room with an ancient weight.

"The Fates are cruel and jealous beings. In each of your past lives, you and Damien have found each other, only for them to tear you apart. Every time, Elira, you have died."

My breath catches in my throat. "I died?"

Veylan's voice softens, a rare flicker of what almost feels like regret in his tone. "Yes. And I was the one sent to fetch your soul each time. It was my duty as their messenger, their harbinger."

"Wait!" Lyric rubbed her forehead. "Are you like...death?"

Veylan doesn't deny, nor does he approve. Well...fuck me.

The room grows colder, the enormity of his words pressing down on me. "So what's different now? Why am I still here?"

Damien's jaw tightens, his hands curling into fists. "And why didn't you tell us this before?"

Veylan's fiery eyes flick to Damien. "Because this life is not like the others. The Fates… they have grown desperate. The force is no longer just a shadow on the edges of their threads; it is unraveling them. This time, they have decided to give you a chance."

My stomach twists. "A chance?"

"Yes," Veylan says, his voice grave. "This time, they did not take you, Elira. They allowed you to live, to stay by Damien's side, because they need you to end this. To help him destroy the force before it consumes everything."

Lyric's sharp intake of breath cuts through the silence. "And what happens if we succeed? If we destroy the force?"

Veylan's gaze shifts to her, unreadable. "Then the Fates will be satisfied. The balance will be restored."

"And you?" Damien asks, his voice low and dangerous. "What's your role in this, wolf?"

Veylan straightens, his massive form casting long shadows across the room. "I am still their messenger, their harbinger. But this time, my duty is not to take Elira's soul. It is to ensure she stays alive until the mission is complete."

The room falls into a tense silence. I stare at Veylan, my chest tightening with a mix of anger and disbelief. "You've known all of this, and you didn't think to tell me?"

"It was not my place," Veylan replies, his tone unyielding. "The Fates' will is not for mortals to question."

Damien's smirk is sharp, cold. "Big doggy loves keeping secrets."

Veylan growls low in his throat, his massive form bristling. "Mind your tongue, King."

Damien steps forward, his grin widening. "Or what? You'll fetch my soul next?"

"Enough!" I snap, my voice ringing out. Both of them freeze, their gazes snapping to me. "We don't have time for this. If what Veylan says is true, then we need to focus."

Lyric crosses her arms, her golden eyes narrowing. "And what if the Fates change their minds? What if they decide they don't need Elira anymore?"

Veylan's gaze softens as it shifts to me. "This won't happen."

The weight of his words presses down on me, the enormity of what we're facing threatening to crush me. Damien's hand find mine under the table and tightens around mine, his grip steadying me.

I look around the room, at the faces of those who have become my allies, my family. Lyric's sharp defiance, Eryndor's quiet strength, Veylan's unwavering presence, and Damien's unrelenting determination.

I get up and step away from the group, my thoughts churning as I glance down at the mark on my wrist. My chest tightens with questions I don't know how to ask. The idea of Damien and me being bound through lifetimes, only to be ripped apart, feels too cruel to comprehend.

I look back at Veylan, my voice quieter now. "Why now? If we were lovers in the past, why give us this life to fight back? Why not before?"

Veylan's ember eyes soften slightly, and he exhales heavily. "Because it was not possible before. Damien's deal with the force changed everything. In every other life, he never made that choice. But in this lifetime, his desperation gave the Fates the opportunity they needed. His pact with the force created a new thread, one they could manipulate. This is the first time the threads have aligned to give you both a chance to fight back."

Damien stiffens beside me, his expression darkening. "So it's my fault."

"It's your decision," Veylan corrects. "And it's the reason we have this chance. Without your choice, the force would have continued its reign unchecked."

Eryndor's voice cuts through the tension. "And Elira's power? Why does she have it? Is it just because of the Fates?"

Veylan's massive form seems to sag slightly, his patience fraying under the weight of our questions. "Yes, and no. The Fates marked her bloodline long ago. Those with black hair and blue eyes were created by them—a preference, a people shaped directly by their will. They were meant to be stewards of balance, wielders of power to counter the force's influence. But as word spread of their abilities, the force turned its focus on them. It hunted them, corrupted them, until they were all but wiped out."

Lyric's golden eyes narrow. "Why? What does the force gain by destroying them?"

Veylan's growl is low, frustrated. "The force thrives on chaos, on breaking the threads of fate. By targeting those with the Fates' blessing, it ensured that the balance would tip in its favor. It made the world—past, present, and future—descend into chaos. Across dimensions, across realms, it turned everything into a battlefield, leaving only destruction in its wake."

The room falls into a heavy silence, the weight of Veylan's words pressing down on us. I look at Damien, his jaw clenched, his gaze fixed on me. For a moment, the enormity of what lies ahead feels impossible.

But then his hand finds mine, his grip firm and steady. "We've come this far," he says, his voice low but resolute. "We're not stopping now."

A World Divided
Damien

Veylan's revelations hang in the space between us, heavy and unyielding, like a chain we're all bound to wear.

I glance at Elira. She's standing tall, her expression as sharp as a blade, but her hands betray her—trembling, curling into fists that shake with the weight of what she won't let herself feel.

I ache to steady them. To steady her. Because I'd carry it all for her if I could. But I can't. The Fates have seen to that.

"So, what's next?" Lyric's voice slices through the silence, her golden eyes narrowing at Veylan. "You've dropped enough bombs on us for one lifetime. What do we do with it all?"

"We prepare," Veylan rumbles, his ember eyes sweeping across us like the judgment of some ancient god. "The Bloodstone is not far from here, but the force will not let you take it easily. It knows you are coming. It always knows."

The force's voice rises in my mind, a sinister, slithering thing that coils itself around my thoughts.

Because I am always with you, Damien.

I clench my jaw, pushing back against the intrusion. It's louder now, bolder. The quiet in my head that I'd started to enjoy was nothing more than a lull in the storm.

"Perfect," Eryndor mutters, his tone dripping with sarcasm as he leans against a shelf. "We're walking straight into a trap."

"We always were," I snap, sharper than I mean to, my voice like the crack of a whip. "This isn't new. What matters is how we spring it."

Elira's gaze cuts to me, her blue eyes sharp and unyielding. "And what about the people here? Relvaris is untouched for now, but if we bring the fight here, we'll destroy that."

I turn to her, my jaw tightening. "You think I don't know that, little warrior? You think I want to bring ruin down on this place, too? But we don't have a choice. The Bloodstone is our only shot. If we don't take it, there won't be a Relvaris left to save."

Her shoulders slump, and the fire in her gaze dims just enough to make my chest ache. Damn it.

I step closer, lowering my voice so only she can hear. "Wildflower," I murmur, the word soft and sharp all at once, "we're playing a game the Fates have rigged from the start. The only way we win is by breaking the board."

Her lips part, the argument on the tip of her tongue dying as her gaze searches mine. There's a moment—just a breath—where she falters. Then, to my surprise, she nods, her fingers brushing against mine.

The touch is electric, setting fire to the raw edges of my control. Without thinking, I reach for her, pulling her into my arms. She stiffens for half a heartbeat before melting into me, her breath shaky against my chest.

I tower over her, her head fitting perfectly under my chin, her black hair soft against my jaw. From this angle,

I can see everything—her long, dark lashes brushing her freckled cheeks, the way her blue eyes flutter closed as she exhales. Her grip on my shirt tightens, grounding me, anchoring me against the chaos roaring in my head.

"I'm so tired, Damien," she whispers, her voice a threadbare thing. "I don't know if I can do this."

"You can," I murmur, my lips brushing against her temple. "You're stronger than any of us, wildflower. You don't have to carry it alone."

Her fingers press harder against my chest, and I can feel the tremble in her. I hold her tighter, as though sheer force of will could shield her from everything waiting outside these walls.

For a moment, I forget the force's voice, its laughter echoing in the corners of my mind. For a moment, it's just her and me, and the world isn't crumbling around us.

She leans back, just enough to meet my gaze. Her cheeks are flushed, her lips trembling. "Don't let me fall," she whispers.

"Never," I promise, my hands framing her face, my thumbs brushing against the curve of her jaw.

The moment stretches, fragile as glass, until Lyric clears her throat, shattering it. Elira pulls back, her cheeks turning an even deeper shade of red as she steps away, her gaze flickering to the others.

The force's laughter creeps back into my head, curling around my thoughts like smoke. Such a sweet, futile dream. You'll break, Damien. You always do.

I shove it aside, fixing my focus on the room.

"Fine," Lyric says, her voice cutting through the tension. "We go for the Bloodstone. But how do we know it'll work? What if we're wrong?"

Veylan growls, low and resonant. "The Bloodstone's power is ancient, forged by the Fates themselves. It is the only hope we have."

"There's always a catch," Eryndor mutters, shaking his head.

Elira steps forward, her voice a blade of steel wrapped in velvet. "What kind of catch?"

Veylan's silence stretches, the weight of it sinking into every corner of the room. Finally, he speaks, his voice heavy with regret. "The Bloodstone severs the force's connection to this world. But to do so, it may demand more than you are prepared to give."

The words hang in the air, unspoken questions clawing at all of us.

"Then we make the most of it," Elira says, her voice trembling but unyielding. "We get the Bloodstone. We destroy the force. And we figure out the rest when we get there. Together."

She looks at each of us in turn, her blue eyes blazing. When her gaze lands on me, the fire in her expression burns something into place inside me.

"Together," I echo, my voice resolute.

Veylan inclines his head, his ember eyes gleaming with something I can't name. "Then we move. The Bloodstone awaits."

As we leave the library, the weight of the world pressing down on all of us, I catch Elira's gaze one last time. The mark on her wrist glows faintly in the dim light, a reminder of everything we're up against.

And everything we stand to lose.

The Past We Bear
Elira

The group begins to move, the echoes of boots against stone the only sound accompanying our hurried steps through the city. The weight of what we've just learned presses down on us, but Lyric lags behind, her gaze flicking between me and the mark glowing faintly on my wrist.

The streets of Relvaris glow softly under the warm flicker of lanterns, a stark contrast to the growing unease gnawing at my chest. The city feels alive in a way the others didn't—families chatting on their doorsteps, the occasional burst of laughter cutting through the night. For a moment, it almost feels normal.

Almost.

"Help! Please, help!" A small voice pierces the air, fragile and trembling.

I turn sharply, my heart leaping at the sound. A little girl stumbles toward me, her cheeks streaked with tears, clutching a ragged doll to her chest. She looks no older than six, her wide brown eyes brimming with fear.

"My brother," she sobs, her tiny voice cracking. "He's hurt. He's bleeding."

I crouch instinctively, my hand brushing against hers. "Where is he?" I ask softly, glancing back at the group. Damien's gaze sharpens immediately, his stance shifting as if sensing the wrongness before I do.

"Just down there," the girl whispers, pointing to a narrow alley that cuts through the city's maze-like streets.

"Elira," Damien's voice is low, a warning. He moves closer, his hand brushing against my arm, his warmth grounding me. "Something's off."

"It's a child," I whisper back, my gaze locking onto his. "We can't just ignore her."

His green eyes darken, his jaw tightening. "I don't like this."

"Wait here, I won't be long," I say, my voice firm as I follow the girl into the alley, my fingers brushing against the hilt of my sword.

The alley narrows, the light fading as the towering buildings close in around us. Shadows stretch and shift, the faint hum of the city fading behind us. My steps falter as the atmosphere grows heavier, colder.

The girl stops abruptly, her sobs cutting off. She straightens, turning to face me with an unsettling calmness in her gaze.

"She's here," she says, her voice eerily steady.

A figure steps out from the shadows ahead, tall and broad, his face obscured by a hood. The girl scurries to his side, her small hand slipping into his.

"Well done," the man says, his voice low and gravelly. My pulse spikes, my grip tightening on my dagger as I take a step back. "What do you want?"

The man laughs, the sound cold and sharp. "You, sweetheart. The woman with the glowing mark. You'll fetch a fine price."

I whirl around, but another figure blocks the exit, his silhouette hulking in the dim light. Trapped.

"You made a mistake," I say, my voice trembling with anger.

The man steps closer, his grin predatory. "Oh, I know exactly who you are. That's why you're not walking out of here."

A feral growl echoes through the alley, low and menacing. But it's not Veylan.
It's Damien.

Before I can process the movement, he's there. His presence is a storm crashing through the narrow space, his green eyes blazing with a fury that sends a chill down my spine.

"Get away from her," Damien snarls, his voice guttural, almost inhuman.

The man doesn't have time to react. Damien moves faster than I've ever seen, his hand snapping out to grab the man by the throat. The sound of bone crunching reverberates through the alley as Damien slams him against the wall, his fingers digging in like a vice.

"You thought you could touch her?" Damien growls, his voice dark, dangerous. "You thought you could take her from me?"

The man gurgles, his hands clawing at Damien's iron grip, but it's futile. Damien's strength is monstrous, his fury all-consuming.

"Damien," I whisper, but my voice is lost in the chaos.

With a savage roar, Damien throws the man to the ground. He doesn't hesitate, his boot slamming into the man's chest with a sickening crack. Blood sprays from the man's mouth as he gasps for air, his eyes wide with terror.

"Please," the man chokes, his voice barely audible. "I—"

Damien doesn't let him finish. He draws his blade, the steel gleaming in the faint light, and drives it down in his eyes with brutal precision. The man's scream is cut short, the blade buried deep in his skull. "You…looked at her." Damien murmur.

A second figure lunges, but Damien is ready. He twists, his blade slashing through the air in a deadly arc. The man collapses, clutching at his throat as blood pours through his fingers.

It's over in seconds.

Damien stands in the carnage, his chest heaving, his blade dripping crimson. His eyes flick to the little girl, who cowers against the wall, her earlier composure shattered.

"Run," Damien growls, his voice like thunder. She doesn't need to be told twice. She disappears into the shadows, her footsteps fading into the distance.

The feral rage slowly ebbs from Damien's face as he turns to me, his green eyes wild but softening. He steps closer, his hand trembling as he brushes a strand of hair from my face.
"Are you hurt?" he asks, his voice hoarse, raw.

I shake my head, my throat tight. "Damien, you—"

"I'll kill anyone who tries to take you from me," he says, his voice trembling with unrelenting conviction. "Anyone. Do you understand?"

His words should terrify me, but they don't. They steady me, grounding me in the chaos. I reach for him, my fingers brushing against his blood-streaked hand.

"I know," I whisper. "I know."

For a moment, the world narrows to just us, the scent of blood and the distant hum of the city fading. His hand tightens around mine, his grip a silent promise: no one would ever take me from him.

"Elira," Lyric calls softly, breaking the silence.

I pause, my fingers still brushing against Damien's arm as if afraid to let go. I turn to Lyric, my expression wary but curious. "What is it?"

Lyric steps closer, her golden eyes softer than usual. For once, the sharp edge in her voice is absent. "Can I talk to you? Alone?"

Damien stiffens beside me, his gaze narrowing on Lyric. "If you have something to say to her, you can say it here."

Lyric raises an eyebrow, her smirk faint but laced with genuine affection. "Relax, King. I'm not planning to hurt her."

I touch Damien's arm, my touch light but firm. "It's fine. I'll be right back."

Damien hesitates, his jaw tightening, but he finally nods, though his glare at Lyric speaks volumes.

The two of us step away, our footsteps muffled as we move toward the edge of the dark street. The faint glow of the city lights casts a warm hue over us, softening the sharpness of Lyric's features.

"Elira," Lyric begins, her voice quieter now. "Are you ok? That was crazy!" She says, her big brown eyes looking frantic. "He moved faster than the big wolf. I mean. That was impressive."
"I'm ok." I simply add with a soft smile to her. She huff a breath, "I owe you an apology."

I blink, caught off guard. "An apology?"

Lyric nods, her expression uncharacteristically open. "I've been hard on you. Distrusting, harsh. And for a while, I didn't think you deserved to lead us—or even to fight alongside us. But after everything we've been through…" She pauses, her gaze dropping to my wrist where the mark pulses faintly. "You've proven me wrong. You're stronger than I ever gave you credit for. And you care more than anyone I've ever met."

My lips part, surprise flickering across my face. "Lyric, I—"

She cuts me off with a raised hand, her smile soft. "You've been through hell. And somehow, you're still standing. That's not something just anyone can do. I respect you for it. And I'm… proud to call you a friend."

The words hang between us, fragile but profound. My eyes glisten, and for a moment, I feel younger, like the weight of the world has been lifted off my shoulders, even if just for a moment.

"Thank you," I whisper, my voice trembling.
"That… means more than you know."

Lyric steps closer, resting a hand on my shoulder. "You're not alone in this, Elira. You've got us. And no matter how dark it gets, we'll find a way through."

I nod, my throat tight. "A way through," I echo softly.

We stand there for a moment, the world around us fading as we share a quiet understanding. Then Lyric smirks, breaking the tension. "Now, let's get back before Damien decides to gut me for keeping you away too long."

I laugh, the sound light and genuine. "He would, wouldn't he?"

Lyric shrugs, her smirk widening. "Probably. Big possessive bastard."

We return to the group, our steps lighter despite the looming darkness. Damien's gaze locks onto me the moment I'm within reach, his eyes scanning me for any sign of harm. I roll my eyes but smile, letting my hand brush against his arm again.

Lyric gives Damien a mocking salute. "Don't worry, King. She's all yours."

Damien huffs, but there's no real malice in his tone. "Glad you finally realized that."

The Ghost That Follows
Elira

The vibe is heavy with the aftermath of Damien's fury, the tang of blood and sweat clinging to my senses like a second skin. The streets of Relvaris seem quieter now, the faint glow of lanterns casting long, uneasy shadows against the stone walls. Each step feels heavier than the last, the weight of what we've just learned pressing down on us all.

But it's not just the force or the looming Bloodstone that tugs at my thoughts—it's Kael. Or rather, what I did to him.

The memory flashes unbidden: the way my blade slid between his ribs, the gasp that escaped his lips—a sound more of surprise than pain. The rush of heat, the surge of power as my mark pulsed in time with

the act, urging me forward. I didn't hesitate then. I didn't falter. And now, in the stillness, I feel... nothing.

Not guilt. Not regret. Just a strange emptiness, like a hollow echo where grief should have taken root.

I clench my fists, my nails digging into my palms. The hot sensation of power itches beneath my skin, a persistent reminder of what I've become. My first kill. Shouldn't it weigh on me? Shouldn't it tear me apart? He wasn't just anyone. Kael was someone I trusted, someone who betrayed me.

"Are you all right?" Damien's voice breaks through the haze, low and rough like a distant storm. His green eyes lock onto mine, sharp with concern and something darker—something protective.

"I'm fine," I say too quickly, my voice brittle, snapping like a dry branch.

"You're a terrible liar, wildflower," he murmurs, stepping closer. His hand brushes mine, rough and grounding, as though daring me to deny the truth again. "It's Kael, isn't it?"

His words hit harder than they should. He knows me too well.

I exhale shakily, meeting his gaze. "I killed him," I say, the words heavier than I imagined they'd feel. "And I don't feel bad about it."

Damien studies me in silence, his expression unreadable but intense. "You shouldn't," he says finally, his voice low, firm. "He betrayed you. He would've killed you if you hadn't acted first."

"But shouldn't I feel something?" I snap, my voice cracking under the weight of my confusion. "He was the first person I've ever—" My throat tightens, and I press a trembling hand to my chest. "Shouldn't it haunt me?"

Damien's hand moves to my chin, tilting my face up so I'm forced to meet his gaze. "The first kill always feels wrong, Elira. Even when it's justified. But that emptiness you feel? That's survival. It doesn't make you a monster. It makes you human."

I swallow hard, the words sinking in like stones. "It doesn't feel human. It feels... quiet."

His green eyes darken, softening at the edges. "That quiet? It's how you protect yourself. Don't let it swallow you whole."
I want to argue, but his words settle something inside me, like a puzzle piece clicking into place. He doesn't just understand—he's lived it.

Before I can respond, my thoughts shift to Kael's betrayal. His ability to open a portal between worlds still gnaws at me. The sheer power it must've taken.

"How did Kael even have access to a portal?" I ask, the question cutting through the air like a blade. "That kind of magic isn't just lying around for anyone to use."
The group halts, their attention drawn by the weight in my voice.

Lyric crosses her arms, her golden eyes narrowing. Eryndor mutters something under his breath, and even Veylan's ember gaze sharpens.

Damien stiffens beside me, his jaw tightening. "It's because of the deal," he says, his voice raw, edged with fury. "Kael wasn't just some opportunist. He was bound to the force, like me."

The words send a chill through me, but before I can press further, Damien falters. He stumbles, his hand clutching the nearest wall.

"Damien?" I rush to his side, my heart hammering as I grip his arm. His face contorts in pain, his scars twisting unnaturally, like they're fighting to break free from his skin.

The force's voice slithers through the air, cold and mocking. *You think you can escape me, little king? You think you're free? You're mine, Damien. Always.*

I freeze as the words twist in my mind. "I can hear it," I whisper, horrified. "Why can I hear it?"

Veylan's voice rumbles like thunder. "The mate bond. You're connected to him in every way now."

Damien collapses to his knees, his hands clawing at his head. His groan of pain is guttural, animalistic, as if the force is trying to rip him apart from the inside.

"Stay with me," I plead, my voice shaking as I crouch in front of him. I cup his face, forcing him to meet my gaze. "Damien, look at me. You're stronger than this. Fight it."

The force laughs, a cruel, echoing sound. *You'll break, Damien. You always do. And when you do, she'll burn for it.*

His green eyes flicker, wild and unfocused. "Kael," he chokes out. "He was mine. The force used him... and now it's furious because he's gone. Because she killed him."

The group falls silent, the weight of his words sinking in.

"It's worse now," Damien says hoarsely, his voice gaining strength as the force's grip loosens. "It's angrier. Because I'm the only one left. Its only host."

My stomach churns. "Then it's more dangerous than ever," I say quietly, the truth settling like a stone in my chest.

Veylan steps forward, his massive form casting a shadow over us. "The force's rage is centered now. Its focus is singular, relentless."

"And so is ours," Damien says, his voice steadying as he stands. He looks at me, his green eyes blazing with resolve. "We'll stop it, wildflower. Whatever it takes." I nod, my hand brushing against his as the group begins to move again. The glow of Relvaris feels way to beautiful for this world full of evil.

The Weight of Fire
Elira

I stick close to Damien, his presence a solid, unyielding anchor in a world that feels like it's cracking apart beneath my feet. Veylan strides ahead, his form a silent warning to anyone foolish enough to approach. Lyric and Eryndor flank us, their weapons drawn, their gazes sharp.

But even with all of us together, the city feels different now. Colder.

"Does anyone else feel like we're being watched?" Lyric murmurs, her voice low but cutting through the quiet.

Damien glances over his shoulder, his green eyes scanning the shadows. "We are," he says simply, his voice like a blade drawn from its sheath.

I shiver, not from the cold but from the creeping sensation of eyes I can't see but can feel. My wrist throbs faintly where the mark pulses, almost as if it senses the force drawing closer.

"Let's not stop moving," Eryndor says, his tone unusually grim. "If we slow down, we're sitting ducks."

I nod, gripping the hilt of my sword tighter as we push forward. The streets seem narrower now, the buildings taller, leaning over us like silent sentinels. Each step echoes faintly, swallowed by the stillness.

"Veylan," I call out, breaking the quiet. "How much farther to the Bloodstone?"

The wolf doesn't turn, but his deep voice rumbles back to me. "Not far. But the closer we get, the more resistance we'll face."

"Great," Lyric mutters. "Something to look forward to."

Damien slows his pace just enough to fall into step beside me, his hand brushing against mine. The contact is brief, but it sends a jolt through me, grounding me in a way nothing else can.

"You're too quiet," he says, his voice low, meant only for me.

"I'm trying to understand, trying to link things." I reply, glancing at him. His face is drawn, the sharp lines of his jaw even more pronounced in the flickering light. "About the Bloodstone. About Kael."

"Kael's gone," he says flatly. "Don't waste your thoughts on him."

"I'm not," I say, though it's only half true. "I'm thinking about what's waiting for us. About what happens if this doesn't work."

His hand brushes mine again, this time deliberate. "It'll work," he says, his voice unwavering. "Because it has to."

Before I can respond, Veylan halts abruptly, his massive form tense. He raises his head, sniffing the air, and a low growl rumbles in his chest.

"What is it?" Damien asks, his hand already on the hilt of his sword.

"Something ahead," Veylan says, his ember eyes glowing in the dim light. "Not human."

The words send a chill down my spine. I draw my weapon, the blade gleaming faintly as we step forward, the group tightening around me instinctively.

The dirt path opens into a wide square, the centerpiece a massive fountain long since dried up. The moonlight casts an eerie glow over the scene, highlighting the figures standing on the far side.

Three of them. Their shapes humanoid but wrong, their movements jerky, unnatural. Their faces are pale, almost translucent, with eyes that shine faintly like the embers of a dying fire.

"Revenants," Veylan growls, his fur bristling.

"In the city. It's not good." Lyric mutters, twirling her daggers.

Eryndor yelled, "Fuck, fuck, fuck. They don't seems friendly."

"They're not," Damien says, stepping in front of me.

"Stay behind me, Elira."

I bristle at the command but don't argue. The air shifts as the revenants notice us, their heads snapping toward us in unison. The sound they make is guttural, a low, echoing growl that reverberates through the square.

"They're fast," Veylan warns, his voice like thunder. "And they don't tire. Stay sharp."

The first one moves, a blur of motion heading straight for Damien. He meets it head-on, his blade slicing through the air with precision. The clash of steel and unnatural flesh rings out, the creature shrieking as Damien drives it back.

The second one lunges at Lyric, but she's ready, her daggers flashing as she moves with deadly grace. Eryndor engages the third, his sword arcing through the air in powerful, controlled strikes.

And then there's me. Standing, waiting, the heat of my mark pulsing stronger now, begging to be unleashed.

"Wildflower, show me your force!" Damien's voice cuts through the chaos,
snapping me out of my hesitation.

I raise my blade just as a fourth revenant emerges from the shadows, its movements disjointed but fast. It's on me before I can react, its clawed hand swiping toward my face.

Fire erupts from my free hand, a blazing wall that sends the creature shrieking backward. I don't stop to think. I lunge, my sword driving into its chest, the force of the strike sending it crashing to the ground.

The battle is over quickly, the revenants reduced to smoldering husks. The square falls silent again, the only sound my ragged breathing and the faint crackle of residual fire.

Damien steps toward me, his green eyes scanning me for injuries. "Are you hurt?" he asks, his voice rough with concern.

I shake my head, unable to find my voice. His hand finds my shoulder, grounding me, and I look up at him, the intensity in his gaze chasing away the lingering fear.

"You did well," he says softly, his hand lingering for a moment before he steps back.

"Let's move," Veylan rumbles, his gaze fixed on the path ahead. "The Bloodstone isn't far."

But instead of striding forward, the massive wolf halts abruptly, his head turning toward a side street. His nose twitches, and he snorts, a sound somewhere between annoyance and command.

"What is it?" Lyric asks, her golden eyes narrowing.

Veylan turns back to us, his giant paws blocking the path like an immovable wall. "You're all filthy, exhausted, and smell worse than the revenants. If you march into tomorrow like this, you'll die before you see the Bloodstone." He jerks his head toward the alley. "There's a hostel. You'll sleep, bathe, eat, and for the love of the Fates, change your damn clothes."

"We don't have time for this," Damien growls, his voice edged with frustration.

"You don't have time not to," Veylan snaps, his ember eyes narrowing. "Rest is not a suggestion. It's survival. You can thank me when you're still breathing tomorrow."

Lyric snorts, folding her arms. "You've got a way with words, wolf."

Veylan doesn't dignify her with a response, already padding toward the alley. The rest of us exchange glances before reluctantly following him. The side street is quieter, the faint glow of lanterns casting soft light on ivy-covered walls and cobblestone paths.

At the end of the lane stands the hostel—a cozy, two-story building with gothic charm. Its pointed gables and arched windows are softened by the warm light spilling from within, casting a welcoming glow against the night.

The wooden sign above the door swings gently in the breeze, the words Willow's Rest carved in flowing script. Smoke curls from a chimney, the scent of burning wood and something sweet—honey, maybe—wafting through the air.

Veylan stops at the door, his massive paw raising slightly before he steps back. "I'll stay outside. Someone needs to keep watch."

Damien arches an eyebrow. "The big, scary wolf is afraid of a little hospitality?"

Veylan's growl is low, rumbling like distant thunder. "I'm sparing you from explaining why there's a beast on your heels. You're welcome."

Before Damien can retort, the door creaks open, and a woman steps out. She's in her late thirties, her black hair pulled into a loose braid over her shoulder. Her soft brown eyes scan us, warm and inviting, and for a moment, I can't breathe. She looks so much like my mother.

"Travelers?" she asks, her voice gentle but tinged with curiosity.

"Yes," Lyric answers quickly, her tone uncharacteristically polite. "We need rooms for the night."

The woman nods, stepping aside to let us in. "Come in, come in. You look like you've been through a storm."

I hesitate at the threshold, my chest tight as I watch her movements—the way she brushes her hands on her apron, the quiet grace in her step. The resemblance is uncanny, and it takes Damien's hand brushing against mine to pull me from my thoughts.

Inside, the hostel is just as charming as its exterior. The main room is cozy, with worn wooden floors and walls lined with shelves of books and trinkets. A stone fireplace crackles warmly, its light dancing across the room. The scent of baking bread and lavender fills the air, wrapping around me like a comforting embrace.

A little girl peeks out from behind the counter, her eyes wide with curiosity. She can't be older than seven, with the same black hair and brown eyes as the woman. When she spots me, she giggles softly, her shyness melting as she steps forward.

"I'll show you to your rooms," she says, her small voice bright against the quiet.

The woman—her mother, clearly—smiles gently. "This is Mira. She'll take care of you."

Mira leads us upstairs, her tiny footsteps light on the creaking wood. She chatters as she goes, pointing out the paintings on the walls and the flowers

set on the window sills. Her innocence is disarming, a stark contrast to the darkness we've been wading through.

When we reach the rooms, she beams up at me. "I hope you like it here."

I crouch to her level, managing a small smile. "Thank you, Mira. It's beautiful. Can you ask your mommy for warrior clothes to be prepped for us by tomorrow morning. We'll pay good."
She simply nods.

Her cheeks flush, and she scurries back down the hall, leaving us in silence. I stand and turn to the room she's shown me—a small but inviting space with a single bed covered in a quilt, its patterns intricate and colorful. A basin of water sits on a wooden stand by the window, steam rising faintly from its surface.

"We need to save this world and all the others Damien."
I absently murmured.

"For all the Mira's out there."

Beneath
Elira

The room is cloaked in a warm, flickering light, the glow of the lantern casting long, dancing shadows across the wooden walls. The faint scent of lavender and soap lingers in the air, mixing with the ever-present smoky aroma of the hearth below.

The quiet hum of the hostel wraps around us like a cocoon, a rare moment of stillness in the chaos that has become our lives.

Damien stands near the basin, his broad shoulders illuminated by the golden light. His shirt is discarded, revealing the scars that crisscross his muscled back like a map of battles fought and survived.

His every movement exudes power, his body carved from the kind of strength that only comes from surviving countless wars. His green eyes flick to mine, sharp intensity softened by something deeper, something meant only for me.

He moves toward me with a predator's grace, the floorboards creaking faintly under his weight. When he's close enough that the warmth of his body brushes against mine, he stops.

His fingers tilt my chin upward, forcing my gaze to meet his. His thumb is calloused but warm, the slight pressure grounding me even as it sends a shiver down my spine.

"What trouble this pretty head of yours?" he murmurs, his thumb brushing over my bottom lip. The gesture is tender, but there's a dark edge to his gaze, a heat that makes my pulse quicken.

"It's about you," I admit, the words tumbling out before I can stop them. "About us. About everything."

His smirk is faint, but it doesn't reach his eyes. "You've had a lot on your shoulders, wildflower. Let me take some of that weight."

Before I can respond, his hands move to the fastenings of my jacket, his fingers deftly working to remove it. I freeze, the vulnerability of the moment catching me off guard. But the way he looks at me, as if I'm the only thing anchoring him to this world, dissolves any hesitation.

The jacket falls to the floor, and his hands find my waist, pulling me closer. His touch is firm, possessive, yet his movements are unhurried, giving me the space to stop him if I want to. I don't.

His lips brush against my forehead, a fleeting touch that sends a shiver down my spine. "Let me take care of you," he whispers, his breath warm against my skin.

I nod, unable to find my voice. He steps back just enough to lead me toward the basin. The water is warm, steam rising faintly in the cool air. He dips a cloth into it, wringing it out before turning back to me.

"Hold still," he says, his tone softer now, almost reverent.

The cloth is warm against my skin as he starts at my neck, the gentle pressure both soothing and electrifying. The texture is rough but not unpleasant, his movements careful, deliberate. He traces the line of my collarbone with the cloth, the sensation leaving a trail of heat in its wake. I close my eyes, letting the moment pull me under.

His hands shift lower, over the curve of my shoulders, the cloth following the contours of my body. When he reaches my arms, he lingers, his touch firm yet tender, as if committing every inch of me to memory.

"You're beautiful," he murmurs, the words so quiet they feel like a secret shared only with me. His jade iris flick to mine, holding my gaze as the cloth moves lower, over the swell of my chest.

My breath hitches, and his eyes darken, the intensity of his focus sending a flush to my cheeks. The cloth drops, forgotten, and his hand replaces it, the warmth of his palm a stark contrast to the cool air. Pinching one of my nipple between two fingers.

"Damien," I whisper, his name a plea on my lips.

He leans in, his lips brushing against mine in a kiss that starts slow, almost hesitant, but quickly deepens. His other hand tangles in my hair, pulling me closer as the kiss ignites something raw and untamed between us. His lips are demanding, his teeth grazing my bottom lip before he pulls back just enough to almost break the skin.

"I can't stop," he growls, his voice rough with restraint. "Tell me to stop, and I will."

I shake my head, my hands finding his bare chest, the hard planes of muscle flexing under my touch. "Don't stop," I whisper, the words a surrender and a command.

His touch is reverent, his fingers tracing the curve of my ribs, the dip of my waist, the soft swell of my hip.

Every touch feels like a claim, a promise that I'm his as much as he is mine. His lips leave a trail of fire down my neck, his stubble grazing my skin in a way that sends sparks through my veins.

"Elira," he murmurs against my skin, his voice low and trembling with restraint. "You undo me."

His lips find mine again, and this time, there's no hesitation. His kiss is fierce, consuming, his tongue teasing against mine as his hands roam freely.

He didn't hesitate and drop his hands with a feral need directly on top of my underwater clenching pussy. I breath in his mouth when he applied pression with his palm while rolling a finger on my sensitive clit.

The world narrows to just us, the rest of the room fading into shadows as we give in to the fire that's been smoldering between us for so long.

His touch is deliberate, his fingers moving with a skill that leaves me breathless. I exhale sharply, my breaths short and uneven as he explores, his movements sending waves of heat through my body. His finger going from my bundle of nerves to my core, entering me with force.

"Damien," I whisper, my voice breaking as he presses just right. He leans in, his forehead resting against mine, his own breath coming in uneven bursts.

"I've got you," he murmurs, his voice rough and filled with something I can't name but feel deep in my chest. "Let go, wildflower. I'll catch you."

And I explode, my orgasm crashing trough me, making my skin unbearably hot. The water seems to boil around me and when I open my eyes, he's looking at me, shocked in his stare.

"You just became impossible to touch, so hot, like you were literally fire. You warmed the water. Didn't you realize?"

"No," I breath, "Come give me what is mine, come here, King." I confidently add. I'm so horny, so needy, I need to feel him pressed against me.

Damien's smirk deepens as he straightens, his sharp green eyes locking onto mine. He moves with deliberate precision, his hands reaching for the waistband of his pants. The faint sound of the fabric sliding down fills the quiet space, and my breath catches as he stands there, his huge cock proudly pointing in front of my faces, utterly unguarded.

He steps into the bath without hesitation, the water rippling around his powerful thighs as he closes the distance between us. The heat of his body mingles with the warmth of the water, and I find myself captivated by the interplay of light and shadow across his muscled form.

His scars seem more vivid now, each one telling a story of pain and survival. My gaze lingers, my fingers itching to trace them, to understand the battles that marked him.

I reach out, my hand brushing against the scar that cuts across his chest. "This one," I murmur, my voice trembling, "what happened?"

Damien captures my wrist gently, his thumb brushing against my pulse. "A lesson learned," he says, his tone both dark and tender.

The water laps around us as I let my fingers trail lower, exploring the hard planes of his body, the ridges and valleys shaped by years of endurance. His breath hitches, the tension coiling between us like a live wire.

"Elira," he growls, his voice rough and low, "if you keep touching me like that, I won't be able to stop."

I tilt my chin up, meeting his heated gaze. "I

don't want you to stop."

His response is immediate, a primal sound rumbling deep in his chest as he pulls me closer. His hands find my waist, his grip firm yet reverent as he lifts me slightly, adjusting my position in the water. He grip his dick and place it at my entrance and let me descend on it at my own pace, slow and torturing. The feel of his length stretching me.

I trail my fingers down his abdomen, feeling the tension in his muscles, the way his body reacts to my touch.
"Do you always have to be so commanding?" I tease, though my voice wavers under the weight of the moment.

His smirk returns, darker this time, as he leans in, his lips brushing against my ear and biting it. "Only when I want to ruin you, wildflower."

The words ignite something deep within me, I lower myself slightly, empaling me to the halt. A load moan escaping me, I use my hands to steady me against his chest as I let my lips trail lower, his chin, his throat. Damien's sharp intake of breath is like music to my ears as I reach him, my hand wrapping around him as I glance up to meet his gaze. His green eyes are ablaze, filled with a raw intensity that sends a shiver down my spine.

"Elira," he murmurs, his voice strained, "you feel so good—"
"I love you," I interrupted, my tone leaving no room for argument.

His head tilts back, a low groan escaping his lips as I take him into my mouth.
"Repeat that?" He asks.

"I love you." I moan loudly bouncing on him like a fucking rodeo, grinding my clit on his pubis when I reach it.

He suddenly grabs violently the nap of my neck and bring my face in front of his.
"I loved you since my first life it seems. And
I'll love you in this one and the next," He says.

The weight of him, the warmth, the way his body trembles beneath my touch—it's intoxicating. I move rapidly, deliberately, savoring every reaction, every sound he makes.

"Fuck," he growls, his hand tangling in my hair as his control begins to unravel. "You're going to destroy me."

The words are both a promise and a plea, and I revel in the power I have over him in this moment. For all his strength, all his dominance, here he is utterly mine.

When I we finally climax together I pull back, his breathing is ragged, his green eyes dark with desire.

He reaches for me, pulling me into his lap as he captures my lips in a kiss that is both tender and feral. "Wildflower," he murmurs against my mouth, his hands gripping my hips as if anchoring himself to me. "You're all I'll ever need. All I'll ever want."

And we stay there, until the water cools and the night stretches on, we lose ourselves in each other, the chaos of the world fading away, if only for a little while.

The Edge of Tomorrow
Elira

The first light of dawn struggles against the heavy clouds, streaks of muted gold and silver barely piercing the gloom.

Relvaris seems reluctant to wake, the mist clinging stubbornly to the gothic spires and cobblestone streets like a stubborn guest overstaying its welcome.

Somewhere, a rooster crows faintly— probably regretting its decision to announce the day at all.

We step out into the street, the faint hum of the morning quiet interrupted by our group pulling up to the front of the hostel.

The kind woman who had greeted us the night before stands ready, a bundle in her arms. When she reveals it, my breath catches—a set of stunning black war clothes, tailored to perfection, and silver armor that gleams even in the dim light. The craftsmanship is exquisite, every detail precise and elegant, as if it were made for a queen.

Damien steps forward, his presence commanding as always, and hands her something that makes me blink in surprise—a slip of paper, neatly folded, with his sharp handwriting scrawled across it. It's a cheque. Or at least, something resembling it. My modern world brain twitches at the sight of it in this ancient, war-torn place.

"This should cover it," he says, his tone brisk but polite. The woman accepts it with a nod, her eyes widening slightly as she realizes the sum written on it.

"More than enough," she murmurs, bowing her head. "Thank you. May the Fates watch over you."

Lyric lets out a low whistle, her golden eyes flicking to the armor. "Well, someone's dressing for the end of the world."

I shoot her a look but can't hide my smirk. "If we're going to do this, we might as well look the part."

Veylan huffs beside me, his ember eyes glinting with something between approval and exasperation. *"You'll need every edge you can get. Including vanity, apparently."*

I ignore him, running my fingers over the smooth fabric and cool metal. It's not just armor—it's a second skin, something that makes me feel prepared for what's to come, even if I'm far from it.

Damien's gaze lingers on me, his green eyes intense. "It suits you," he says, the words soft but weighted.

"Let's hope it holds up," I reply, my voice steady despite the nervous energy thrumming through me.

The mist hangs low as we leave the city behind, the cobblestones giving way to a dirt path framed by gnarled trees. Their twisted branches stretch overhead, forming an almost oppressive canopy that filters what little light remains. The air feels heavier here, each step carrying us closer to the Bloodstone and whatever nightmare awaits.

Damien walks ahead of me, his broad shoulders cutting through the haze like a beacon. He moves with an effortless strength, his green eyes scanning the path ahead for threats. Occasionally, his gaze flickers back to me, and I catch glimpses of something more in his expression. Concern. Determination. Love. I feel my chest tighten every time our eyes meet.

I'm struck by how beautiful he is, even now. His scars tell stories of battles fought, his sharp jawline and striking features softened only slightly by the misty light. He is my anchor, my reason to keep pushing forward. I can't imagine facing what's ahead without him.

"Still admiring my undeniable charming face?" Damien says without turning, his voice a low rumble that sends warmth coursing through me.

I straighten, clearing my throat. "Just making sure you're still alive."

He smirks, glancing over his shoulder. "You'd know if I wasn't. The world would feel colder without me."

"And quieter," Lyric mutters from behind us, earning a laugh from Eryndor.

"Enough," Veylan growls, his massive form halting abruptly. He sniffs the air, his ember eyes narrowing. "The force knows we're coming. We'll face resistance soon."

"Wonderful," Lyric says, twirling her daggers. "I was getting bored."

Damien's hand brushes against mine briefly—a silent reassurance.

"Stay close," he murmurs, his voice meant only for me.

"I'm not a child," I reply, meeting his gaze. "I can handle myself."
"I know," he says, his lips quirking into a smirk. "But you're not dying today, wildflower. Not on my watch."

The path opens into a clearing, the ground littered with ash and charred branches. The scent of smoke lingers, acrid and sharp, and the air itself feels charged with tension. Veylan stiffens, his hackles rising. "They're here," he rumbles.

The shadows around us writhe, twisting into grotesque forms. The revenants are larger this time, their movements unnervingly fluid as they emerge from the darkness. Their glowing eyes lock onto us, and a guttural growl rises from their ranks.

Damien steps in front of me, his sword gleaming in the faint light. "Stay behind me," he commands, his voice firm.
"Not a chance," I reply, my magic sparking to life under my skin. "We do this together."

The first revenant charges, a blur of motion heading straight for Damien. He meets it with lethal precision, his blade slicing through its torso in one fluid motion. The creature howls, collapsing into ash, but more take its place.

Lyric moves with deadly grace, her daggers flashing as she dances through the fray. Eryndor's strikes are powerful and deliberate, each one landing with devastating force. Veylan charges into the chaos, his jaws snapping shut on a revenant's neck with a sickening crunch.

I focus my energy, the heat building within me until it bursts forth in a fiery arc that consumes a cluster of revenants. The flames illuminate the clearing, casting eerie shadows as the creatures scream and disintegrate. My magic leaves me breathless, but I push forward, refusing to falter.

"Behind you!" Damien's shout cuts through the noise, and I whirl just in time to drive my blade into a revenant's chest. Its form flickers, then collapses into ash.

Despite our efforts, the revenants keep coming. Their numbers feel endless, their coordination unsettling. My arms ache, my breaths come in ragged gasps, and yet we fight on, bound by a shared determination.

Finally, the onslaught slows. The remaining revenants hesitate, their forms flickering as if unsure whether to retreat or attack. Damien steps forward, his sword raised, his presence commanding.

The revenants dissolve into the shadows, their forms scattering like smoke. The clearing falls silent, the only sound our labored breathing as we survey the aftermath. Damien's gaze locks onto mine, his green eyes softening.

"Are you all right?" he asks, his voice low.

I nod, though my hands tremble from the exertion. "We need to keep moving," I say, my voice steady despite the exhaustion weighing on me. "The Bloodstone's waiting."

Veylan steps forward, his ember eyes narrowing. "It knows we're coming," he says gravely. "This was only the beginning."

Together, we press on, the path ahead shrouded in mist and uncertainty. But as we move closer to the Bloodstone, one thing remains clear: we're not turning back.

The Path of Reckoning
Elira

The mist clings to the ground like it's hiding something, swirling faintly as we step into the clearing. Damien is just ahead of me, his shoulders broad and unyielding. Every so often, his green eyes flick back, catching mine. His gaze holds for a heartbeat too long before snapping forward again.

I can't stop looking at him. He's battle-worn and beautiful, the harsh lines of his face softened only slightly by the quiet intensity he always carries. My stomach twists—not with fear but something else entirely.

"Wildflower, if you keep staring, I might start to think you're plotting my death," Damien murmurs, his voice low enough for only me to hear.

"Maybe I am," I shoot back, forcing a smirk. "It's crossed my mind in the past."

He chuckles, a dark, rich sound that sends warmth through me. "If anyone could manage it, it'd be you."

Ahead, Veylan halts, his ember eyes narrowing as he sniffs the air. He doesn't say anything, but the way his hackles rise is enough. We all draw our weapons, the tension coiling tighter with each passing second.

And then it hits.

A wave of pressure slams into us, invisible but heavy, like a giant hand pressing down. My legs wobble, but I manage to stay upright. Damien doesn't.

He collapses to his knees, his sword falling from his grip as his hands clutch his head. "No," he snarls, his voice raw. "Get out of my head!"

The force's laughter echoes in the distance of my consciousness, a sound that sends chills racing down my spine. *You can't escape me, little king. You never could.*

"Damien!" I cry, rushing to his side. My fingers brush his shoulder, but he flinches away, his whole body trembling.

"Stay back," he grits out, his teeth clenched. "It's trying to… stop me. Use me."

I grab his face, forcing him to look at me. His green eyes are wild, unfocused, but they lock onto mine, and for a moment, the force's grip seems to loosen.

"We're here," I whisper, my voice shaking. "Stay with me. Don't let it win."

Veylan growls, his massive body bristling as he moves to shield us. "The force is angry. It knows we're close."

"What's it doing to him?" Lyric demands, her daggers glinting as she spins to face the shifting shadows.

"Trying to break him," Veylan rumbles. "And if it does, we're all dead."

In the distance, faint flickers of light catch my eye. At first, I think it's dawn breaking through the mist.
But then I see it.
Flames.

The town is burning.

"No," I breathe, horror twisting in my gut. Relvaris, untouched by the force for so long, is alight. The smoke rises in thick plumes, the faint screams of people carrying on the wind.

"It's punishing them," Eryndor says, his voice tight with rage. "For helping us."

Damien roars, his hands clawing at the ground as he struggles to rise. "You'll pay for this," he growls, his voice barely human. "You'll burn before I let you win!"

The force's laughter grows louder, cruel and mocking. *You're nothing, Damien. A pawn. A failure. She will die, and you'll watch it happen again. And the fire, wasn't me. It's HER!*

Horror shocked me to the bone. I look at myself like a mad man, and I'm glowing. Glowing with rage and fire.

Everyone's staring and tears escape my eyes. "What…What did I do."

Without wasting time, I grab his face again, my voice firm this time. "Damien, look at me!"

His gaze snaps to mine, and for a moment, the madness recedes. "We need you," I say, my tone unyielding. "I need you. Don't let it take you."

He exhales sharply, his body sagging against mine. "It's strong," he whispers, his voice trembling. "Stronger than before."

"Then we get stronger," I say, forcing steel into my voice. "We push forward."

Veylan's growl cuts through the moment. "It's coming," he warns, his ember eyes fixed on the shifting shadows. *"You need to calm down, Elira, you need to breath, calm the fire."*

The revenants emerge around us, their grotesque forms slithering from the darkness like nightmares made flesh. Their glowing eyes fix on us, and their movements are eerily deliberate, like puppets on strings.

Damien finally rises, his sword back in his hand. "Stay behind me," he orders, his voice steady but seething with rage.

"Not this again," I snap, magic sparking to life under my skin. "We do this together."

The ugly revenant lunges, and Damien meets it with a ferocity I've never seen. His blade cleaves through its torso in one brutal strike, black blood spraying across the ground.

Another comes for me, its claws outstretched, forcing my flames here, I send it towards him consuming it before it gets close. The heat scorches the air, illuminating the chaos as the battle begins.

The revenants are relentless, their numbers endless, their fury unmatched. Damien fights like a man possessed, each strike filled with unbridled rage. His movements are precise, deadly, but there's a wildness to him now—a barely contained feral energy that makes my chest ache.

"Damien!" I call out, my voice cutting through the din. "Focus!"

He doesn't respond, his blade cutting through another creature with savage efficiency.

Lyric and Eryndor hold their own, their movements sharp and coordinated. Veylan is a blur of fur and fangs, tearing through revenants like they're paper.

And me—I let the fire consume me. It burns hot and wild, my magic fueling every strike as I send waves of flames crashing into the horde.
But the revenants don't stop.

They keep coming, their grotesque forms filling the clearing, their howls drowning out the world.

Then Damien's voice cuts through the chaos, a roar that shakes the ground. "ENOUGH!"

His sword glows faintly, his green eyes blazing as he drives it into the ground. A shockwave ripples outward, tearing through the revenants and sending them screaming into the void.

When the dust settles, the clearing is empty.

Damien falls to his knees, his breathing ragged. I'm at his side in an instant, my hands cupping his face.

"We're not done," he says, his voice hoarse but steady. "Not yet."

"No," I agree, my voice soft but firm. "But we're closer."

Veylan steps forward, his massive form towering over us. "The force isn't done either," he says grimly. "This was only a taste of its wrath."

I glance at the distant flames, the town's screams still faintly audible. My chest tightens, but I force myself to stand, pulling Damien to his feet.

The Burn
Elira

It smells of scorched earth and blood, an acrid blend that clings to my throat and fills my lungs. The distant flames consuming Relvaris are a constant, terrible glow on the horizon. My chest feels tight, my breaths shallow and unsteady.

I did that.

My hands tremble as I look down at them, the faint shimmer of heat still radiating from my skin. The power that surged through me moments ago was primal, unstoppable—a wildfire I couldn't control. And the price was steep.

Damien stands beside me, his sword still in hand, its edge gleaming faintly in the dim light. He's watching me, his green eyes sharp, his expression unreadable. There's no judgment in his gaze, but there's something else—concern? Fear?

"Wildflower," he says, his voice rough, dragging me out of my thoughts.

I swallow hard, forcing myself to meet his gaze. "Did you see what I—"

"Yes," he cuts me off, stepping closer. His hand reaches for mine, his touch grounding. "I saw."

"I burned the town," I whisper, my voice cracking. "I didn't mean to. I didn't—"

"You didn't burn the town," Damien interrupts, his tone firm. "The force pushed you. It wanted you to lose control."

"But I—"

"Enough." His voice sharpens, and he steps even closer, his presence like a shield against my spiraling thoughts. "You're stronger than this. Don't let it win."

Veylan's deep rumble breaks through the tension. "She needs to learn control," he says, his ember eyes flicking to me. *"Quickly. That fire won't just destroy your enemies, Elira. It'll consume you too."*

I nod, unable to find the words. He's right. I feel it—the dangerous edge of my power, the way it pulls at me, relentless and untamed.

"We need to move," Lyric says, her voice tight. She glances back at the distant flames, her golden eyes hard. "If the force is trying to break us here, it's because the Bloodstone is close."

Eryndor steps up beside her, his jaw set.

"What's the plan? Do we even have one?"

Veylan exhales sharply, his massive frame bristling with tension. "The Bloodstone lies at the heart of its domain. If the force pushed Elira to this, it means we're close enough for it to feel threatened."

Damien's hand tightens around mine, and I glance at him. His gaze is steady, unyielding. "We don't stop," he says simply. "We push forward."

"Just like that?" Lyric asks, her tone dripping with skepticism. "No strategy, no backup plan, just walk straight into whatever trap it's set for us?"

"Sometimes the only way out is through," Damien replies, his smirk sharp and humorless.

Lyric mutters, rolling her eyes. "Love a good death march."

I can't help but huff a breath of laughter, though it's hollow and shaky. The group starts to move, the remnants of the battle fading behind us as we press on.

Damien stays close, his hand brushing against mine occasionally, a silent reminder that he's there. I cling to that touch, to the steady strength he radiates. But inside, I'm a storm.

The power that burned through me feels like it's still there, lurking beneath the surface, waiting for another moment to escape. I flex my fingers, trying to shake off the lingering heat, but it doesn't fade.

"Veylan," I call out, breaking the silence. "What if I lose control again?"

The wolf's ember eyes meet mine, his gaze heavy. *"Then you'll learn from it,"* he says simply.

"That's not comforting," I mutter, my frustration bubbling up.

"It's not meant to be," he replies, his tone unyielding. *"The force thrives on fear and doubt. It will use them against you every chance it gets. Control your fire, Elira, or it will control you."*

Damien's hand finds my wrist, his thumb brushing over the mark that pulses faintly beneath my skin. "You're stronger than it," he murmurs, his voice low but firm. "Stronger than all of this."

His words settle something in me, a flicker of resolve cutting through the storm.

"We're almost there," Veylan says, his voice a rumble that carries through the oppressive silence. "Prepare yourselves."

Ahead, the trees thin, revealing a jagged, rocky outcrop that seems to rise out of the earth itself. At its center is a faint glow, pulsing like a heartbeat—the Bloodstone.

But the air shifts again, and my pulse spikes. The shadows around us ripple, twisting into grotesque forms. The revenants are back, their movements faster, more deliberate, their glowing eyes fixed on us.

Damien draws his sword, his green eyes narrowing. "Stay with me," he commands, his voice sharp.

"I'm not going anywhere," I reply, my magic already sparking to life.

The battle is immediate and brutal. The revenants swarm, their numbers endless, their claws and teeth tearing through the air. My fire burns hotter this time, a controlled blaze that cuts through the horde. But it's not enough.

The force's voice echoes in my mind, dark and mocking. You'll fail. You'll all fail.

Damien's roar cuts through the chaos, his blade flashing as he carves a path through the creatures. His movements are precise, deadly, but I can see the strain in his jaw, the way his body tightens with each strike.

"Damien!" I shout, my voice cutting through the din. "Don't let it take you!"

His gaze snaps to mine, and for a moment, the world narrows to just us. He nods, his grip tightening on his sword as he pushes forward.
The Bloodstone glows brighter, its pulsing light a beacon amidst the darkness.

"We're close!" Lyric shouts, her voice strained as she drives her daggers into a revenant's chest.

But the force doesn't relent. The revenants keep coming, their fury unending. My fire wavers, the strain of the battle beginning to take its toll.

Then Damien is there, his body a shield as he steps in front of me. "Focus, wildflower," he growls, his voice steady despite the chaos. "We're almost there."
I nod, drawing strength from his presence. Together, we push forward, the Bloodstone's light growing stronger with every step.

And the force's laughter grows louder, its fury palpable.

"You can't stop us," Damien snarls, his voice carrying over the battlefield. "Not this time."
The Bloodstone awaits, the path to it bathed in blood and fire.

The Stone's Claim
Elira

The battlefield is chaos incarnate, every step toward the Bloodstone harder than the last. My body feels like it's dragging through molasses, the force pushing against us with an unrelenting presence that grows stronger with every pulse of the stone's glow.

The revenants are endless, their grotesque forms writhing out of the shadows like maggots from a rotting corpse.

"Keep moving!" Damien shouts, his voice cutting through the chaos like a blade. His sword is slick with blackened blood, his movements feral and precise. He is rage incarnate, a king fighting for his kingdom, his queen.

And as his green eyes catch mine for the briefest of moments, I see it—a promise that he'll die before he lets this fight end without victory.

My fire burns bright, the heat of it coursing through my veins as I scorch through the horde. But the drain is immense, the weight of the power making my arms heavy and my vision blur. I stumble, and in an instant, Damien is there, his hand gripping my arm to steady me.

"Elira, stay with me," he growls, his voice low, fierce.

"I'm fine," I bite back, shaking off the weariness. "Focus on them."

His gaze lingers a moment too long before he nods and turns back to the fight. I hate the concern in his eyes almost as much as I crave it.

"Don't fall behind!" Lyric's voice cuts through the chaos as she spins, her daggers slicing through a revenant's throat. The golden glint in her eyes burns with determination. "The damn stone's right there!"

The Bloodstone looms ahead, its light flickering like a dying star. The ground around it is jagged, broken as if the earth itself tried to reject its presence. The pulsing glow seems to call to me, a siren's song that wraps around my mind and tugs at my chest.

It's close. So close.

But the force isn't letting us take it without a fight. The laughter in my mind is louder now, a cruel symphony that digs into my skull.
You'll fail. You'll lose him. Just like always.

"No," I snarl, slamming my fire into a group of revenants. The blaze engulfs them, their shrieks filling the air as they disintegrate into ash.

Damien's roar follows, a guttural sound that shakes me to my core. I turn just in time to see him drive his blade into the ground again, a shockwave tearing through the revenants around him. The strain in his face is evident, the lines around his mouth tight with pain, but he doesn't falter.

Veylan charges past us, his massive form colliding with a revenant that dared get too close. His jaws snap shut with a sickening crunch, and the creature falls limp. "Move!" he barks, his ember eyes blazing. "The stone won't wait for you!"

Eryndor is beside Lyric now, the two of them carving a path toward the Bloodstone with synchronized precision. Their movements are seamless, deadly, but even they are slowing. The force's pressure is too much, a weight that threatens to crush us all.

"I've got this," Damien says, his voice rough as he pulls me forward. His hand wraps around mine, his grip strong, unyielding. "Don't stop. Don't look back."

I don't argue. I can't. The mark on my wrist burns brighter with every step closer to the stone, the heat of it merging with the fire coursing through me. It feels alive, like a living entity bound to my very soul.

And then we're there.

The Bloodstone is massive, its surface jagged and raw, glowing with a light that's both beautiful and terrifying. The hum of its power is deafening up close, vibrating through the ground and into my bones.

Damien pulls me forward, his green eyes locked onto the stone. "This is it," he murmurs, his voice low, reverent. "The beginning of the end."

"You think you've won?" The voice echoes all around us, dark and mocking, resonating deep within my chest. *"You've done nothing but march into your own graves."*

A figure materializes from the shadows, grotesque and monstrous, its eyes glowing with a sickly light. It's the force made flesh, a manifestation of everything we've been fighting against.

Its form shifts and writhes, like it can't decide what shape to take.

Damien steps in front of me, his sword raised. "Not today," he growls, his voice steady despite the fury in his eyes.

The force laughs, a sound that makes my skin crawl. *"You'll break, little king. Just like you always do."*

"No," Damien says, his voice low but unshakable. "Not this time."

He moves first, his blade slicing through the air as he charges the manifestation. The force meets him head-on, its claws swiping toward him with unnatural speed. Their clash shakes the ground, the impact sending shockwaves rippling outward.

I don't hesitate. My fire flares to life, and I hurl it toward the creature, the flames engulfing its form. It shrieks, the sound piercing and inhuman, but it doesn't stop.

Lyric and Eryndor join the fray, their weapons striking with precision and force. Veylan circles the creature, his growls low and menacing as he waits for the perfect moment to strike.

The battle is chaos, a blur of fire and steel and shadows. The force is relentless, its laughter echoing in my mind even as we fight to push it back.

But we don't stop. We can't stop.

The Bloodstone pulses behind us, its light growing brighter with every passing moment. It's close, so close, but the force isn't giving up without a fight.

Breaking Point
Damien

The Bloodstone's light pulses erratically, brighter and brighter, until it seems to burn against my vision like a second sun.

My grip tightens on my sword as the force presses harder against me, a searing weight that digs into my mind, clawing, tearing. My knees threaten to buckle, but I grit my teeth and force myself to stay upright.

This is wrong.

"Elira!" My voice cracks through the chaos, desperate to reach her. She's standing too close to the Bloodstone, her hands outstretched toward it as if she's trying to pull something from its depths. The glow wraps around her like a living thing, coursing through her veins, igniting her mark into a brilliant, blinding light.

"It's not working," Lyric yells, her daggers clutched tightly as she surveys the battlefield. "Why isn't it doing anything?"

The force laughs, low and cruel, its voice reverberating through the clearing, worming into every corner of my mind. *Because it was never meant to save you, little king.*

"Elira, get back!" I shout again, but she doesn't move. Her wild eyes are locked on the Bloodstone, her breaths coming in frantic gasps. The air around her shimmers with heat, and the ground beneath her feet begins to blacken.

"Damien," Veylan growls, his voice sharp in my head. "She's losing control."

"I can see that," I snarl back, my mind racing as I take a step closer to her. The heat rolling off her makes it almost unbearable to approach. "Elira, listen to me! It's enhancing you, but it's not stopping the force!"

Her head snaps toward me, her blue eyes glowing with an unnatural brilliance. "I can feel it," she says, her voice trembling, her body vibrating with energy. "I can stop this—I have to—"

"You can't!" I bark, the desperation in my voice cutting through the din. "It's not helping us. It's feeding off you."

The force's laughter grows louder, a mocking symphony that drowns out the sound of my heartbeat. *So close, little warrior. So powerful. Do you see now? You're not the savior. You're the storm.*

"Elira," Lyric calls, her voice wavering. "You have to step back. It's not safe."

The Bloodstone pulses again, and this time, the light lashes out, a shockwave that sends all of us staggering. Elira cries out, clutching her head as the force presses harder, its voice curling around her like poison.

You were born to destroy this world, it whispers, its tone dripping with venom. You could burn it all, every corner of existence, until there's nothing left but ash.

"No!" she screams, her hands clutching at her temples. "I won't let you—"

But you will. Or he will. The force's attention shifts to me, its presence tightening like a vice.

I've waited lifetimes for you, little king. To wield you, to break you. You'll watch her burn, and then you'll be mine.

My body jerks as if shackles have wrapped around me, holding me in place. I try to move, to fight against the invisible chains, but they're too strong. The force's voice snakes through my head, its tendrils rooting deep in my thoughts.

"You can't have me," I spit through clenched teeth. "I'm not yours."

"Elira!" I call out, my voice raw. She's trembling now, her hands glowing with fire, her magic spiraling out of control. The clearing quakes under the pressure of her power, the air thick with heat and the scent of burning earth.

"Veylan," her voice cuts through the chaos, frantic and desperate. She's not speaking aloud, but in my head—our heads.

"What happens if we stop it?" she asks, her mental voice breaking. *"If we kill the force, will my world... will it be beautiful? Will my mom be okay?"*

The silence that follows her question is deafening. Even the force pauses, as if savoring her uncertainty. Veylan's ember eyes meet mine, they seem frantic, for the first time.

He panics.

His massive form shuddering under the strain of the force's weight. He growls low, his answer deliberate but strained.

"Yes," he finally says, his mental voice rough. *"If the force dies, the worlds will heal. Your world, your mother—they will be safe. They'll thrive."*

Her relief is fleeting, her breath hitching as he continues.

"*But*," Veylan growls, the regret in his tone cutting deeper than any blade, "*you won't be her daughter. You won't exist in that world. You'll be someone else. Perhaps.*"

Her power falters, the fire around her flickering for a moment before roaring back, stronger than ever. Her voice shakes as she speaks, her words trembling with both fear and resolve.

"If it means saving them, I'll do it."

And as her words settle in the air, the force laughs, its malice wrapping around us tighter than ever.

I looked at her, and I know.

To Be Found Again
Elira

The world is collapsing around us.

Fire and shadows twist together in a dance of destruction, devouring everything in their path. The screams from Relvaris pierce through the suffocating roar of flames, each one sharper than the last, like jagged glass tearing into my chest. The ground quakes beneath my feet, cracks spiderwebbing out from the Bloodstone's base, and the force's laughter fills my mind, cruel and unrelenting.

It's all too much.

"Damien!" I scream, my voice breaking as I search for him through the chaos. The glowing embers of the Bloodstone throw jagged shadows across the battlefield, and when I finally see him, I feel the air rush out of my lungs.

He's on his knees, his sword slack in his hand, his body trembling under the weight of the force's power. It's wrapped around him like chains, twisting and pulling, trying to drag him down. The sight of him—my strong, unyielding Damien—brought so low makes something inside me snap.

I run to him, tears streaming down my face, the heat of the fire I've unleashed burning at my back. The moment I reach him, I drop to my knees, my arms wrapping around his shoulders, pulling him into me. His warmth is familiar, grounding, but his body is trembling, his breaths shallow and ragged.

"Damien," I choke, my fingers tangling in his hair as I press my forehead to his. "I'm here. I've got you. Please, stay with me."

"Elira," he whispers, his voice hoarse and broken, his green eyes flickering with pain and love.

"I'm so sorry. I couldn't stop it—I couldn't stop any of this."

"It's not your fault," I sob, my tears falling onto his cheek. "None of this is your fault. We're going to fix it. Together."

His lips find mine in a desperate kiss, and for a moment, the world fades. His hands grip me like I'm the only thing keeping him tethered, and I cling to him just as fiercely, pouring every ounce of love, fear, and desperation into the kiss. The chaos rages on around us, but here, in his arms, I find a fleeting moment of peace.

When we finally pull apart, his forehead rests against mine, his breath mingling with mine. "I love you," he says, the words trembling on his lips. "In every life, in every world, it's always been you."

My heart shatters, and I nod, my tears blurring my vision. "I love you too, Damien. Always."

Veylan's voice rumbles in my mind, soft and filled with something I never thought I'd hear from him: pride. *You've done well, little one. You've fought harder than anyone could have asked. You've been everything the Fates dreamed of.*

But his voice falters, a weight settling in my chest as his next words come. *You know what must be done.*

I glance at the Bloodstone, its light dimming but still pulsing faintly, feeding the fire that rages within me.

The force's laughter grows louder, mocking, as if it knows I've realized the truth.

Not thinking I'm capable of it.

"Elira," Damien says, his voice pulling me back to him. He's looking at me now, his green eyes soft but resolute. "You feel it, don't you? The only way to end this."

I nod, a sob catching in my throat. "If the force dies, the world will heal. My world, your world... everyone will be safe."
"But it will cost us," he says quietly, his hand brushing my cheek. "Both of us."

I press my face into his palm, my tears soaking his skin. "Damien... if we do this... if we die..."

"We'll find each other," he interrupts, his voice firm despite the tremor in it. "In the next life, where there's no evil. Where there's only us."

My chest tightens, and I pull him into another kiss, this one slower, filled with every word I can't say. When we part, my fingers trace the scars on his face, memorizing him, every line and curve, every mark of the man I love.

The force's voice slices through the moment, sharp and cruel. *You think this will stop me? You think your pathetic sacrifice will make a difference? She'll destroy the world before she saves it, and you'll watch her burn.*

I look at Damien, my heart breaking as the truth sets in. "It's time."

He nods, his hand finding mine and gripping it tightly. "Together."

Veylan's voice trembles in my mind, heavy with grief. *The world will heal, Elira.*

I close my eyes, my tears falling freely now.
"That's enough," I whisper. "That's enough for me."

The Bloodstone pulses again, brighter this time, as if responding to my resolve. I channel every ounce of power within me, the flames building, consuming me from the inside out. The force screams in protest, its grip tightening, but I push through the pain.

"Damien," I say, my voice breaking as I look at him one last time. "I'll find you."
"I'll be waiting," he replies, his green eyes filled with love as he squeezes my hand. "Always."

With a final surge of power, I unleash everything. The fire erupts, engulfing us and the Bloodstone in a blinding inferno. The force's screams are deafening, its presence tearing away piece by piece until there's nothing left but silence.

And then, darkness.

Reborn
Veylan

The field stretches endlessly before me, a sea of wildflowers swaying gently in the breeze. The air is warm and sweet, filled with the scent of blossoms and the hum of life. The horizon glows with the colors of a setting sun, casting the world in a golden light. This place, untouched by darkness, is the world they fought for—a world they gave everything to create.

Your burial was beautiful.

The thought lingers, unspoken but heavy in my mind. Their ashes—Elira's and Damien's—are buried together beneath the tallest tree in this field. Its branches stretch toward the heavens, its leaves glinting like emeralds in the sunlight. At its base, a simple stone marker rests, inscribed with words that carry the weight of their sacrifice:

**_For the King and His Wildflower— The Ones Who
Ended the Dark._**

I pause before the tree, the flowers brushing against my fur. Ember eyes scan the horizon, taking in the laughter of children chasing one another through the meadow, the warmth of families picnicking under the shade of the trees, and the soft murmur of peace that has settled over this place.

This is what they wanted.

The world is free now, unshackled from the malevolence that had poisoned it for so long. The skies are clear, the rivers run pure, and the people—those who once lived in fear—now move with joy and ease. But even as I witness the beauty they created, a pang of loss cuts through me.

You should be here to see it.

The breeze shifts, carrying with it the faintest whisper of their voices, like a memory too delicate to hold onto. I close my eyes, letting the sounds of the field wash over me—the rustle of leaves, the ripple of grass, the laughter of the living. They're echoes of the new life they gave to this world.

Their burial was not just an ending; it was a beginning. The ashes of their sacrifice nurtured the soil, gave strength to the tree that now stands as a symbol of their love and their legacy. People gathered here to mourn, to celebrate, to remember. They brought flowers, tokens, stories. They sang songs of gratitude and grief. And when the crowd dispersed, leaving only the quiet of the field, I remained, standing sentinel over what they left behind.

Now, I walk among those they saved, my massive form towering over the people who no longer flinch at the sight of me. They've come to trust me, to understand my purpose. And though I carry the weight of their memory, I also carry their hope.

The crowd gathers again today, their voices a murmur of anticipation. They look to me, their eyes bright with curiosity and reverence. I pause before them, the weight of the moment settling over me.

"They were more than heroes," I begin, my voice deep and steady, carrying over the meadow. "They were the light that burned away the darkness. They were the fire that forged this new world. They were everything we needed—and more."

The people bow their heads, their silence a testament to the love they hold for Elira and Damien. The tree stands tall behind me, its shadow stretching over the crowd like a protective embrace.

I lift my head, my voice rising with conviction as I shout to the heavens, to the people, to the earth itself:

"Long live the King!"

And as the sun sets on this day, casting the world in a fiery glow, I turn my gaze to the horizon. The world is safe. The people are free. And somewhere, in the threads of fate that stretch beyond my sight, I know they've found each other again.

Together. Always.

ABOUT THE AUTHOR

Step into the captivating world of Maryse Marullo, a Canadian author who masterfully blends passion, darkness, and forbidden desires into her stories. Maryse's tales explore the fine line between love and obsession, immersing readers in worlds where danger and romance intertwine. With a talent for crafting raw, emotionally charged narratives, she delves into the shadows of the human heart, revealing the beauty found in the unexpected.An unapologetic lover of dark, taboo, and forbidden romance, Maryse invites readers to lose themselves in her hauntingly beautiful tales. Follow her on Instagram, TikTok, and Goodreads for exclusive updates, behind- the-scenes glimpses, and sneak peeks at her latest releases.

BY THE SAME AUTHOR

- Say Sorry (A second chance romance novella)
- StepPsycho-Tangled hearts, Twisted fates Duet#1 (A dark-forbidden romance)
- Ruins and shadows (A enemies-to-lovers romantasy)
- Sleep my dear – The Godsland Book One (A dark romantasy)
- Long Live The King (A dark romantasy)